Praise for *The Core of the Sun*

'A chilling tale reminis̶ent of M̶a̶r̶g̶ ̶̶̶̶̶ ̶̶̶̶̶̶̶ ̶̶*naid's Tale* . . . a fascinating s̶ o̶ı̶

Post

'As a mirror held slantwise̶ ̶̶̶̶̶̶̶̶̶ ̶̶̶ ̶̶o̶ften convincing, and rarely withou̶ ̶̶̶̶̶ ̶l̶ever and comical. Likewise, as a repudiation of the e̶ alitarian gloriousness of the 'Nordic model,' it's a thing we rarely behold in America: a feminist novel that propels you forward to its terrifying, pulpy conclusion.'

Flavorwire

'There's a streak of scathing satire to the book's fragmentary science fiction, and in that sense it sits somewhere between Margaret Atwood and Kurt Vonnegut – but Sinisalo crafts a funny, unsettling, emotionally charged apparition of the present that's all her own.'

NPR

'Johanna Sinisalo's dystopian *The Core of the Sun* is a stunningly evocative novel about the great literary theme of identity, brilliantly rendering the complex struggle between society's norms, our innate personal qualities, and the transformative substances of the physical world. Sex, drugs, and bureaucracy: What could be more compelling?' Robert Olen Butler

'Will inevitably bring Margaret Atwood's *The Handmaid's Tale* to mind, but the narrator's funny, sad, punk voice could fit right in to the stories in Kelly Link's *Get in Trouble* and is as unforgettable.'

Library Journal

'Sinisalo . . . m̶ ̶̶̶̶̶̶̶̶̶̶ ̶̶̶̶̶̶̶̶̶̶̶̶̶̶ . A̶n unusual and fun s̶tory ̶̶̶̶̶̶̶̶̶̶̶̶̶̶̶̶̶̶̶̶̶̶̶̶ ̶̶̶̶̶̶.'

Publishers Weekly

The Core of
the Sun

Also by Johanna Sinisalo

Troll: A Love Story
Birdbrain
The Blood of Angels

The Core of the Sun

JOHANNA SINISALO

Translated from the Finnish by
Lola Rogers

Grove Press UK

First published in the United States of America in 2016 by Grove/Atlantic Inc.

First published in Great Britain in 2016 by Grove Press UK, an imprint of Grove/Atlantic Inc.

This paperback edition published in 2017.

Originally published as *Auringon ydin* by Teos Publishers (Finland)

English edition published by agreement with Johanna Sinisalo and Elina Ahlbäck Agency, Helsinki, Finland

The translation of this book was subsidized in part by FILI.

F I L I FINNISH LITERATURE EXCHANGE

1 3 5 7 9 8 6 4 2

A CIP record for this book is available from the British Library.

Grove Press, UK
Ormond House
26–27 Boswell Street
London
WC1N 3JZ

www.groveatlantic.com

Paperback ISBN 978 1 61185 526 5
E-book ISBN 978 1 61185 957 7

PRINTED AND BOUND BY NOVOPRINT IN BARCELONA

Dedicated to the Freedom Trust Conglomerate
(you know who you are)

Teach me, chile, and I shall Learn.
Take me, chile, and I shall Escape.
Focus my eyes, chile, and I shall See.
Consume more chiles.
I feel no pain, for the chile is my teacher.
I feel no pain, for the chile takes me beyond myself.
I feel no pain, for the chile gives me sight.
> —Transcendental Capsaicinophilic Society,
> "Litany Against Pain"

My boat is light and swift.
> —Chukchi shaman Ukwun

PART I

The Cellar

VANNA/VERA

October 2016

I lift my skirt, pull aside the waistband of my underwear, and push my index finger in to test the sample.

The seller's eyes go wide. The maple tree's branches and sparse leaves splash shadows over his face, the whites of his eyes flash, and I can see his Adam's apple jump as he swallows.

He exudes a sour smell, a mixture of tar and spirea blossoms. Fear, confusion, disbelief: he's an amateur, probably a closet capso, hooked on capsaicin, trying to feed his addiction by dealing. He's trying to keep his face neutral, but he flinches at this habit of mine. A beginner. Probably shocked by the glimpse of my pubic hair, too. Maybe that's something he's never seen before.

I pull my hand out of my panties and let the waistband spring back into place. *Snap*. I lower my skirt. Press my thighs together to let the sample take effect. Flash a calm smile.

The lower lip doesn't lie.

"This will take a second," I say, looking at the sky, or rather at the branches swaying above us. "Looks as though it might drizzle."

The seller opens his mouth but no sound comes out. I can sense a whiff of hostility, the kind that happens when someone's slightly anxious, when he's lost control of a situation. Understandable. If you're engaging in illegal activity in the wee hours of the night in a corner of a cemetery, you don't want to run into surprises like me.

"I guess we should expect the first snow pretty soon," I say. That's when the stuff starts to kick in.

First the burn spreads across my lower body, my labia and vagina turning hot as glowing embers. The first drops of sweat form under my eyes, then along the edge of my scalp, then down my neck. The blood rushes in my ears. The stuff thrums a dredging bass note, almost an infrasound, with fantastic dark brown tones in its burn.

I take a deep breath and smile wider than I should. "I'll take the whole load."

The lower lip doesn't lie.

This is the real stuff.

The seller has been holding the score in his hand the whole time and gives it to me now. About a hundred grams, and if it's all like the stuff that's in my coot right now, it's incredibly strong. I twirl the transparent plastic bag in my hand and check to make sure the dried flakes aren't cut with bits of plastic or crepe paper or red flower petals. It doesn't look adulterated.

He claims it's Naga Viper, but it could just as well be some variety I've never heard of. Judging by its potency, it's about a million scovilles. This is one of the strongest scores ever.

The capsaicin is roaring so loudly through the blood vessels in my ears that it's hard to concentrate on closing the deal. I fish the agreed-upon sum out of my bra. The seller stares at me as I do this, his eyes like saucers. The whole transaction is probably starting to seem to him like a cock tease, with me flashing first my pubes and now my bosom. But if he's got any experience at all with this stuff and even a little sense in his head, he knows that under no circumstances should he try to go poking his dick into a vagina where Naga Viper is waiting to bite it. The nerve endings of a woman's genitals are sparse for an erogenous zone—and, of course, I scrupulously avoid letting the sample touch my most sensitive spots—but if a man got a dose of capsaicin around his urethra it would be quite a jolt.

The seller takes the money, counts the bills out twice—separating them with mind-numbing exactness—finally nods, and stuffs the cash into his breast pocket. I give my head a jerk: "Get lost." He raises an eyebrow, runs his gaze up and down my body. He's putting out a candy-flavored smell, a tinge of something almost like burnt sugar. I look him in the eye without blinking and cross my arms over my chest in a firm negative. He shrugs and leaves, pushing the branches out of his way and strolling down the gravel path toward the cemetery gates with purposeful slowness.

When I'm sure he's far enough away, I stuff the bag into the waist of my skirt and tug the hem of my blouse over it. The blouse is a bit too tight to cover the lump, but it's not likely to show up in a surveillance video.

I wait a few more seconds and then slip out of the grove of trees. I walk briskly down the path in the opposite direction. There aren't many cameras at the cemetery, and they check the film only when they know something suspicious has happened. There are also rumors that most of the cameras are just empty cases. Still, I try to look as if I have a purpose. If someone asks what I'm doing in this particular cemetery, and why I'm here in the middle of the night, I have an excellent explanation.

Hearing Transcript (Extract)

October 9, 2016

Hearing supervisor [hereafter HS]: Let it be noted that FN-140699-NLP [Vanna Neulapää, hereafter V], owing to her legal status, was questioned in the presence of witness Jare Valkinen.

Questioner [hereafter Q]: Why did you come to Kalevan-kangas cemetery?

Jare Valkinen [hereafter J]: To watch my girlfriend, Vanna Neulapää. I knew she was going there to visit a grave.

Q: Which grave?

V: My sister's.

Q: Why did you go there?

V: Well, um, she died just a short time ago. And I just can't sleep because I keep turning it over in my mind! [witness begins to cry]

J: Vanna's sister's death was a great shock to her. The grave is an important, beloved place for her.

Q: Why were you watching Vanna?

J: Elois are so easily led astray or pressured into things that I thought it best to be on the safe side and sort of look after her.

Q: As well you should. Is the other witness able to speak now?

V: Yeah. I think so.

Q: Did you know the man who attacked you?

V: I sure didn't!

Q: Did you know him, Valkinen?

J: No. I suspect the man may have been following Vanna for a long time and saw her go into the cemetery and thought it a good opportunity.

Q: Both the witness and the attacker spent several minutes in a location that is obscured in the surveillance footage. Was there at that time any kind of provocation or enticement?

V: Of course not! I was . . . I needed [said in a whisper] to pee. Because I'd drunk at least six cups of a kind of herb thing that's supposed to help you sleep, but it just made me . . . need to tinkle . . . sorry. So I wanted to sleep but I couldn't, and I went to the cemetery, but then I really had to go.

Q: So you purposely went out of sight because . . . you needed to do your business?

V: The man who came up to me must have been spying on me from someplace while I was peeing! I should have tried to find a restroom, but it was awfully urgent! [witness begins to cry again]

Q: So the attacker, having seen . . . this activity . . . followed the witness?

J: I assume that's what happened.

Q: And you were hiding near the grave, because you wanted to know what your girlfriend was doing when she went out at night?

J: Exactly. When the attacker got there, I thought at first that he had come there to meet her, but then he attacked her and tried to sexually assault her.

Q: Right. From the tape we can see that the man tried to tear off the witness's skirt.

J: I went to help her, of course, and I struck the attacker in the face. I assumed that he had been knocked unconsciousness by the blow, and I turned to see if Vanna was all right. Then the attacker ran away. When I saw that Vanna wasn't seriously injured, I quickly went to the nearest social disturbance alarm and pushed the button. Has the man been caught? If so, I can try to help identify him.

Q: For investigative reasons we are unable to provide any information about the progress of the case at present.

V: Can we go now?

Q: Speak when you're spoken to. I consider the matter settled. You may go, but first you must both sign the record of this hearing. Your name underneath, miss. Chop-chop. There's no time for you to work out what the whole thing says. Your manfriend will get a copy later and tell you what it all means.

VANNA/VERA

October 2016

I buy a bouquet of chrysanthemums from the cemetery kiosk in the pale October morning light.

At the grave, I carefully unwrap the flowers from their paper. I try to still my trembling hands but the paper crackles like the frost under my feet. I put the paper down with feigned nonchalance next to the stone flower vase sunk into the ground. I shove the chrysanthemum stems deep into the pot and feel around the bottom of the vase with my fingertips.

A cold surge jolts through my stomach.

I try to move naturally, take more flowers from the bouquet, and pretend to arrange them. But no matter where I place my fingers against the cold, rough inner surface of the vase I can't find the little plastic bag. The vase is empty.

Empty.

My heart starts to pound. The mere thought of ending up back in the Cellar makes my pulse race.

Just a few hours ago I had a bag of Naga Viper in my possession. My share of it would have been enough to last for weeks. Really potent stuff.

The thought is crushing.

I pretend to arrange the last of the chrysanthemums carefully in the pot. They're purple and yellow, Manna's favorite colors.

I wad the wrapper in my fist and stand up. I had planned to slip the stuff from the vase into the paper and carry it away as if I were going to throw it in the trash.

I lean against Jare and he wraps his right arm around me. I put my head on his shoulder as if I'm weak with grief. I don't really have to pretend. I speak quietly, from the side of my mouth.

"It's gone."

Jare's body stiffens. A slow breath seeps out of him into the air. "Shit."

"It was that double-crossing dealer. It couldn't be anyone else."

"Not such a brilliant hiding place, then."

"I was sure nobody would dare to come and search the grave. They go over the night footage with a magnifying glass after an alarm."

"But somebody came and got the stuff without being seen. We wouldn't be walking free if they'd caught the guy."

True.

I look at the grave and the chrysanthemums. When I hid the bag the night before I had pretended to arrange some dried violets that were in the vase. They were scattered every which way over the grave in the tussle. Now there are only a few stray violet petals lying on the ground.

"The groundskeeper," I whisper to Jare. "Somebody must have pretended to be him and cleaned up the grave. Took away the old flowers and picked up a little something else while he was at it."

I take a deep breath.

"Let's go."

I pull carefully away from Jare's consoling embrace and twist the paper in my hands until my fingers hurt. I stand for a moment to look at the gravestone and the text.

MANNA NISSILÄ
(NÉE NEULAPÄÄ)
2001–2016

My knees give out. I don't know whether it's because of my mental anguish or my need for a fix. They're all mixed together. Black water is rising in the Cellar, and it's already reached the threshold, stretching its dark, wet fingers into my thoughts. It was supposed to be such a good idea to use Manna's grave for a drop spot. A place where it would make sense for me to go often, even at unusual hours, because of emotional ties that the authorities have no interest in.

But coming to the grave is always so shattering that I need a much larger dose than usual afterward. It's a vicious circle.

I turn away from the grave, my eyes wet. I take a handkerchief from my skirt pocket, remember the cameras, and carefully dab the corners of my eyes so I don't smudge my makeup. I shouldn't forget these little gestures even momentarily.

At the cemetery gates I drop the flower wrapper into the trash can. When we get to Jare's work-issued car I bend over double and start shaking. There's a rush of black in the back of my head. The Cellar door is starting to open.

"Can you make it home?" Jare asks worriedly.

I have to.

Dear sister!

There are things that are difficult to talk about with anyone. I don't have Aulikki anymore. I have some girlfriends, but of course I can't tell them everything. Aside from you there's only one other person I can open up to who would probably listen, but he doesn't have the same points of memory that I have, like you do. Mascos have a way of always trying to find a solution for any problem you present to them, even if all you want is to share your worries. And solutions to my problems aren't that easy to find.

So I decided to write to you.

You'll probably never see this letter. But I have to tell you what happened from my own point of view. I have no idea how much you even remember of all this, or how much your memories were colored by your own experiences. There are also a lot of things you didn't necessarily know about. Or didn't really understand. In many ways, we were sisters but we didn't have the same childhood.

I'm so worried about you. I'd be glad to get news of you, however terrible it might be, if I could just know for sure. Once you've hit bottom, you're at the bottom, after all; you just have to push off from there. I might get over the grief and pain as the years go by, I might even have the mercy of forgetting. But for now I have no way to heal, not when I don't know for sure what's happened to you.

You disappeared once before.

I remember it vividly, even though I was only six years old. Aulikki was in the garden and we were playing by the swing— the board swing that Aulikki had hung from a branch of the big birch tree. You loved swinging, and I was carefully building up your speed with pushes on your back. Your long blond hair was blowing and you were squealing and giggling because the swing made your stomach tingle. I remember I was a little upset that you didn't know how to give me a push yet, even though you got to enjoy my help. But it didn't matter. You were my little sister and Grandma Aulikki had left me to take care of you.

The phone rang inside. Aulikki straightened up from weeding the carrots, wiped her hands on her apron, and strode into the house. A bird flew into a young spruce tree on the other side of the vegetable garden. The unusual color of the bird aroused my curiosity. Later—quite a long time later—I looked in a book and learned that it was a jay. I'd never seen a bird like it at the time and I crept to the edge of the vegetable patch so I could see it better.

I got so close, in fact, that I could make out the fine turquoise stripe on its wings and grayish-red feathers and the black streaks like whiskers coming from its bill. I stood there for at least a minute watching it turn an acorn against the bend of the branch with its bill. I tried to get an even closer look, but I stepped on a twig and it snapped under my foot and the jay flew away with the acorn in its mouth.

I sighed and turned around.

The swing was empty, swaying faintly in the light and shadow of the birch leaves.

I didn't see you anywhere.

I heard a muffled voice from the house that told me that Aulikki was still talking on the phone. I thought you had sneaked into the house. Aulikki wouldn't want you to bother her during a telephone call. I ran to the door and peeked inside. You hadn't gone to get Aulikki's attention; she was still in the middle of a conversation about the potato harvest. I hurried to our room and looked inside. You weren't there, either.

I went back out into the yard, my heart racing. Where could you have gone? I didn't want Aulikki to know I'd been so terribly careless.

The yard at Neulapää didn't have a fence, but it was surrounded by a thick stand of spruce on two sides, and I didn't think you would have wanted to struggle through there. If you'd gone down the gravel driveway that led into the yard you would be visible. The only possibility was a little path that led behind the sauna to the woods and the spring.

You liked the spring. The clear stream of water bubbled up between the stones and formed a little pool with fine sand on the bottom. You liked to make your little hands swim in water that was ice-cold even in the hottest weather and to watch the narrow, gurgling spring that wound down to . . .

The swamp.

I took off running.

No sooner had I passed a couple of turns in the path than I heard your voice. It was a scream, telling me unequivocally that something was seriously wrong.

I tore down the path, oblivious of the roots and pinecones ripping the soles of my feet bloody. I could see a flash of Riihi Swamp through the trees, its surface covered with a bright blanket of sunbathed yellow-green moss, white tufts of cotton grass drifting on the wind. Riihi Swamp was a pond swallowed up by a bog. The layer of moss on its surface was a beautiful, deceptive shell hiding the airless black depths below.

I saw a flash of red—the red stripe around the collar of your dress—and then I saw you. Only your head and shoulders were above the layer of moss. The rest of you had sunk into the mouth of the bog that had suddenly opened up beneath your feet. You were holding on to the tufts of moss with both hands and yelling at the top of your lungs, and I saw that you were sinking a little more every moment as your weight sucked the sodden moss with you toward the bottom.

I was heavier than you, but I'd seen on television what to do in the winter if someone is on thin ice. Instead of trying to walk over the treacherous surface, I threw myself on my belly over the floating layer of moss and wriggled toward you. I tried to keep my voice steady, to calm you, but as I got closer you started to thrash and struggle, trying to get to me, your hope of rescue, and you lost hold of the moss and your head sank completely into the dark brown water.

I was quite close to you by that time. I thrust my hand into the black jaws of the swamp, felt something with my fingers, and wriggled backward, tugging with all my might, and I could feel, then see, that my fingers were gripping your hair, and your head popped up to the surface and you opened your mouth and let out a howl that stabbed my ears. I don't know how I had the strength to do it, but I got you close enough to me to get my arm under your armpits, and then partly rolled and partly crawled back to the edge, tugging us both to where the moss was thick enough to support us.

We were both wet and dirty and muddy and you were still screaming like something was eating you alive as I led you back to the house. Aulikki came running around a bend in the path toward us with a horrified look on her face, the sour smell of fear swirling around her.

The entire time that she was washing us up in the sauna, putting our muddy clothes in a bucket to soak, checking to see if you were hurt anywhere, dabbing medicine onto the cuts on the soles of my feet, she muttered and grumbled, not just at you but at me, too. I know now that she was letting her fear out, but at the time I formed a crystal clear picture that I had to look out for you.

I always look out for you.

I don't wonder at all that you went to explore the swamp. You just wanted to see the spring—it was a trip that had always fascinated you, although you didn't much like walking in the woods otherwise—and when you saw the swamp shining in the rays of the sun with fairy-tale colors, an almost perfectly round field in the middle of the dark green of the forest, I'm sure you thought that it was like a golden meadow in a story, where fairies and princesses held their secret dances.

In your world, it's always a surprise when there's something deceptive, evil, destructive under the pretty surface.

That's why I have to look out for you.

Aulikki built a gate in front of the path later, but it wasn't necessary. You never wanted to go near the spring after that.

I'll never leave you alone again.

Your sister,
Vanna (Vera)

VANNA/VERA

October 2016

When the door to my apartment closes behind us I kick off my high-heeled shoes and run—no, sprint—to the sleeping alcove, climb like a squirrel along the shelves (going to fetch the step stool would take too long), and pound at the top of the back wall with my fist until the board tilts and reveals the secret cache with its emergency stash. I grab a jar, jump down, get a jolt through my shins when I hit the floor, and start unscrewing the metal cap.

It's stuck, immovable as death.

"Fucking hell!"

I flop onto the bed. Tears are pushing straight up from the Cellar and I don't have anything to say about it, nothing to close it off, dam it up—it just gushes out like vomit.

Jare is beside me. He takes the jar from my limp fingers and twists the top with his deft masco fingers and strong hands; he turns it once and I hear the delicious click of the lid.

I tear the jar away from him, push a finger into the salt water and start scooping the green slices into my mouth. The top of the jar is too small to get my whole hand in so I pour the jalapeños straight into my mouth, letting the blessed broth pour over my face and down my chest and onto the pink bedspread. I swallow the peppers almost without chewing them. I know that the scovilles in jalapeños are pathetic, and they taste pretty much like dill pickles to me, but just knowing that there's capsaicin in those scrunchy little slices makes my hands begin to stop trembling. A couple of minutes later the coal black of the Cellar has receded a little, lapping just barely below flood level in my brain now. The meager kick of the jalapeños is weak, blue-gray, a pale noise from between the stars at the edges of hearing.

I drop the jar onto the floor. It falls with a thud but doesn't break—it's strong glass, foreign made. I get up and go to the kitchen, turn on the tap, don't bother to look for a glass, just shove my face under the cold, trickling column of water—my head half in the sink, my neck tilted painfully—and drink greedily, then stand up and wipe my mouth with the back of my hand. It leaves two streaks of lipstick across my cheek.

"Good God those are salty," I say to Jare. He looks at me and I can see the edge of his mouth twitch. Then he laughs himself almost into a knot.

"I'm—I'm sorry . . . I know there's nothing funny about it, but . . . if somebody came in here . . . it would sure make them wonder."

Now that I've had my fix, poor and basic as it is, a trace of a smile tries to find its way to my lips. I stroll to the full-length mirror with a purposely loose stride. Jare's right. I look like a living caricature. Tears and jalapeño juice have smeared my mascara down my cheeks; my hair, carefully curled in the morning, hangs in two wet hanks on either side of my face; and the remains of my lipstick spread around my mouth look like some kind of awful rash. My foundation has failed, too, and the ugly traces of the struggle at Kalevankangas cemetery show through on my temple and cheek.

Jare comes out of the alcove with the wet bedspread and jar. "Should we mop the floor?"

I wipe up the splashes of salt water. Jare stuffs the bedspread into the washing machine. I hate the color of the bedspread—it's garish and shows every spot—but the decor has to look right. I help Jare turn on the machine and point to the jar.

"What should we do with that?"

I look at the label. It looks like it came from Turkey. Jare turns on the tap and starts to fill the jar with warm water. I nod. I let the jar soak in the stream of water for a moment and then scratch off the label in pieces and carefully mix them into the compost.

I hand the clean jar to Jare. He gets the canvas shopping bag from the coat rack, puts the jar in the bag, and zips it closed. He slams the bag as hard as he can against the leg of the table. The glass cracks into pieces, the noise covering our speech.

"Do I know the guy you got that from?"

"I think it was before you came around. He's dead now."

"They're thinning out."

"That's why I gave that guy a shot yesterday. It's been such a long time since there's been any new blood."

"What if they catch him?"

"If he's still got the stuff and they recognize him as the same guy, there could be problems. Otherwise no. It was just an attempted assault. Nobody's going to waste society's resources on that kind of investigation."

Crunch. Crunch. Jare keeps knocking the bag against the table leg. "They wouldn't tell us for investigative reasons whether the attacker was caught, which is another way of saying that nobody's interested. There's nothing about it that points to any other illegal activity. To the police it's just a routine case. A stupid eloi in the wrong place at the wrong time, and luckily her boyfriend stepped in to rescue her."

I form the words "Health Authority" with my lips.

Jare shakes his head. "Someone just wanted to have his cake and eat it, too."

There's no more crunching noise coming from the bag, just the tinkle of splinters of glass, but Jare keeps hammering it furiously against the wood, grunting with each blow.

It's actually almost a miracle that this situation has never come up before. I know the screws are getting tighter all the time. It was inevitable somebody would eventually start playing dirty and sell the same stuff over and over, because there's not enough of it to sell.

The black water in the Cellar sloshes and rises a millimeter higher again, licking at the threshold in the dark back of my mind. I sit down—almost fall—onto the flowered cushion of a kitchen chair.

"We might be in a tight spot."

Part of the score was supposed to be for Jare. He was supposed to get a lot of money for it. Part of it was for me. For my own use.

Jare nods. He spreads a copy of *State News* on the table and pours cold, shining grains of glass out of the bag in a pile, then wraps the paper around it in a tight packet.

MODERN DICTIONARY ENTRY

eloi — A popular unofficial vernacular word, first entering the language in the 1940s, for what is now properly called a *femiwoman*. Refers to the sub-race of females who are active on the reproductive market and are distinguished by their dedication to the overall advancement of the male sex. The word has its roots in the works of *H. G. Wells*, an author who predicted that humanity would be evolutionarily divided into distinct sub-races, some dedicated to serving the social structure and others meant to enjoy those services. *Plural:* elois. *Examples:* "A typical eloi has light hair and a round head." "Elois can legally reproduce."

Manna,

I remember.

My sister of a different race. My fair-haired sister. My sweet-natured sister.

Round head covered in platinum curls, cute little turned-up nose, narrow shoulders, full breasts, curving waist. Tush like a peach.

When we were children we played children's games. "Aa," I said, when the block had a letter for that sound on it. "Aa-aa," you said, rocking the block in your arms, lifting it gently to your breast.

I plucked the comb like an instrument; you drew it through your hair with flirty strokes. I painted a sunset with red watercolors; you smeared vermilion on your lips. I put the pail on my head as a helmet; you took it from me to make a play salad in. For me a pen was a conductor's baton; you used it to poke a disobedient doll and then blew on the spot to make the pain go away.

Oh, my sweet, gentle sister. Your heart was made of chocolate, you hands were full of comfort, your brain was full of pink fluff.

Do you remember our games?

"I'm the princess."

"I'm the shepherd girl."

"The prince comes and proposes to the princess."

"The shepherd girl puts on a disguise and carves a sword for herself out of stone. She tames a wolf and rides it into battle and conquers the kingdom and . . ."

Then you burst into tears.

"I'm afraid of wolves."

"There isn't any wolf. Not really. It's just a story I made up."

"Good. I'm the princess."

"You were already the princess."

"Now the princess is going to the ball and she is the most beautiful one of all. And everyone wants to marry her."

"Didn't the prince already propose?"

"Another prince comes, and he's handsomer and richer."

"The shepherd girl comes to the ball with her stone sword in her hand. And she challenges the prince to a battle for the kingdom!"

"I don't like your sword."

"It's my turn to make it up."

"I don't want to have a sword. It's not real. It's just a story you made up."

"Your prince isn't real, either."

"Grandma Aulikki. Vanna's teasing me!"

You ran sniffling to your grandmother's arms, and Aulikki looked at me over your flaxen hair, and she smelled angry and sad at the same time. She comforted you, my sweet sister, stroked your hair, hugged you, kissed you, let you go, and gave me a pointed look. I knew what that look meant. It wasn't your fault that we were different.

You came back to me and the smile returned to your face, and it made me want to be the handsome prince and bring a jeweled gown to the princess as a present.

We played and we played and we danced a wedding waltz. You were the princess and I was the prince, and the evening sun came through the window and lit up your hair as if it were made of golden fire.

I miss you so much.

Vanna (Vera)

VANNA/VERA

October 2016

The need for a fix is gnawing at my insides like a ferret. The door to the Cellar is open all the time, ready to swallow me up in its maw. After the incident at the cemetery the flow of the stuff has practically dried up completely.

We've heard about a lot of arrests. Even shots being fired.

Jare finds something every now and then—a jar of sambal oelek or some vindaloo paste—but all the real stuff is off-limits. You can't open the jars—they have to be sold whole; you can't take a cut for yourself.

It won't kill me.

But the Cellar's sucking blackness is seeping out, so greedy that I can hear its rustling, night-colored breath.

The Cellar was created by an explosion.

A blazing hot, violent nuclear charge that instantaneously melted a chamber in the gray matter of my head. It left a smooth-walled hollow, a ghostly, echoing cave with a darkness deeper than the space between the stars.

The darkness of the Cellar lives because it gets its strength from death. The Cellar is where my sister's negation lives, wrapped in a swirl of ink and pitch and coal and soot and the stifling scent of earth.

The door to the Cellar is in the back of my head.

Sometimes the door to the Cellar is made of solid steel with clunking metal bolts and rusty, creaking hinges—heavy. Sometimes it's made of rotten wood, sometimes gauze that flutters in the wind. Sometimes there's no door at all, and the ice-cold wind blows out of it.

That wind brings with it a fist, wet with black fog, a crushing grip that clenches around my mind like the hand of a sadistic child, a cruel child who wants to hear the tortured squeak of a rubber toy when it's squeezed again and again.

At the bottom of the Cellar, dark, ominous water splashes. It seeps out of openings the size of molecules through walls sealed with nuclear fire. I can bear the black wind, the merciless mist, but when the deep water starts to lap at the threshold of the Cellar and threatens to flood the rooms in my head, I know how close I am to drowning. The water's pitch-black surface shining like molten metal rises, and soon a thin, horrible snake of liquid will trickle over the threshold.

I have only one way, one bag of sand to stave off the flood, one method of trying to shove that steel door closed, to slap temporary planks on the rotting wood.

> *Teach me, chile, and I shall Learn.*
> *Take me, chile, and I shall Escape.*
> *Focus my eyes, chile, and I shall See.*
> *Consume more chiles.*
> *I feel no pain, for the chile is my teacher.*
> *I feel no pain, for the chile takes me beyond myself.*
> *I feel no pain, for the chile gives me sight.*

Dear sister!

Just today I felt a vast longing for you.

I'm sure you have no mental image of Spain, because you were so little then. I don't remember much, either, but I do remember that one day our mother and father didn't come home anymore, and everything was confusion and commotion and sadness. A drunken truck driver was driving too fast at an intersection and crushed our parents' car. Things like that can happen only in hedonistic countries. Because we didn't have any relatives in Spain, we were sent to Finland. I was four years old then. You were just a sweet little two-year-old.

I remember how you shrank from Neulapää on that first day, the new smells and strange furniture, the wrong kind of light, the trees in the yard that were too big. You were forlorn and teary-eyed and I tried to comfort you, even though I was worn out from homesickness and the hard journey and everything that was scary and new. It wasn't a simple thing to move from a suburb of Madrid to a little farm in the middle of the Finnish woods.

Aulikki was probably nearly seventy then. She was our only close relative. We had almost no relatives because our father had been an illegitimate child. Aulikki had never married. Maybe

27

our father's father was a minus man or some other shady type. That would explain a lot. I never dared to ask Aulikki about it.

Many other things about Aulikki dawned on me only later. They probably never occurred to you. Aulikki was sent to Sweden as a war refugee in the 1940s, and that was why she was away from Finland when the final sex decree was made law. Her biological parents both became seriously ill when she was about twenty. Her father had kidney disease, her mother cancer. They were both about to die, because the Health Authority said that their illness came from unwholesome, wrong ways of living, so they weren't allowed any treatment by the state. They didn't have any money for a private doctor, and Aulikki returned to Finland in 1954 to help them. I don't understand why she came back. They were both going to die anyway.

But she did come back. She had Swedish citizenship in addition to her Finnish citizenship, so when she decided to stay and take care of Neulapää, she was living under a strange sort of diplomatic immunity that reserved her full citizenship rights. She was even allowed to act as an employer. That's why she was able to hire a young masco graduate from the agricultural school every summer.

Aulikki harvested enough from the vegetable garden to keep her own cellar full and also sell potatoes and other vegetables to a local farmer, who in turn sold them, along with his own berries and apples, at the Tammela Market. We got by as well as we could, and Aulikki got some state child-care money and did sewing in the winter for extra income.

The strongest of all my early Neulapää memories is from when we first got there. We had already started to get used to our new home, to the too-bright nights and the strange sounds of nature. We were playing in the yard when Aulikki came and led us over to the storage shed, and as we got near it she put her finger to her lips. She gestured for us to crouch down and peek under the shed. How delighted we were when we saw a pair of bright, startled eyes staring back at us. A stray cat had had kittens under the shed. Aulikki told us that she'd seen the homeless cat wandering around the edges of the property and thought that it would be good to keep the voles in check, but she hadn't realized it was going to have kittens. The mother cat had managed to keep the litter a secret, but now the kittens were opening their eyes and learning to walk, and Aulikki had found them when she heard a scratching sound and a faint mewing from under the building. The mother cat was away, probably out hunting. One of the kittens stumbled toward us, curious. Its downy fur and clumsy walk, its trembling little tail stuck straight up like an antenna, and its round little head with its almost too-big ears and eyes—its whole soft and delicate and yet intensely energetic presence—flooded me with a deep, sweet anguish.

Later when I looked at you or remembered you, I would feel a splash of that same feeling.

Aulikki promised that we could keep one of the kittens, but just a couple of days after we found them, the litter and the mother cat disappeared. Aulikki said the mother must have become nervous after the nest was discovered and moved the kittens someplace else.

Of course when I got a little older I understood that there were also a lot of foxes in the woods at Neulapää.

Another very powerful early memory is from almost right after we got to Finland, when we had to have our final gender specified. I was already very late because they didn't have rules like that in Spain, of course. The Health Authority sent two child welfare workers to test us.

First they examined our appearance. Round heads, small noses, large eyes, light hair—it all seemed clear. They took photos of us. Then they started the tests.

They showed us pairs of pictures. There would be a tractor and a baby, or an airplane and a flower, or a hammer and a kettle, and we were supposed to choose which picture we liked better. I remember very well how you grabbed the picture of the baby and made your voice even more soft and childish than it really was. "Ooh, ooh, baby, ooh," you babbled. You glanced at me now and then, and I chose the baby, too, to encourage you. "Pretty baby, nice baby," I cooed, more to you than to the social worker. I thought the tests must be to find out if we were good sisters. Maybe something bad would happen if we were too different, if we didn't agree. So I chose some pictures even before you did, the ones I thought you would like better. I didn't know at the time how pivotal this would be.

Then the social workers took some toys out of a big suitcase. There was a wooden fire truck painted shiny red that I loved at first sight. There was a doll the size of a real baby dressed in pink. There was a stuffed cat, and they put a tin train engine down next to it. There were blocks with letters and numbers on them and sparkly stickers with pictures of hearts and smiling wedding couples. There was a wonderful wooden wrench and a pretty little ladle decorated with roses. A conductor's hat and a frilly apron. Little bright-colored rectangles that you could connect by pressing them together—the social worker showed us how to do it. You could build anything you wanted out of them, castles and cranes and airplanes.

They told us to choose the toys we liked. You immediately toddled over and hugged the cat—I'm sure your memory of the fluffy, adorable creature toddling out from under the shed was still quite fresh—and then you ran over with the cat in your pudgy little hand and pushed it into the arms of the baby doll and said happily that the baby liked the kitty. I was entranced with the fire truck, and I couldn't help running over to it first and picking it up to look at it. Then I noticed the social workers' response: as if a whiff of tar or smoke had drifted in on the air, like a distant forest fire somewhere off in the woods.

Something wasn't right.

I let go of the fire truck and it fell to the floor with a thud. I even kicked it a little, as if I'd just realized that, in spite of its bright color, it was a cold, dull thing. The smoky smell cleared up immediately and started to change into something more like the smell of a warming sauna, pine soap and dried birch whisks. I noticed that the nice smell they were exuding grew stronger and lingered when I rejected the tools and trucks and put on the apron and picked up the ladle. I built a circle of letter blocks and threw the little plastic bricks in the middle and mixed them around with the ladle and said I was making oatmeal. I scooped up a ladleful of bricks and offered them to the doll you were holding and told her to be good and eat her porridge.

I saw how one social worker looked at the other one and there was a hint of metal in the air. One of them gathered up all the dolls and stuffed toys—you protested so loudly!—and left the fire truck and the wooden wrench and the bricks and the conductor's hat.

You immediately knew what to do. You were a little copycat, and you put the bricks in the conductor's hat with your chubby hands and started mixing them with the wrench. I was left with the fire truck. It had a folding ladder and real wheels that rolled. I picked it up again.

Grandma Aulikki took a little breath and I could smell something faint, sharp like lemon juice. The social workers' eyes were cold, waiting.

Then I knew what to do.

I pulled the fire truck to my breast and rocked it. I said, "Aa-aa."

I saw the looks on the social workers' faces and my grandmother's face, and there were two completely different kinds of smells in the air: a sweet, almost overripe smell around the social workers, and a smell from my grandmother like the freshness of laundry dried in the sun.

That was the first time I heard someone use the word "femiwoman." The other social worker used the word "eloi," but they were both talking about us.

The social workers didn't give us another glance as they wrote on their papers. They told Aulikki that we would need new names, and that for simplicity's sake they would use the same first letters. I'm sure you don't even remember that you were once Mira and I was Vera. After that we were Manna and Vanna.

The new smell around our grandmother got stronger, like the cleaning fluid you use to scrub the bathroom, but she nodded and smiled and murmured her agreement that the names suited us perfectly.

The social workers gathered up the toys and I was tense, wondering if they would remember the little tin train engine, which had rolled out of sight under the table. They did, and I was terribly disappointed, so disappointed that I was afraid they would notice the dark, earthy smell coming from me.

After that Aulikki called us Vanna and Manna. That same day I named your dolls Vera and Mira, to at least keep our real names that way.

Aulikki didn't care in the least about how she was supposed to raise elois, but I realized that only much later. When I turned seven and was supposed to go to school, she asked for permission to homeschool me. It was a long way from Neulapää to the nearest school, she didn't have a car, and the state school transport would have been an extra expense to society because there were no other houses in the area with school-age children. So she had no trouble getting permission.

Just before the education inspectors came to Neulapää, Aulikki asked me to change out of my overalls and sweater into a dress and patent-leather shoes. She took my erector set and books and wooden train set into the shed and hid them behind the firewood. I was old enough by then that she didn't hide the seriousness of the situation. She told me to sit at the kitchen table and looked me in the eye.

I remember every word of that conversation. "Vanna, there's something I have to ask you to do. I want you to not tell the nice men that you know how to read and count. When they come here I want you to play house with Manna and be polite and smile and be very good and agreeable. Copy everything Manna does."

"Why?"

She started to laugh. The pear smell of amusement mixed with the lemon of worry. "Never, ever ask 'why' when they're around. You see, those men don't like little girls who are too smart and curious. Remember the story about the feisty shepherd girl who was really a princess under her ragged clothes?"

"I remember."

"Now think the other way around. Pretend that you're a clever shepherd girl, and you're just dressed up in pretty clothes, and you're trying to make everybody believe that you're a spoiled, empty-headed little princess. So no one guesses that under your

33

clothes you're a brave shepherd girl who climbs trees and chases away wolves with your staff."

A fun, challenging game. I nodded enthusiastically.

"I know you can do it, sweetheart. Even the little girl in the story must have found it very useful to know how to be a fancy princess sometimes and a clever shepherd girl at other times. She had to be the most capable shepherd of all when she was with the shepherds, and the kind of princess who demanded ten mattresses to sleep on a pea when she was in a palace."

The inspectors found two little flaxen-haired, pink-swathed darlings. They inspected our toy box with a single glance, watched for a little while as we played house. I was the mother and you were the child and the baby doll was the other child and the teddy bear was another and the sofa cushion was the daddy, who went to the sofa to go to work. The inspectors nodded with satisfaction and smelled as sweet as jelly. They gave Aulikki a thick stack of booklets and notebooks with instructions for early eloi education.

When they had left, Aulikki put the notebooks and booklets aside and took a key out of her pocket. She went to the wide cabinet with the glass cupboard on top where she kept the good china. She unlocked the lower doors of the cabinet. All the books were kept there, out of sight. She gave me permission to touch the books again and read them. But all the toys I liked best had to be kept in the barn loft from then on, and I could play with them only where you couldn't see me.

It surprised me for a moment, but then I understood. "If Manna accidentally tells someone then everyone will know that I'm a shepherd in princess's clothing."

A smile spread over my grandmother's face and her eyes shone.
"Vanna, you might be the smartest little girl in Finland. And I mean that literally."

Her tears smelled like a warming sauna.

I didn't want to keep secrets from you. I didn't want to treat anyone wrong. But I trusted that Aulikki knew best.

I miss you so much.

Your sister,
Vanna (Vera)

MODERN DICTIONARY ENTRY

morlock — A popular unofficial vernacular word, first entering the language in the 1940s, for what is now properly called a *neuterwoman*. Refers to the sub-race of females who, owing to physical limitations (infertility, etc.), are excluded from the mating market. The word has its roots in the works of *H. G. Wells*, an author who predicted that humanity would be evolutionarily divided into distinct sub-races, some dedicated to serving the social structure and others meant to enjoy those services. The morlocks are a disposable segment of society whose use is limited mainly to serving as a reserve labor force for routine tasks.

Dear sister!

Do you remember the tests? There were two of them each year at the little school in Kaanaa.

We sat side by side at shiny, varnished desks with slanted tops that opened on hinges. The pupils who attended regularly could keep their pencils and notebooks inside.

The tests were exciting and fun. I got to play princess. I wrote in poor penmanship and purposely forgot my spelling and pretended not to understand the questions. We wrote shopping lists and read them aloud, said the names of plants and mushrooms and fish on classroom charts, remembered what temperature to use to wash wool or cotton. We calculated how to alter a recipe for four to feed six. I'd heard that some elois never learned to read, but they could listen to their recipes on recordings. You were a good learner. You were smart for an eloi. I always thought of those delicate, lively little kittens as I watched you toil over your notebook, writing down the numbers, and sometimes you erased them so many times that you almost wore through the paper. Sometimes I peeked at your paper and copied your mistakes.

The eloi class had a room where we practiced making beds and washing windows. We boiled potatoes, made gravy, mixed bread dough, scrubbed grass stains out of fabric. We knew how to darn a

37

sock and sew on a button. I was older, so I learned to iron a man's shirt, too. It wasn't a skill I particularly needed at Neulapää, but you had to show you could do it to pass the class. The higher levels of education like child care weren't taught until we were at the eloi college, the National Institute of Home Economics.

We had both learned the basics of planting, watering, thinning, and weeding the garden; hilling and harvesting potatoes; staking pea vines; and drying onions from Aulikki. Do you remember how little you liked those things? Sometimes when you had to put your hands in the dirt you would hesitate, as if there were dangerous things that could bite under the ground.

I, on the other hand, enjoyed many of the garden chores, like grafting the apple trees. It was magical to me that one tree could grow several kinds of apples if you wanted it to.

But school and chores didn't take up all our time. When Aulikki didn't need our help in the kitchen or the garden and was sure we knew everything that would be asked on the test, we could use our time as we wished. Do you remember the little porcelain tea set with roses and lilies of the valley on the saucers? You never tired of setting out meals for your dolls on those plates. In the winter we slid down the little hill on our sleds and I built a lantern out of snowballs and Aulikki put a candle inside it in the evening.

I remember so clearly one fall evening when we were sitting next to each other on the sofa in the living room. Aulikki was sitting in her favorite chair listening to music. She had a small collection of records, mostly classical music and jazz records she'd brought from Sweden. She didn't care for the state music.

I was ten. You had just turned eight in August. Aulikki was listening to Mozart's Requiem.

I had a heavy encyclopedia in my hands.

The Concise Encyclopedia *was my favorite thing to read, although the books my grandfather had left at Neulapää included plenty of books on individual subjects as well. I was most interested in biology and botany, but I also read about physics, geography, and world history. I muddled through the basics of French and English for fun and learned the table of elements by heart. Aulikki had brought a collection of European and American literature with her to Neulapää, and the worlds it described were as strange to me as the alien cultures in my father's old science fiction novels.*

I was sitting there with volume M through P of the Concise Encyclopedia *in my lap. The pounding, stirring music had awakened a desire in me to know more about Mozart.*

You were holding a copy of Femigirl *magazine.*

It was sent to all elois' homes when they turned six. It had romantic stories, written in the simplest sentences, about elois competing for the same masco, and one girl would always get him in the end through feminine wiles. There were pictures of elegant weddings and instructions on ladylike behavior and proper dress. Your lips moved when you read, painfully, slowly making your way through the stories, but you waded through every issue again and again.

I understood for the first time—sharply, painfully—the depth of the difference between us.

I couldn't help noticing that for a long time your favorite game was wedding.

I wasn't the prince or the knight in our games anymore; I was the groom. You would don a pillowcase veil and clutch a crumpled bouquet of dandelions and cow parsley, but the light in your eyes showed how real it all was to you. You didn't see a sister beside you; you saw a future where you would be supported and safe, sheltered by undying love.

I'm sorry I couldn't give that to you.

Your sister,
Vanna (Vera)

"LITTLE REDIANNA"

Eloi Girls' Best-Loved Stories
National Publishing (1951)

Once upon a time there was a very pretty, very good little girl who was always obedient and kind to everyone. She liked pretty clothes, and she especially liked the color red. That's why everyone called her Little Redianna.

One day Little Redianna's mother asked her to bring some medicine to her grandmother, who was sick. So Little Redianna put the medicine into her basket and set off for her grandmother's house. On the way there she met a wolf. The wolf told Little Redianna that she was the prettiest girl he had ever seen. He said he wanted her to be his wife.

Little Redianna told the wolf she couldn't marry him because she liked her grandmother very much and she wanted to bring her some medicine. Then she continued on her way. But the wolf found a quicker way to the house, and when he got there he ate her grandmother up. Then he put on her grandmother's nightgown and lay down in the bed to wait for Little Redianna.

When Little Redianna arrived at her grandmother's house with the medicine, she noticed that her grandmother looked strange.

"Grandmother, what big eyes you have," Little Redianna said.

"The better to see you with, my dear," said the wolf.

"Grandmother, what big ears you have," Little Redianna said.

"The better to hear you with, my dear," said the wolf.

"Grandmother, what big teeth you have," Little Redianna said.

"The better to gobble you up and make you a part of myself and keep you as my own for the rest of my life," said the wolf.

Then the wolf leaped out of the bed and threw off his wolf's skin, and Little Redianna saw that he wasn't a wolf at all but a handsome prince.

"Because you didn't obey me and agree to be my wife, and decided to bring medicine to your grandmother instead, I'm not going to marry you," said the handsome prince, and he left Little Redianna at her grandmother's house, and she never, ever got married.

The End

Dear Manna,

It was inevitable that we would grow out of our games.

You won't remember this because you weren't there. I was twelve and I was working in the garden on a hot day, wearing a bikini. I noticed Aulikki glancing now and then at my bikini bottoms and it was obvious that there was something she wanted to say.

"Well, what is it?" I finally asked.

"It's, um . . . that."

I looked down at my crotch. Aulikki pointed at the little curls of blond pubic hair peeking out of my bikini. I thought it was interesting that it was curly when the hair on my head was naturally straight.

"You have to shave," Aulikki said.

"Is there something wrong with hair?" I asked.

I had seen Aulikki in the sauna, and she didn't shave her own body hair. Aulikki looked uncomfortable and fumbled for words. She said we had to be careful in case someone dropped by on a hot day and noticed it.

At first I didn't understand, and then I did and rolled my eyes. It was another one of those eloi things that kept popping up more and more every year. This new rule about hair was inconsistent, though. I was supposed to let the hair on my head grow long so no one would mistake me for a morlock. And I was supposed to wear a bikini in the summer because elois liked to wear bikinis in the summer. So if the hair on my head was so sacred, why should the hair farther down have to be kept out of sight, particularly when I was supposed to wear clothes that were obviously going to show it?

Then Aulikki suggested I shave my armpits as well, and I asked if I should shave off my eyebrows, too. I meant it as a joke, but Aulikki said that it might be a good idea to start plucking them now, and I should keep my leg hair under control, too.

I marched inside to do some research. According to one book, a person's individual smell was an important factor in mating. The hair in the armpits and on the groin traps special odors that exude their scent to those close by. This made shaving seem even more stupid than I'd thought. Why purposely destroy a physical characteristic specifically linked to the survival of the species?

Judging by the pictures and the mascos I'd seen, they weren't required to trim anything except their beards and the hair on their heads, and even that rule seemed to be loosely interpreted.

Then it said that hair on the groin and armpits was a visible sign of sexual maturity. That in ancient human societies it may have helped to identify whether another individual was of mating age. If elois were required to shave off this identifying characteristic, did that mean that mascos actually wanted to mate with children?

Another book said that armpit and pubic hair also had a health function. It protected the extremities from chafing during movement, provided cushioning, and promoted air circulation.

But I was supposed to shave it off.

There were many, many more bizarre aspects to the world than I could have imagined. I realized I'd been stupid. It wasn't enough anymore to be a brave shepherd girl inside. My body was betraying me, turning me into a princess against my will.

We both were going to become narrow-waisted, big-breasted, long-legged elois, but you were the only one who approached the change with curiosity and excitement. You started to talk more and more about entering the mating market and the debutante ball you would have when you turned fourteen.

I was so jealous of you, Manna. You grew and developed such poise, like a young tree, but I was afraid and filled with angst about the unknown life ahead of me.

Luckily, Aulikki saw that.

Aulikki was already nearly eighty when I reached the age of coming out. Because of her age and lack of resources, she got permission to put off my debut for two years so the two of us could come on the market at the same time. That meant I could spend two more precious years at Neulapää.

I never told you how important it's been to my whole life to have a sister like you. I would never have learned how to behave, how to talk to strangers, if I didn't have you.

With eternal gratitude, your sister,
Vanna (Vera)

MODERN DICTIONARY ENTRY

masco — A popular unofficial vernacular word for the majority of males. Used to distinguish these men from so-called *minus men*, a minority of men who, because of their limitations (such as chronic illness or serious physical deficiencies), are designated as outside the mating market.

Dear Manna,

Sometimes, for no reason, just to torture myself, I wonder when it was that things took a wrong turn. If I could turn back time, of course, our parents would never have died. But if I stick to things that I might have been able to influence, I would go back to the spring of 2011.

I had reached the age of coming out, but my debut had been postponed, so there shouldn't have been anything special about that year. The snow had melted; it was time to do the spring sowing, and a new farmhand had to be hired—an April like any other.

Aulikki had asked us to get out some clean sheets for the bed in the barn. Remember how we went out to pick pussy willows from the side of the brook and put them in a vase on the little bedside table? That was your idea. It was exciting that we were going to have a stranger at the house again, and you and I were speculating about what kind of person the new farmhand would be. Would he be grumbly and untalkative, or would he make jokes all the time? Would he be athletic, always doing chin-ups on the birch tree in the yard, or studious, shutting himself up in his room with his textbooks after his day's work was done? Would he like the food we made for him? Would he be as thoughtful as one farmhand we'd had, who would go fishing on his time off and bring Aulikki his catch to add to dinner?

The new hand was seventeen and was studying food science. Aulikki showed him around Neulapää. He would be sleeping in the barn, washing up in the sauna, and eating his meals in the kitchen. Aulikki introduced us, too. We curtsied and said our names. He asked which one of us had put the pussy willows in his room. You giggled and blushed when I told him it was your idea.

There was always a lot of work to do at Neulapää in spring and early summer. So we helped Aulikki as well as we could. She had to save her strength for instructing and supervising the farmhand; she couldn't manage heavy physical labor anymore. Since I was already fourteen I took responsibility for the meals. Your cooking skills still needed a lot of work then, but you helped me peel the vegetables and you knew how to poke the potatoes to see if they were done and set the table and carry the food out. The farmhand couldn't come into the house except at mealtimes, and even then he could come only into the kitchen, because you and I weren't officially of mating age and any fraternizing that could be associated with mating was not allowed.

But a smell like fresh-cut grass started to float around you nevertheless, growing stronger whenever you saw the farmhand. Your cheeks would flush, and you read your Femigirl magazine stories more and more greedily.

I mentioned this to Aulikki. She sighed and said that every eloi starts practicing falling in love at some point before she reaches mating age, and that you were obviously directing these feelings at the farmhand. She also said—rather cruelly, I thought—that it was good that your feelings weren't returned because every eloi

48

has to start competing for mascos eventually, and it's better that she have some experience with disappointment from the beginning. But maybe it would be best if you didn't help with serving the meals anymore.

You cried and threw a tantrum at that, but Aulikki wouldn't budge.

Do you remember that day?

I brought the farmhand dinner by myself. He didn't seem to notice that anything was different. He ate, thanked me, and left. I washed the dishes and went to my room. When I got to the doorway, I stopped.

On the floor was one of my favorite books, Native Plants of the Nordic Countries. *A wonderful picture book. It had been cut up with scissors. I burst into tears. My library was so small and pitiful; I couldn't bear to lose even one of my books. I'd read through them all many times, but they still gave me a lot of happiness, and there wasn't really any way to get anything new to read about subjects that interested me. Aulikki could order books by mail about plant care or sewing, of course—those were things appropriate to her life—but it would have been difficult to explain a sudden interest in natural science or history without arousing suspicion. She was a full citizen, so it wasn't officially forbidden, but she thought you could never be too careful.*

I knew, of course, that you were the one who'd cut up my book. But I couldn't understand why. I went to your room. You weren't there, but there were scraps of paper and scissors and pages of the book on your desk. Next to them was a sheet of paper with a clumsy drawing of a bride and groom. The bouquet in the bride's hands was a clump of plants cut from the book and glued to the paper. You'd chosen wild roses, twinflowers, lilies of the valley, and several other lovely spring flowers. Under

49

the bride you'd written "Manna" and underneath the groom it said "Jare."

I left your room. Maybe you remember that I never mentioned that book, or your picture. I didn't blame you. I understand why you did it.

Sometimes I wish I could find you just so Jare could tell you what really happened. Maybe you would believe him.

I hope you aren't really mad at me.

Missing you, your sister,
Vanna (Vera)

JARE REMEMBERS

July 2011

I cut my hand making stakes for the peas. The cut wasn't that deep and I hoped it wasn't serious, but it bled like hell, dripping on my clothes and onto the ground. I couldn't keep working until I'd put a bandage on it. I didn't have a first aid kit, just some bath things in the sauna. I took off my shirt, found a clean spot on it and wrapped it around my hand to stop the bleeding, then ran over to the main house. I knocked on the living room door, hoping the old woman would be there—and be awake, since she was often napping. There was no answer, so I opened the door a crack and peeked into the room. I grimaced; the blood was already soaking through the shirt. I had to find a bathroom and see if there was something I could use there, maybe a towel I could borrow to use as a bandage—it was an emergency, after all. I pushed open the first door I came to.

The older eloi, Vanna, was sitting in the room alone. It seemed to be her room. There was a bed and a young eloi's clothes—but also a pile of books on the table and on a small shelf on the wall. Vanna looked up and saw me and leaped to her feet, a book falling from her hand. Seeing any kind of book in an eloi's hands was unusual, but this book was titled *Astronomy and the World Today*. She quickly tried to kick it under the chair where I couldn't see it.

An eloi might flip through a book for fun, of course, especially if it has pretty pictures in it. But that didn't seem to be the case here, and the strange part was that she was so afraid that I would see what she was reading. If she had just been innocently looking at the book out of curiosity she wouldn't have panicked.

And then her whole demeanor changed. Her sharp gaze dropped and turned soft and hazy, and she thrust out her breasts, cocked her hips, raised her hand to her chin as if she were embarrassed, her lower lip trying for a sweet little droop. She batted her thick eyelashes. "Oh! You can't come in here. I'll get my grandmother," she cooed.

Then she noticed the bloody shirt wrapped around my hand and suddenly her eloi mannerisms disappeared again. Her eyes brightened, her posture straightened, the submissive simper went out of her voice. "Yikes. We've gotta do something about that." She came to the door, took hold of my arm and led me through the living room to the other side of the house. We went through a small passage to the bathroom. She turned on the light, told me to sit on the toilet, and held my hand in the air as she rummaged in the medicine cabinet. She found a bottle of disinfectant and a bag of cotton balls, told me to unwrap the shirt from the cut, and quickly washed the wound. She got out gauze and a roll of bandage tape, deftly wrapped my hand, and secured the bandage with a few strips of the tape. "I'm sure it won't bleed for very long. Do you think you can change the bandage every day if I give you these, or would you rather come to the house and have one of us help you?"

I didn't answer.

Her eyelashes started to flutter again, her lower lip thrust out.

I touched her hand. "Stop that."

She pulled her hand away. "Now, now, young man," she cooed, looking up at me with her head cocked to one side. "Just because I was a good girl and fixed up your boo-boo doesn't mean you can start getting fresh."

I touched her hand again briefly to make her look at me. "It's quite obvious you're not an eloi, or at least not an ordinary eloi, even if you do look like one. But if you want to keep it secret that you're a . . ."

"Morlock." Her voice had lost all its flirty chirpiness. The word fell between us cold as a stone.

"Right. I won't tell anyone. It's none of my business. Or anybody else's business. What would I gain from it? You and your family haven't done anything to me."

Vanna bit her lower lip.

"I wonder what Aulikki has to say about it."

The next moment we were standing in front of the old woman, who had just awakened from her nap. Vanna explained in a few quick sentences what had happened.

I watched their conversation with a fearful amazement. It was like hearing two parrots that I'd thought could only repeat the phrases their master taught them suddenly start exchanging observations on the theory of relativity.

"Should we kill him?" Vanna asked, in the same tone she might have used to discuss changing the drapes.

When the old woman pursed her lips, apparently giving this idea serious consideration, I turned cold. "Hmm. I don't know. What do you think?" she said, and looked me straight in the eye, and it was crystal clear to me that even though I was talking to an old woman and a half-grown . . . something . . . I had reason to fear. They had a lot to lose, and the two of them allied was chilling.

I spread my arms. "I have no way to prove I won't turn you in, but if I did I would lose a good summer job reference. The reward for reporting gender fraud wouldn't be enough to make up for that."

They looked at each other, the understanding flying like sparks between them.

"It's true that he wouldn't gain anything by it," Aulikki said. I was admiring her more every moment, the way she didn't seem to take any notice of the fact that the topic of discussion was standing half a meter away, shifting from foot to foot. "And if he tried, you're so good at acting like an eloi that he'd be a laughingstock and get a fine for wasting the authorities' time. We could claim that he had a crush on you and made the story up when he couldn't get anywhere with you."

Vanna nodded. "On the other hand, what if he keeps it a secret and I get caught later on? Will he get in trouble? Will they think he was in on it?"

"No, not if he claims he didn't notice anything unusual about you."

As I watched and listened to their conversation, I realized for the first time what it's like to have people talking about you, talking over you, past you. Deciding your fate, chattering about this and that—could he be useful somehow or should we dispose of him?

I thought through my options. Should I run away? But how? On the old girl's-style bike in the yard? And where was I supposed to go?

Maybe the best tactic was to attack. The best defense is a good offense.

No. There were no neighbors close by, they had me out-numbered, and after what I'd seen that day I wouldn't have been surprised if the old woman had a pistol under her mattress. If I suddenly vanished, nobody would suspect an elderly woman and two sweet little elois.

The best thing to do was to not get cocky, and to watch my cards.

"Forgive me for prying, but how is this even possible?"

"I was born this way. Genetic lottery. Like a family where the great-grandfather was white but his descendants reproduced only with black people. Everyone in the family will have African characteristics, but then out of the blue a baby with rosy cheeks and freckles pops into the world." Vanna dropped this terminology like an educated masco.

"Morlocks have such a small, dark corner reserved for them in this world that an eloi's life—even though it's limited and regulated, too—is positively carefree by comparison," Aulikki said.

"I don't think Jare wants to mess up our lives," Vanna said. I could have hugged her when she said that.

Aulikki looked at me for a change.

I nodded. I swallowed. I nodded again.

Aulikki smiled, but her eyes showed only flinty calculation. "Let's work on the assumption that something good could come of this."

Her expression changed. She was looking at me now, seeing me as a person, an individual, not just weighing me like a chunk of meat. There was even amusement in her eyes.

"Jare, have you ever thought you might like to order a few books to read here over the summer? Just for your own edification and education?"

At first I was perplexed. Then Vanna laughed out loud and slapped her grandmother on the shoulder. They looked at each other and slapped their thighs.

Then I understood.

GENDER FRAUD IN FINNISH LAW

1. § Any person who deliberately misleads state authorities with regard to officially defined sexes by altering an inborn neuterwoman's appearance to resemble that of a femiwoman, whether through surgery or other cosmetic means, shall be charged with aggravated gender fraud and making a mockery of the state. If the neuterwoman herself is guilty of the abovementioned activities, both subject and perpetrator are legally responsible. Punishment for this offense for the subject of the fraud is a term of labor in state rehabilitation facilities and possible confiscation of family property. Punishment for the perpetrator who carries out such a crime is as outlined in applicable Criminal Code on Social Sabotage, § 220, subsection 6.

2. § Any person who deliberately misleads state authorities with regard to officially defined sexes by altering an inborn femiwoman's appearance to resemble that of a neuterwoman, whether through surgery or other cosmetic means, shall be charged with aggravated gender fraud and making a mockery of the state. If the femiwoman herself is guilty of the abovementioned activities, both subject and perpetrator are legally responsible. Punishment for

the perpetrator who carries out such a crime is as outlined in applicable Criminal Code on Social Sabotage, § 220, subsection 6. Should a femiwoman be found guilty of gender fraud there is no designated punishment, because of the rarity of the crime. Instead the subject shall be referred to a mental health facility.

Dear Manna,

Jare and I were co-conspirators , that's all. You understand that, don't you? Nothing more.

Although being discovered by Jare may have been an unavoidable accident, one that was exceedingly useful to me, it was also a problem. In your mind it gnawed at the bonds of our sisterhood. It never even occurred to me that anything could cause a break between us. To me you were always the sweet little sister I loved, and you always will be.

Because of our shared secret, Jare and I became closer than we had intended. It happened almost by accident. Although Jare continued to obey the rules—living in the barn, washing up in the sauna, eating in the kitchen—the packages of books sent to him every week were like little Christmases for me. Jare would pick the books up from the postman's truck and leave them on the porch of the house, and as soon as he and I had time, we would admire the books together. Some of them interested Jare, too, especially books on botany and biology, his own subjects. I noticed that every time we looked at the books together a scent that was new to me would hover faintly around him—something like lavender, and rosemary warmed by sunlight, with a tang like pine sap underneath.

Of course you noticed.

Of course you drew conclusions.

Of course you did, even though I tried to be careful. I was cool and neutral toward Jare whenever you were around, but in some things you were very perceptive. Your intelligence was almost entirely social intelligence, quickly recognizing mating rituals and the movements of other people's relationships, skillful at reading nonverbal communication. You added up the laughter and smiles, made note of the quick exchange of looks that hid secrets, observed the simultaneous absences.

I have those typical eloi abilities, too. I can pick up people's unconscious emotional signals, wishes, mental processes. I just do it in a different way from how you do. I might be better at it than you are, even though I'm not a real eloi—or maybe precisely because I'm not, because I can analyze and tabulate my observations, use those vague sensations to create a true sense.

You made careless, quick-tempered, overly general interpretations, followed a false trail. You built a romance between Jare and me.

That happened because in your logic there was nothing else but love, human relationships, and a future marriage. For you there was no such thing (why would there be? it would have been an impossible thought to almost anyone) as a friendship or spiritual connection between a masco and an eloi.

Your heart was broken for the first time.

When you looked at me there was a sharp stink of resentment floating around you.

My heart was scraped raw.

That was the first time. And how many times after that did I let you down?

I'm sorry.

Your sister,

Vanna (Vera)

LOVE STORY

Excerpt from *Femigirl*
National Publishing (1958)

"No, I could never consider Elanna as a spouse," Torsti said in a firm voice, pulling Nanna into his manly embrace. Nanna trembled in the tight hold of his strong arms. "You're much nicer and prettier. And Elanna is . . . well, she's careless of her freshness."

"No!" Nanna gasped. "Poor Elanna! I feel sorry for her. Every femiwoman should know how important freshness is."

"I think I fell in love with you the moment I noticed how wonderful you smelled, Nanna," Torsti said. He bent toward her and pressed his passionate, powerful lips on hers. Nanna shivered under the bliss of that kiss.

As they pulled away from each other for a moment, Torsti looked deep into Nanna's eyes. "Nanna, will you be my wife?"

"Gosh! Of course I will!" Nanna exclaimed, her voice trembling. "Oh, Torsti, I'm so happy! I have a feeling I have Fresh Scent to thank for this!"

Torsti smiled. "The most important thing is your sweet, humble nature—but I must admit that Fresh Scent may have had something to do with it!"

* NOTICE *
*The sweet smile of a real eloi
will bring a husband pride and joy.*

But to attract a handsome gent
you also need a nice Fresh Scent!

Be dainty-fresh when love is near
and a sweaty smell you need not fear.
Fresh Scent will make you clean and nice,
and at such an easy price!

So buy some Fresh Scent and don't tarry
if you ever wish to marry.

FRESH SCENT
THE FIRST CHOICE IN FEMI-FRESHNESS
Fresh Scent is a registered trademark of the State Cosmetics
Corporation. Available from all well-stocked chemists.

VANNA/VERA

October 2016

I shout and rage at Jare. It gives me a moment's relief from the adrenaline.

Then I collapse and cry, and the black water in the Cellar splashes over my chilled feet. My knees. My thighs. My stomach. My heart.

Especially my heart, because the water seeps in from every side and chills me to the core.

I shout and rage at Jare. *Why don't you do something? Why don't you help me? Why don't you act? Why isn't anything happening? You could at least do something!*

Even though I know that there's nothing he can do.

Manna. Manna. Manna.

If I could just *know* what happened to her!

Or if not, at least get a fix, from somewhere.

I shout and rage at Jare in sheer powerlessness.

I wish I could harness all my intelligence, all my cleverness, to find out what happened to Manna. Or to find some dope. But I live in a glass box.

The walls of the box are transparent, the world is almost within reach—I can almost touch it. The sun is shining in the sky, trees are swaying in the wind, the horizon glimmering in the distance, but when I try to take a step in any direction my head hits a glass wall. I can pound it, kick it, try to scream through it, but it doesn't budge, doesn't even tremble. It's there to protect you, the builder of the box says. You'll never be cold, never feel the wind, never wander out and get lost in the dangerous world. Plus you'll always be handy if I happen to need you.

And all I can do is press my nose and my hands against the smooth transparence until it hurts, all I can do is bang my fists against the immovable surface, tear my own nails out against the sheet of tepid ice, shout and rage and curse and shriek, cry and berate and rebuke the smothering hothouse I'm trapped in.

Some of the people who live in the glass box don't even notice it, can't even begin to imagine life outside it.

And then there is the Cellar, where just trying to keep my nose above the water takes so much energy that every little thing that comes along almost crushes me. If a spoon falls on the floor when I'm eating my oatmeal in the morning I burst into tears. If my mascara clumps again on my lower eyelashes I slam the brush on the counter. I'm jumpy and irritable; things my classmates do make me shudder, demands crowd in on me, and there's nothing I can do about it. I've been in eloi school for a year and I should be used to certain things, but they stretch my nerves to the breaking point.

Makeup, for one thing. Of course I understand that life is full of unpleasant things that you have to do again and again. You have to get food every day, even if you ate a huge meal the day before. That's understandable. Your body needs fuel continuously.

But the way an eloi has to darken her eyelashes every morning, cover her skin with colored cream, powder her nose and forehead all day so it doesn't shine, freshen her lipstick over and over, and then take it all off at night. It's like the myth of Sisyphus in Hades, rolling the rock up the hill just to watch it roll down again.

Just for fun I once calculated that by spending an hour every day on this stuff, in two years' time I would have wasted an entire month of my life.

If the point of it is to fool mascos, the logic of it falls apart. Of course the mascos know. Cosmetics are advertised in magazines, on the radio, on television, and mascos see those same ads. They know my eyelashes aren't really thick and black and my eyelids aren't naturally blue. They can see elois going into the restroom and coming out with redder lips; they can see the traces of lipstick on the edge of a drinking glass. The same goes for hair. Curling and fluffing and spraying.

Who do the elois think they're fooling? Each other?

Of course the state cosmetics industry makes a tidy profit from this farce, but I simply can't imagine that mascos really think elois always look the way they pretend to look. Even if elois are secretive about it, even if almost every outfit has a belt or a ruffle with a hidden pocket so you can keep your makeup on hand when you don't have a purse with you.

I've tried to think of makeup as a kind of evolutionary feature. Even if the deception is obvious, maybe mascos think that the more effort an eloi makes to attract them, the more eligible she is. Like those species of birds that demand elaborate mating rituals and display behaviors from prospective mates to show that they're committed. Or birds that are influenced in their choice of mate by gender markings like larger head crests or more colorful plumage, even though those traits have nothing to do with an individual's basic fitness—like whether he can find worms for the chicks.

I guess you can't compare humans to birds. Humans are rational beings. They're not just creatures without any sense of responsibility, ruled by drives and instincts, as our teachers at eloi school keep impressing upon us. Human beings are the pinnacle of creation, able to use rational, organized methods to place themselves outside nature, to control nature. But no sooner have they said that than they start invoking what is "natural," and to whom, and how such and such is the "natural order" of things. And for some reason these definitions are almost always applied to elois.

MODERN DICTIONARY ENTRY

eusistocracy — The social order of Finland, the "reign of health." Derived from the Latin *eu* (good) and *sistere* (remain), literally "to remain in good condition." See *eusistentialist, eusistence. Example:* "In a eusistocratic society the government's most important task is to promote the overall health and well-being of the citizens."

REPORT

Social Studies 101
Vanna Neulapää 1B
October 15, 2016

Why Finland Is the Best Country in the World

We live in a eusistocracy. A eusistocracy is the only Society where all the people really have a good life. Eusistocracy is the system of Finnish Society. The highest governing body is the Health Authority. Eusistocracy means the people always knows what's best for them and how they should be if they want to live healthy and a long time. That's why it should be the Health Authority who tells us how to eat and do other stuff.

The opposite of Eusistocracy is Hedonist Democracy, and it has lots of things wrong with it. People choose to do things that aren't Good for them. They even choose to do things that are dangerous. For instance in Decadent States you can drink Alcohol and buy it from Alcohol stores even though it's poisson. And theres other poisson things like Caffeine and Nicotine. So if there's no Health Authority then people won't know how to take care of their health and then they get all kinda diseases and Decadents in their body and that's the greatest resource to the Society. If we don't take care of our Physical Body then the whole world will degenerate like a pencil that isn't sharpened and just makes a mess.

The most important thing for a person in a Eusistocracy is to keep useful to the Society and that's why Eusistocracy is the best way to live in the world and that's why Finland is the best place in the world to live.

Teacher's Notes: *Excellent content, but pay attention to your grammar. The comparison to a pencil sounds like something you might have heard from someone. Remember—a well-mannered eloi never presents another person's idea as her own. 8/10 points.*

VANNA/VERA

October 2016

Every time I go out for a walk the realities of an eloi's life are breathing down my neck.

When I got home from school I washed my makeup off and brushed the hair spray out of my hair. Now if I want to go out I have to build the whole disguise again.

But I just can't bring myself to do it all. I make do with as little as I can—wrap my hair in a loose bun, put on just a little eyeliner and lipstick, leave my corset at home.

I don't remember ever having such a long dry spell.

Jare has good, reliable contacts. He's been skillful at locating shipments coming on the market, knows where to find sailors on freighters willing to take risks, people who are planning a trip abroad or foreigners visiting Finland for some reason, people with diplomatic immunity or enough connections in government that their bags aren't searched too thoroughly at customs. But some new kind of net has closed tight, some new step has been taken. The authorities are always learning more about users' behavior, the smuggling channels, the methods the mules use. It wasn't very long ago that you could supposedly depend on the customs officials not even knowing the difference between canned cherry tomatoes and whole cayenne peppers. Now it seems that nothing gets through their filter.

Jare heard a rumor that another mule was killed in a raid a week ago. The same seller who robbed me at the cemetery. I don't know if I should be afraid or glad.

I walk as quickly as I can in an eloi's shoes, trying to make my stride seem purposeful, to look as if I have some errand to run—some shopping to do—or a date. Stopping for even a moment would be a signal to any masco that I wanted company.

I cross Hämeenkatu into the park, and go around the block of wooden houses. Some of the oldest houses are scheduled to be torn down to make room for modern three-story cement buildings. When I get to the corner of Rongankatu I freeze.

A bulletin board.

A primitive means of communication but effective, perhaps for that very reason.

The wall of a building slated for demolition is covered with obscenity, typical pubescent masco drawings of genitalia, dirty words, and initials. Among the swamp of filth, you sometimes find messages that mean something quite different from what they seem to say.

My eyes immediately fix on one of the drawings. It's childish looking, a cartoonish scribble of a hedgehog wearing a hat, and underneath it says in crooked letters "Dandy" and "Oct. 18, 2016."

I can see that it was drawn several days ago. The rain has smeared the lines a bit; the marks of the felt pen are slightly faded.

Today is the eighteenth.

There's no way for me to get in touch with Jare. He's working in the field somewhere outside town.

This is the first shipment I've heard of in a long, long time, and I can almost taste the satisfying heat in my mouth; my salivary glands activate at the mere thought of it.

I check how much money I have on me. A pretty paltry amount even if I wanted only a gram for myself, but maybe I can make a contact. Reserve a batch and swear that he'll get a good price for it.

But this isn't my turf. That scares me.

What if the seller is jumpy when I approach him and know the code? Whenever I'm around dealers Jare warns them well ahead of time that he has an eloi for an assistant.

But what could the guy do? Call for a policeman?

The thought almost makes me smile. And another thought. Maybe I can get a sample.

Even just a little one.

The Hedgehog refreshment bar is just a couple of blocks away.

A hedgehog.

Wearing a hat.

I step into the bar and glance around at the customers. Many of the mascos have their hats on a corner of the table, but only a few are sitting alone; the rest have eloi companions. I buy a cranberry juice and look around like I'm trying to find someplace to sit. Just then a couple of new masco customers come in, and one of the men in the bar starts to rub the brim of his hat, as if in thought.

Got it.

I walk up to his table. In a low, flirty voice I say, "Hi there. That's sure a nice hat you've got. You must be quite a *dandy*." I breathe the last word in a sexy whisper.

The masco's eyes snap open. I'm startled by his reaction—almost too surprised, the smell of fear spitting into the air—but then I realize he's looking past me, over my shoulder, and a firm hand from behind me grabs my arm and moves me aside, sloshing my cranberry juice.

The masco with the hat has risen to a half-standing position and is looking around in a panic for an escape route, but there is none; the two mascos who've just come in are blocking his way. One of them takes a blue card out of his pocket and shoves it in front of his face.

The Authority.

The Authority.

My knees are knocking so hard that I collapse into a seat at the next table. One of the mascos takes out a pair of handcuffs; the other deigns to look at me and gives me a lecherous wink.

"Sorry, sweetheart. This fellow's off the market."

When they've left, I sit for about a minute before my heart-beat settles down.

My thoughts are racing.

The seller must have thought—has to have thought—that my use of the password was pure coincidence. But he still might mention it when he's questioned, so maybe it's a good thing I wasn't wearing my normal makeup. They probably won't be able to connect me with the usual public me.

There is a risk, though. I can't just put it out of my mind, can't just forget.

The net is tightening.

I can't tell Jare about this.

JARE SPEAKS

November 2016

I've sifted seeds out of bags of flake, soaked them, tried to rub the tough husks off between two pieces of sandpaper. I've watered them, kept the pots on the brightest possible windowsill, achieved seed leaves, then seedlings with stems. A couple of times I've even gotten them to flower, and once, my heart pounding with hope, I saw a flower's petals fall and at the base of the bud a little green bulge the size of a pea. But that's as far as they've gotten.

Maybe I'm not watering them right—sometimes the pot gets moldy; sometimes the plant is clearly suffering from being too dry. I think the problem is in the amount of light. The little windows in my apartment face east and west, so even in the middle of the summer the place doesn't get much sunlight. I can't put the pots outside even for a minute, not even on my little balcony. When friends come over I always put them all in the back of the closet and I'm on my guard the whole time, afraid someone will open the wrong door by accident.

I can't do it. I don't know enough. I've tried using what I've learned about farming other nightshades like tomatoes and potatoes. But since I can never be sure what variety I'm trying to grow, I always have the wrong temperature, or the wrong kind of soil, and especially the wrong light. Chilis are anything but straightforward—there are varieties that grow in near-desert conditions, some that like damp river valleys, and some that grow high in the mountains where the night temperatures drop below freezing.

But it seems that growing the plants is the only way I'm going to get my hands on any capsaicin these days.

When I come home from work, the door of my apartment is open.

There's someone here.

For once I'm glad of this dry spell—there's no stuff in the apartment, not even in the stash. But there is one spindly chili plant drooping on the windowsill.

If it's the Authority, the game is up. Even if I turned around right now and hopped on the next train, I would be arrested before I got to the Russian border.

I hear a clang of metal. Then the gurgle of water.

I carefully open the door a crack. Peek into my little kitchen. A man in coveralls is puttering around the sink. I recognize him— the building maintenance technician.

The situation is still anything but safe.

I walk in with a proprietary air, stomp loudly, shout a noisy hello from the doorway. The maintenance man turns, recognizes me, and says hello. He dries his hands on a rag.

"The drain's clogged upstairs. I came to see if this one was stopped up, too."

"Ah. It's been working fine."

I take off my shoes, trying to think of what to do about the plant, but it's too late for that. The maintenance man comes into the main room with his toolbox and is clearly curious, in a slightly malevolent way.

"Your plumbing seems to be working fine. Watering plants and everything." He looks pointedly in the direction of the windowsill.

Oh God. I can't tell him it's a houseplant. That's a minus man's hobby.

"Basil. Excellent seasoning."

I whip off a leaf, shove it into my mouth, and chomp on it, practically drooling over the thing. I pluck another leaf and hold it out to him, even though my heart's beating a mile a minute. "Have a taste!"

Luckily he's an old-fashioned guy, the kind who thinks dill and parsley are too exotic. "That's not really my . . . What's a young guy like you doing messing around with seasonings?"

Easy. I tell him that it's for work, that the Food Bureau is researching the possibility of producing Finnish herbs for export. This explanation suffices.

The chili leaf tastes surprisingly good. I thought it would just taste like grass, but it's tough and fibrous.

Tough like my failure.

My failure to help V.

The net is tightening.

I thought I would be earning money a lot faster than this.

I thought I would be able to get out of the country before Harri Nissilä got out on parole. He might get out any day. Sentences like his are always getting shortened for good behavior or some other reason. Nissilä's had time sitting in a cell to think, to put two and two together. He had time to figure out too many things *before* he went to jail. When they release him he'll do whatever he can to even the score. And if we come under investigation we're sure to get caught. Just like Harri did.

It doesn't matter that much for me. But V.

I can't tell V about it. I can't add to her burdens.

VANNA/VERA

November 2016

As if to torture me, they're presenting a special unit on dangerous substances at school.

I'm already shaking.

NATIONAL INSTITUTE OF HOME ECONOMICS INSTRUCTIONAL FILM

Social Responsibility 102

A middle-aged masco sits at a table. He's pale, hollow cheeked, sweating. His hair is mussed and poorly cut. He's wearing a suit that looks as though it doesn't belong to him; the collar's too big and the shoulders are baggy. Someone off camera gives him a signal and he nods, licks his lips, and begins.

Masco: In the beginning it was just innocent curiosity. And besides, there was so much false or incomplete information going around. People said chili was just a spice, a kind of food. They said that enjoying it in potent concentrations was just a harmless competition between men, testing your limits. Like seeing who could jump off a high rock into the water or who could climb the highest tree. I didn't know how insidious it was.

The masco lowers his eyes for a second, takes a deep breath, and lifts his head again.

Masco: Back then there was still quite a bit of chili, all kinds of it, coming into the country. It was like alcohol before prohibition. You could get various kinds, various strengths, if you just knew where to look. A friend of mine who'd been to one of the decadent democracies—to Spain—had played a game there called "Spanish roulette." You played it with green Padrón chilis. You roasted them quickly in a pan with oil to give them a little color, then you rolled them in salt and put them on a plate. Each player took turns picking one up and eating it in just a couple of bites. They called it roulette because the heat in Padrón chilis varies a lot. One might be no hotter than a pea pod and the next one might be so incredibly strong that it was painful to eat it and it left you panting and burning for a long time afterward. And of course dozens of kinds in between, from just a tiny bit of spice to unbearably hot. About one in eight was very strong. You could get Padrón chilis in a lot of grocery stores back then. They were imported from Spain. They were in demand for masco stag parties, things like that.

The masco closes his eyes as if remembering some important turning point in his life.

Masco: The truth dawned on me when I'd been doing chili for a couple of years, with different chili products. I was participating in another one of these games of Spanish roulette, and every single one of the padróns I ate was really mild. They just tasted like salt and sweet peppers. At first I thought it was just luck, that the real firebombs just happened to always go to the other guys. Then I started to think it was actually bad luck—after all, it was exciting to get a really strong chili in your mouth; it was an intoxicating experience. I started to envy my friends with their faces all red, gasping for air and trying to cool their mouths off with ice water. I went out and bought a whole bag of padróns as a test and roasted and salted them just for myself. I ate them all. Not one of them tasted hot. One chili, maybe two at the most, gave me a tiny little burning feeling, just a pale shadow of what I'd felt before. I started to suspect that the stuff that was coming into the country was milder than normal for some reason. About a month went by and I kept playing roulette off and on, and every time I would get just mild chilis. I bought another bag. Same result, except this time not one of them had any bite at all. The next roulette night I went to I watched my friends. When one of them took a bite out of a chili and started to cough and pant and grimace, I grabbed the other half of it, acting like it was a joke, and tossed it in my mouth. I chewed it up and waited for the heat to spread over my tongue and palate. But nothing happened. Nothing at all. It was just a pepper.

The masco looks directly into the camera.

Masco: It was clear to me now. I was building up a tolerance for capsaicin. Back then I didn't even know the name of the substance, but I do now. There's a lot of things I wish I'd known then, before I started experimenting—like the fact that it's a nerve toxin. A toxin that demands higher and higher doses.

He glances around, as if looking for reinforcement.

Masco: I started to look for different kinds of chilis at the store, the hottest ones I could find. Fresh, canned, dried, processed into hot sauce. I'd had no idea how much of the vile stuff there was available. I tried all of them: put chili in my food, mixed different kinds of chilis. I put fresh bird's-eye chilis in my soup and topped it off with a dash of Tabasco . . .

A figure in a Health Authority uniform comes into the frame, touches the masco's shoulder. The person's head is outside the shot, but I can hear his voice saying, "Let's leave out any too specific details." The masco nods, looking frightened, and the official steps out of the picture.

Masco: All the while I thought that it was just a game. I was just like a kid, testing my limits, looking for excitement, for extreme experiences. Nothing could happen to me. I was young and healthy; I thought I could control myself. But the poison had gotten into my blood and cut a swath through me. It was like having a demon inside me, whispering, *More, I have to get more capsaicin, stronger and stronger doses*. I just had to think about chilis and my mouth would water and my whole body would be screaming for that flood of fire on my tongue.

From off camera I hear, "Side effects." The masco nods, takes a moment to focus.

Masco: We'd studied the effects of alcohol in school. I knew that one of the nastiest side effects of alcohol poisoning— if the poisoning wasn't so bad that it killed you—was what was called a hangover. When you use alcohol there's an inevitable aftereffect where you have a terrible headache, fatigue, shaking, nausea. If what I've said about chilis up to now sounds interesting or fascinating, maybe I can shed some light for you.

The masco takes a deep breath, seems to be gathering courage.

Masco: Using chili causes critical damage to the digestive system. It's most obvious in stomach pain and cramping, but can also take the form of powerful diarrhea. Chili addicts lose control of their bowels. They wake up the next morning lying in their own shit!

I hear an audience off camera gasp in shock and horror. This is clearly the climax of the story.

Masco: There's nothing heroic or manly about using capsaicin. It will literally get you into deep shit. The symptoms of capsaicin addiction are just like symptoms of the most revolting venereal diseases, like painful and humiliating burning with urination or defecation. If somebody offers you capsaicin, remember what I've told you. If you find some old chili products that are illegal now in the back of a family cupboard, bring them straight to the authorities.

The masco looks up and to the left and is apparently given permission to end, because he nods and turns back to the camera.

Masco: I'm eternally grateful that I got caught and the Health Authority rehabilitated me. I'm also grateful that the awful, nasty stuff is illegal now. Capsaicin addiction is forever—you can't ever get away from it—but now I have a life worth living.

Meaningful pause.

Masco: In clean pants.

End of film.

VANNA/VERA

November 2016

The horrified murmurs of the elois around me tell me that the message of the film has hit home.

Jare has heard from his customers that when chilis were first banned even some respectable families dared to break the rules sometimes. The secret high point of a dinner party might be a recipe seasoned with a dash of Thai sweet chili sauce from the back of a cupboard, a daring treat, like decades earlier when people would end a meal by passing around a Marlboro Light someone had gotten somewhere. But the transition had been complete for a long time now, and the young brides in training who had just watched the film would most certainly never let a speck of capsaicin anywhere near their darling husbands or their happy homes.

The film would have been more effective if the capso's speech hadn't sounded so coached. But he had really been a capso; there was no doubt of that. He knew what he was talking about. A Health Authority propagandist wouldn't have known to bring up Spanish roulette.

Using diarrhea as the clincher was shrewd. Even I know from experience that a good fix can give a beginner stomach trouble. But with regular use I built up my tolerance and calmed my digestive reaction considerably. The film gave the impression that using chilis basically weakens the sphincter muscles. And a person might easily believe it if he saw the film, still stubbornly decided to try capsaicin, and got a shock in the bathroom the next morning—tried the stuff just one time and got some kind of toxic sludge coming out his rear end. And it surely stung.

Very clever, Health Authority. Very clever.

HOMEWORK

Social Responsibility 102
Vanna Neulapää 1B
November 9, 2016

Why Is Capsaicin Dangerous?

Capsaicin when you eat it you need more and more and it give you the runs. Capsaicin is kind of like venereal disease. If somebody eats Capsaicin you should call the authorities right away.

Teacher's Notes: *You have not provided very much information, but your central themes are fairly well presented. Pay attention to spelling. I would like to see more insight on how an eloi can combat capsaicin, for example, in her home management and food preparation responsibilities. 7/10 points.*

Manna dear,

I'm writing these letters partly to myself. I haven't sent a single one of them, after all. Where would I send them? Even if you are alive, I don't know your address.

I'm also writing them because they keep me momentarily sane when the Cellar is at its darkest and the water starts to rise.

Reminiscing about these things is painful, but it cleanses me. Everything gets all tangled up inside my head, and if I write it down it wraps up in a tidy thread, even if it is ugly black barbed wire.

I've thought way too many times that everything could have been different if I had tried harder. If I had stifled my dangerous, antisocial tendencies.

I could have at least tried to be a real eloi. Really made an effort to like the things elois like, studied them systematically. Trained. You may not like a food the first time you try it, but you can learn to like it.

There were many times when I thought I was learning. I like beauty the way any elois would. It's obvious to me that a bunch of flowers in a vase can make a room more colorful and pleasant. But I don't really like merely decorative things. For an eloi, beauty and decorativeness are the same thing.

I was interested in makeup as a child, too. It was exciting to change the way I looked by spreading different colors on different parts of my face. When you wanted and got the Femigirl *Sample Pack for your birthday and let me borrow it, I had fun painting my face like a mask or putting leopard spots on my forehead. You were upset with me. I was playing it wrong. I played a lot of things wrong, even though I tried to follow your rules as well as I could.*

I sat with you and watched one television show after another that ended in marriage. "Elois" flouncing around in beautiful gowns, heavily made up, wigs on their heads, padded in the right places. They couldn't use real elois—that would have been a real job, would have required memorizing lines, concentration, perseverance. The mascos dressed as elois on the TV shows tittered and giggled and fluttered and swung their hips and stuck out their lips and used an exaggerated caricature to show how an eloi should look and sound. I had read in one of Aulikki's books that in old American movies, white people painted their skin black to portray Negroes. I wonder if some dark-skinned people who watched those movies thought that they were supposed to speak in simple sentences and roll their eyes and be childish and superstitious.

I couldn't be a real eloi because I had a horrible, selfish rebelliousness inside me that only caused trouble and sorrow later on. I know there's absolutely nothing to envy about the depravities of a decadent democracy, but sometimes I find myself thinking that at least in a place like that nobody ever has to wonder about these things.

I think of you every day. Every single day. I just know that I'm going to find out what happened to you. It's the least I can do for you after all we've been through.

Your sister,
Vanna (Vera)

SERVICE COMMENCEMENT ORDER

Neulapää, Vanna
FN-140699-NLP

You are ordered to appear for mating market commencement under the following terms of service:

Mating Market Region: Northern Pirkanmaa

First Day of Service: June 1, 2015

Location: The Mating Palace, Hämeenkatu 30, Tampere

This service commencement order will serve as a travel pass on state railways and bus routes in transit to your designated regional station.

Failure to arrive at the appointed time will be considered a punishable infraction. Those in financial need may apply for state wardrobe assistance.

Dear Manna,

This memory comes back to me over and over. It comes to me in dreams as vividly as if it had happened yesterday, and I wake up in a cold sweat.

Aulikki had brought us up to the attic at Neulapää. I still remember the spring sunlight coming through the grimy little window at the end of the house, the smell of old beams and dust and heat and insulation under the roof.

It was May.

The debutante balls are always held on the first of June.

We needed dresses. There were certain rules for what prospects should wear—nothing anyone had ever officially written down, but tempered by custom until they were as hard as iron.

The dress should be low cut and show your legs and arms. If the weather was cold you were allowed to wear some kind of light wrap or lace shawl.

It all had to do with the old saying "A mating man needs to see what he's getting," but of course it doesn't stop anyone from putting padding here and there, wearing underclothes that puff you up or squeeze you in. Asking for state wardrobe assistance was something even the poorest families would avoid if at all possible—the state dresses were always years out of style and had a cloud of industrial cleaner clinging to them. People called them "bulletproof dresses" because they were made from the sturdiest possible materials. And you couldn't customize them in any way; you had to return them to the state wardrobe supply exactly as you'd received them.

Aulikki led us to the end of the attic where there were old rolled-up rugs and winter coats hung from the rafters for the summer. She showed us a row of dark blue, zippered garment bags and said she'd saved some of her old dresses in them. We could save some money by altering them to fit and using them for our prospect dresses.

You hated that idea and stomped your feet, remember? You weren't going to put on some hundred-year-old rag. You'd rather wear a state dress! But when Aulikki opened the first dusty old bag, you changed your mind. It was a bright red gown, bright as a glass ball on a Christmas tree. It had an open collar with an indescribable downy red cloud along the border— "Ostrich feathers," Aulikki said—and the narrow waistline was made even more elegant by sparkling sequins that radiated down the skirt. Aulikki told us almost apologetically that in Sweden she had spent a couple of years as a ballroom dancer, and she hadn't been able to bring herself to get rid of her costumes. Your eyes shone with excitement and admiration.

Now I was eager to see the dresses, too. I opened one zipper after another and found more and more treasures: emerald green, electric blue, dark gold, amethyst purple. Embroidered hems, ruffles, bows, feathers, silver glitter. Each dress was more wonderful than the last. You were so enchanted with the first dress we found that you hardly glanced at the others. You were smitten by the red color and the sequins, your fingers stroking the ostrich feathers over and over.

I opened the last garment bag. It was a white floor-length gown. Not bright white but slightly silvery. It was made of a heavy, flowing, silky fabric, very simply cut. The strapless top was like a corset, covered in delicate lace.

White, simple, unobtrusive—the kind of dress you could blend into the walls in. It was the opposite of all the other dresses.

The idea came into my head at that second.

I could finally do one good thing for my little sister. I wasn't the tiniest bit interested in what impression I made at the ball, but it was extremely important to you. You imagined I'd taken Jare away from you. Now was my chance to give you something in return.

At the ball you would be a glittering bird of paradise, and I would be beside you looking like a seagull at the landfill.

I looked at Aulikki and asked if I could wear the white dress.

Aulikki looked at the dress with her lips pursed, and at first there was a slight smell of turpentine and mud. But then she relaxed and said, "Why not? Finally get some use out of it." It was a wedding dress, but the wedding never happened.

When she mentioned a wedding you were immediately interested and started examining the dress. You didn't think it looked like a real wedding dress at all. You waved your hands around showing how a bridal gown ought to have a wide hoop skirt with lots of tulle and brocade embroidery and little fabric roses and a train behind it. This didn't even have a veil. It was just boring. Ugly.

Your opinion strengthened my decision. It was a perfect plan.

I wore my hair in a simple chignon, as close to my head as I could make it, ascetic and cold. Not a single alluring curl, no ringlets dangling in front of my ears, every strand of hair sternly *plastered down and wrapped tight against the back of my head.*

I didn't want any jewelry. For shoes I found some low-heeled white pumps at the store—I could use them later for summer shoes. You chose twenty-centimeter heels—you'd always liked walking around in those ever since you were little, trying not to trip. You knew how to stride from the hip, half tiptoeing, half in a swinging stride, as if you'd been wearing a skirt that was too tight around your knees all your life.

You did your hair in a pile of curls peppered with little artificial flowers and topped off with a fountain of satin ribbons. You smelled like lilacs and lily of the valley and musk, your carefully grown fingernails painted to match your dress and decorated with gold flourishes (I did those, and they were quite good, if I do say so), your makeup smoky and heavy, your lips lacquered red to match.

You were—as they say—a darling debutante.

I was wearing a nearly colorless lip gloss and a little bit of mascara. I wouldn't have worn makeup at all but Aulikki warned me about it. A real eloi should be made up. Always. She helped me put it on so I looked like I had perhaps tried to make myself up but only done a halfway job, because of my inexperience. Makeup to inspire pity, but not suspicion.

When I looked at the two of us in the mirror, it was like a red baroque canopy bed and a white puff of smoke, side by side.

I was extremely pleased.

At home you had seemed dazzlingly decked out.

When you stepped into the banquet hall, I saw the strain in your face.

You grew up in the country. You had no idea how tough the competition would be, how in this context more really was more. To an almost sickening degree. Dresses cut so low that nipples peeked out with the slightest movement. Skirts slit nearly to the waistband. Shoes with heels so high that they made you walk on pointe like a ballerina. Eyelids so plastered in gold or turquoise that they could hardly stay open. False eyelashes two inches long, artificial fingernails as long as the fingers they were glued to, unnaturally tiny waists in cinched corsets. The quantity of perfume in the air made my eyes water, made me cough.

In this carnival of peacocks and puppets, things went absolutely the wrong way. I did stand out from the crowd. But I stood out like a graceful white gull soaring among a flock of fluttering, cawing, scratching birds of paradise piled with plumes to the point of collapse.

I spent the whole evening on the dance floor, though I'm a bad dancer. Aulikki was a good teacher when it came to this important eloi skill, but it simply never interested me much. I preferred to listen to music rather than move to its rhythm, and when I did, I danced alone. Nevertheless, no sooner would one dance end than more mascos would shove themselves in front of me, jostling, shouting witticisms, each one trying to get me to choose him for the next dance. And while we danced they pressed their lips against my ear and called me "ice princess" and "snow queen" and "moonbeam" in a whisper, complimenting my daring, distinctive, exciting style of dress. Now and then I caught glimpses of you over their shoulders.

I'd never felt so disappointed in my life, so sad, so powerless and helpless.

My whole body ached as you stood in a row of rejected girls, waiting to be asked to dance, trying to thrust your chest out even farther, batting your eyelashes as if you were trying to fan the whole room, swinging your hips as suggestively as you possibly could, and when I caught your eye, it was burning with emotion.

Hate.

Jealousy.

Pain.

Inferiority.

Sadness.

Fear.

Every time the water in the Cellar starts to rise, I remember that moment, remember the look in your eyes.

Or rather, when I remember the look in your eyes, the water starts to rise. Black, shining, ready to drown me.

I have to stop now.

Vanna (Vera)

VANNA/VERA

November 2016

I've had to use two jars of jalapeños from my secret stash to keep the Cellar door closed. Luckily fitting in at eloi school isn't particularly demanding. When the black water starts to splash in the back of my head, calculating the calories, cholesterol, and salt content of a sample meal is about as difficult for me as it is for the average eloi. I don't need to pretend to make mistakes.

Right now I'm having an extremely hard time concentrating on the lecture on "A Crying Baby and a Harmonious Marriage," because my mind is seething with all kinds of other questions.

Why have our sources dried up?

Has the Authority improved its methods that much, or are there more middlemen in the market? And if there are, why haven't we heard about them?

Is there some large organization that's grabbing up control of the capsaicin market?

And most important, where will I get my next fix?

"Vanna, if your child is continuously crying because of colic, perhaps, or an earache, what do you do?"

I'm startled by the teacher's question. He's a family masco, already in his forties. He enjoys his work; it's a personal triumph for him whenever an eloi graduates to marriage.

What in the world was he just talking about? I didn't hear a word he said.

Do I throw the baby out the window?

"Um, I'd try to protect my husband from the noise."

"How, specifically?"

"I'd sorta take the baby away from where he was sleeping. Or give him some earplugs."

The teacher looks at me in surprise. "So, Vanna, you were listening after all."

I wasn't listening. I was deducing.

Dear Manna,

Maybe it was good that you hated me.

When I inadvertently put you out of the game at the debutante ball, it aroused your anger to a peculiar intensity. But Jare upset you even more.

You fell in love. That was your nature. You're not to blame for that.

In the life of an eloi there are certain rules and ways of thinking, and I wasn't even conscious of all of them. They dawned on me in all their bleakness only after I met other elois at school in Tampere.

If two elois are in competition for the same man, whoever is more charming or manipulative wins. Any feeling of friendship or empathy for the other person is a handicap. If a more attractive eloi is asked to dance, the wallflower has only herself to blame. Sometimes taking a masco from another eloi is just a display of superiority. Any attachment to the masco in question is irrelevant—the act of conquest is reason enough.

From your point of view this is exactly what happened. I got Jare's attention, but when he went back to town in the fall, I wasn't crying in my pillow. I didn't want him, but I couldn't give him to you, either. I had, in other words, behaved in a perfectly normal, acceptable manner.

You had to show your anger through some means other than sulking or arguing. But you were incapable of hiding it.

It hurt. But maybe you weren't afraid to hate me because you knew very well that I would still love you, unconditionally, no matter what you did. Like a little child who can shout at her parents and say she wishes they were dead and still trust that they will never abandon her.

I will never abandon you.

There was so much preparation and bustle and excitement about the coming-out ball that we completely forgot what it really meant.

It meant moving to the city. It meant leaving Neulapää.

It meant leaving Aulikki.

It meant going to eloi college.

For you, coming out was an exciting adventure, your entry into the mating market. For me it meant entering an utterly strange and hostile world.

Aulikki was solemn as we gathered up our few possessions. I could smell her sadness, and I asked her if there was anything else bothering her aside from our departure. She said, almost angrily, that she wondered if she had made a terrible mistake about me. She might have been able to make me almost an eloi if she had set limits on my expectations since I was little. I might have learned to believe in them myself.

I squeezed her hand and said that regardless of the circumstances, I wouldn't have wanted us to do it any other way. It was easy to say because it was true.

Aulikki smiled and a scent of relief floated around her. But I could also tell that she wasn't completely convinced. I tried to cheer her up, told her that if she'd raised me to be an eloi I would have been a cat in a doghouse eventually anyway, at the very latest by the time I was in eloi college. But this way I would know exactly what to hide and what to emphasize. "When dogs wag their tails it's a gesture of friendship; when cats do it they're about to attack. I would have been waving my tail around in all the wrong situations if I hadn't been aware of who I really am."

Aulikki hugged me long and hard. She told me that there were two loose floorboards under the large pantry cupboard. Underneath there was a little space above the foundation where she could hide the books that Jare had brought me. No one else would know about them, and I could read them when I came to visit Neulapää. I smiled and nodded, although I thought the situation was more complicated than Aulikki realized, or wanted to realize.

When we got to the city you didn't want to live with me anymore. Living alone is better for advancing your mating prospects, but many elois prefer to live with other elois anyway, to share chores and borrow clothes and support each other in crises and, naturally, to lure mascos away from one another.

I told you that it was your decision to make, that I would still support you and always be close by and easy to reach. You shrugged your slim shoulders with an indifference that stung me to the heart. I hadn't realized how much I'd hurt you.

Aulikki had hired a large moving van and driver. Between the two of us we had a couple of suitcases and a few curtains, lamps, rugs, and knickknacks that Aulikki thrust upon us, not enough to begin to fill the cargo space.

When you were already in the van, your lips pursed and your seat belt fastened, Aulikki took me by the arm and asked me to call her often. I promised I would call every day if I could.

Aulikki stuck her hand into her apron pocket. Remember how you used to hate aprons? In spite of the fact that an apron is a handy thing for an eloi to have around the house, a sign of a good homemaker. It protects you while you do your chores, you can wipe your hands on it, the pockets are handy for keeping things, and you just take it off when company comes. I can't even count the times I've pressed my face into Aulikki's apron in moments of desolation or happiness.

Now a bit of paper appeared from that apron pocket and Aulikki handed it to me. "If you ever feel really lonely or defenseless . . ."

I unfolded the paper. Just one word and a telephone number.

"He knows what you are, and he's promised not to tell anyone. But use your own judgment, and be careful."

I nodded and put the paper in my purse.

When we got to the city you didn't lose any time.

I don't know how you did it, how you managed it so quickly.

We were classmates at eloi college. I saw you every day in the yard or hallways, always with a group of friends. You always greeted me with a little wave, but then you would turn your back and never come and talk to me. I made a few superficial friendships, too. Hanna, Janna, Sanna, Leanna, and I spent time, in various configurations, at refreshment bars, dances, the movies, one another's apartments. We gossiped behind each other's backs in suitably subdued whispers. We talked about makeup and clothes and dieting and mascos. Mascos, mascos, mascos.

For you, it wasn't just talk.

You had a round head covered in platinum curls, a cute little turned-up nose, narrow shoulders, full breasts, a curving waist. Tush like a peach.

And a whole lot of seething, pent-up desire to prove yourself.

We had been in town for only a couple of weeks when you called and told me you were engaged and had already set a wedding date.

It all happened much too fast.

Whenever the water starts to rise in the Cellar I remember that feeling.

Or rather, I remember that feeling, and the water starts to rise. Black, shining, drowning me.

I met your fiancé, Harri, the day after your phone call.

Harri Nissilä was an ordinary, nondescript, brown-haired, not particularly bright masco who worked in heating and air-conditioning. He was apparently ready to be led by his hormones into marriage in his early twenties. He had so little charm, looks, personality, or sense of humor that it was no wonder he'd chosen the first eloi who paid him any attention.

You could have done better, but you were in a hurry. This was your chance to show me up.

Oh my dear, dear Manna.

The diamond on your ring was surprisingly large considering what I presumed were Harri's means. It was a classic cut stone surrounded by the tiniest of sapphires. In the blink of an eye you adopted the body language of an eloi engaged—you walked, moved, drank your herbal tea, did every little thing so that your left hand was as visible as possible at every moment. I imagined you sitting on the toilet and wiping your ass with your right hand while keeping your left hand, especially the ring finger, nonchalantly raised for the admiration of an invisible audience.

There was something indescribably touching about that. You really thought that ring on your finger was a magic charm that would let you live happily ever after.

You got straight to the point.

"There has to be money somewhere at Grandma Aulikki's house. Harri says old ladies like her sock their money away like jam," you said with a shake of your curls. "And it's not as if she has any use for the money anymore. She's going to die soon." That's what you said. Those very words.

You asked if I would ask Aulikki for the money for your wedding.

I'm sure I was visibly surprised, although I knew as well as anyone that the bride's parents or other relatives were expected to fund a wedding. But Aulikki had barely managed to support herself and us with child-care assistance payments and money from sewing and selling vegetables. Now that we were officially debutantes she was no longer receiving child-care assistance, and she couldn't do very much sewing anymore. Her eyesight had started to weaken because of a rapidly worsening case of glaucoma (which I'm sure you didn't know about), and the public health services wouldn't provide any expensive treatments for a woman past childbearing age. What mainly surprised me was that you wanted me to ask her. Why not ask her yourself?

"Because you're Aulikki's pet."

That was a horrible jab. Resentment wafted around you like the smell of the swimming hall. I hadn't expected that.

Aulikki had always treated us equally, whether it was food, treats, clothes, or who got to sit in her lap. The only difference *was that she had educated me, half in secret, set aside time for conversation, for building my double identity. For you it had meant whispers and secrets, time set aside for one of us but not the other. An inner circle that excluded outsiders.*

You thought I had taken Aulikki's love away from you, too.

I, your own big sister, was the worst, cruelest villain in your short life.

I considered my attachment to you so obvious that I didn't do enough to prove it to you. We were two kittens from the same litter. There was nothing, no one, that could break that bond.

I couldn't say the things I wanted to say with Harri there. Shocked, I said I would see what I could do, but I couldn't promise anything.

You wrinkled your adorable nose and said that you'd gotten only a lousy hundred for Aulikki's gowns. You had called her and asked her to send her dance costumes, since she wasn't doing anything with them. I felt a stab in my heart. Those dresses were Aulikki's history. Luckily I had packed the dress I wore to the ball and brought it with me when I moved.

Under no circumstances did I want Aulikki to send every last penny she could scrape together to pay for your wedding—which she would have tried to do if I'd done as you asked me to. She might have even sold the land or furniture from Neulapää. Actually, your mistaken belief about Aulikki and me was a blessing in disguise because you hadn't yet told her about your engagement. You wanted to wait until I'd felt out the situation. That gave me some time to think of ways for an empty-headed eloi—or someone who looked like one—to make a little extra money. I would happily use it to pay for your wedding. Who else could you turn to if not me?

I knew that the state bordellos hired staff, but I had no idea how to apply to work there, or whether it even paid. I made discreet inquiries about it among my classmates. One of them had heard a rumor that the staff was made up of fallen elois working to repay their debt to society. Such a fall could happen to anyone. Neglecting your home, violent opposition to a husband, adultery. Shoplifting from a state store.

Unpaid work was not an option.

I went to look in the cookie tin that I'd brought from Neulapää full of little objects and mementos. And the folded piece of paper Aulikki had given me.

I can't write any more.

Vanna (Vera)

Do You Dream of a Summer Cottage? A Gorgeous Car?
Does Your Wife or Lady Friend Wish She Had Jewelry, Flowers, Cosmetics?

THE STATE LOTTERY can make your dreams come true!

Just six little dots could make your dreams for you and your family come true. At the cost of mere pocket change you could fill your bank account with hundreds of thousands of marks!

THE STATE LOTTERY can change your life in one stroke. You can be the envy of your neighbors, be even more adored by your wife. Toys for your children—stylish clothes—protection from illness!

THE STATE LOTTERY—depend on it.

VANNA/VERA

November 2016

The doorbell rings.

Jare.

I let him in, although we haven't agreed to our normal smoke screen meeting. On Wednesdays and Saturdays we go out, visibly hand in hand, to places where other couples our age go. Our other meetings are strictly business. I don't know how Jare meets his own sexual needs—he probably visits the state bordellos and gets the young bachelor's discount.

I have only six jars of jalapeños left in my stash. Jare put them here without saying a word and hasn't made a move to sell them.

I'd thought about going to the body-perfecting salon, although the pitiful endorphins I get exercising there are like trying to sate an elephant's hunger with a single pea. I really don't want any company right now. The black water's been rising in the Cellar all day. I hardly have the strength to even wash the eloi icing off my hair and face, and I had hoped that going to the bodywork salon would tire me enough that I could get to sleep a little early. I lean limply against the wall near the front door and wait for Jare to tell me why he's come, but he doesn't say anything. I scowl.

"Well?"

I see an expression on his face, a promise in his eyes; I sense the aroma of excitement, expectation, and my pulse starts to race.

I'm already grabbing him by the hand and dragging him into the kitchen, almost jumping up and down, like a dog whose owner has a treat for her. I almost forget to turn on the radio to fill the room with noise.

"How much? Where'd you get it? Is it jar, bottle, chunk, flake?"

"None of those."

My shoulders slump. It's some kind of cruel joke. Everything on the market is either chopped and in jars, mashed into a bottled sauce, powdered, or—the best kind—dried flakes.

Jare pulls a bag out of his pocket. "Fresh."

My mouth hangs open.

Fresh chilis. I've never seen fresh chilis.

Habaneros, no less. Not anywhere near the strongest kind, but still, more than 200,000 scovilles. A fantastic score.

A bag of little red- and orange-tinged, paprika-shaped *fresh* habaneros.

Three thoughts come into my mind, in a very particular order.

One. I am about to be buzzed.

Two. There's stuff on the market again.

Three. Someone's growing it. And that someone isn't far from here.

I make us something to eat. Now that I'm assured of my fixes, and that they're really, really good fixes, I can wait half an hour and maximize my enjoyment. I have enough food on hand to make us a sort of thick ragout: tomatoes, onions, garlic, carrots, green beans, salt, pepper. I simmer the chopped vegetables for fifteen minutes and then dump half of them into another pan. That's for Jare—the best dealers never touch the stuff themselves.

I put on some latex cleaning gloves to chop the habaneros. Although I've never handled the fresh stuff, I assume that touching it with your bare hands—touching any fresh chili—could be a big risk. Even if you wash your hands carefully afterward, they can still have capsaicin on them. I know that from handling the flake. You accidentally rub your eyes or your nose and it can be really painful. Really strong stuff can even injure the skin on your hands. *The way of the chili is not the way of the finger.* They don't say that for nothing.

Although I want a really, really good fix, I also know what this score might be capable of doing. So I'll pace myself. One whole chili should be enough. The aroma of the minced habanero is something new, intoxicatingly fruity and pungent. My mouth begins to water so much that I have to swallow. I pour the pieces into the pan meant for me. Just ten more minutes.

I don't ask Jare where he got it. Not now. That's beside the point right now.

JARE REMEMBERS

November 2016

I'd been out looking at the bulletin boards one more time. Nothing new had turned up in quite a while, as you know. But I went to look anyway; it was better than just waiting around, antsy and uncertain.

Then a couple of days ago I got a surprise. I saw a new bit of graffiti in among the old, on the side of a house that was scheduled for demolition. This new mark didn't follow the rules. It didn't have a date or a key word, just a picture of an elongated, slightly crooked heart with a little flame-like shape nestled on top between its two curves. It couldn't be anything but a chili pepper. The picture seemed to be purposely vague so that if any random law-abiding citizens looked at it they would think that it was in fact a heart, with a little flame on top, a scrawl put there to express some lovestruck person's feelings. Of course my first thought was to wonder if there was a refreshments bar or another public place in Tampere that had a heart or a flame in its name, but I couldn't think of one. Still, the drawing gave me hope—it was a reference to chilis, so somebody might have some.

I went to look at all the bulletin boards again over the next few days. Then yesterday, in the pedestrian underpass at the railway station, the very same drawing appeared on top of the old scribbles, small and unobtrusive, but there it was, and it was quite fresh.

My head was humming with the thought of it as I walked back to work. How could I follow this trail? And was it a trail? I was mulling this over when I passed a group of mascos at the central market square, guys about my age, perhaps a little younger. They had somewhat long hair and more colorful clothes than you usually see. They were talking to passersby and handing out leaflets, smiling brightly at everyone, but it was a little odd that they didn't try to talk up any of the elois walking by. None of them whistled or shouted anything or tried to take any eloi's arm or pat her on the butt, although several good-looking specimens walked past. People were taking the leaflets; most of them took one a bit reluctantly and tossed it into the next recycling bin they came to. I took one, too, mostly out of politeness, and shoved it in my pocket without reading it. Then I forgot about it until I was back at the office, getting ready to go to lunch, and I reached in my pocket for some change and found the leaflet. It was ordinary, cheaply printed, like those sheets people hand out in the central square on Independence Day with the program schedule and the words to the songs on them. I read the first few lines. Then I understood why those mascos looked peculiar—they were members of some kind of religious sect that I'd never heard of, so it made perfect sense that they looked a little odd. The leaflet had some complicated babble about transcendence and Gaia, but it also said something about "oneness with nature" and talked about "the spirit of the soil" and "wisdom of growth." The kind of thing the authorities don't bother with, probably some harmless sect promoting vegetarianism. I was about to put it in the recycling bin on the office wall when I happened to get a glimpse of the paper with the light behind it. It looked as if there was a grease stain on the paper. But when I looked more closely I saw that the stain was actually a little watermark. The same mark I'd seen on the bulletin boards.

My heart started to pound and I quickly stuffed the paper back into my pocket. That same stylized heart with a flame, just the kind of symbol that a religious group could use to send the message "We offer warmth and love." But to me it said that this group must have something to do with chili. There was no other reason for it to be drawn on two separate bulletin boards.

It could have been a trap, but I figured the idea was too complicated and clever to be something the Health Authority had cooked up. It was bait, an invitation, and it was meant to be seen only by those who knew how to look for it.

After work I went back to the market square with the leaflet in my pocket. The group had gotten out an assortment of drums and stringed instruments, and one person had a flute. Some of the instruments looked homemade; some were rebuilt or assembled from parts of old instruments. I stopped to listen to the music. The songs were simple: stuff about plants and trees and sunshine and how Gaia's skin is green. I clapped politely after each song. The musicians even had half of a gourd where people had tossed them some coins—a few tenpenny pieces at most.

I approached a dark, hook-nosed fellow in a striped, hand-knit sweater and asked something trivial about the instruments, and he started to introduce the group enthusiastically with a friendly smile. I showed him the leaflet. I said I wanted to ask them a bit more about their religion, and I could buy him a drink in return. He immediately shook my hand and said that his name was Mirko and he would be happy to tell me more. We went to the nearest market refreshments bar and I ordered two carrot juices. Mirko was babbling something about a bioaura, but I wasn't actually listening to him at all. I just turned the paper over in my hands and then pretended to suddenly notice the watermark. I asked him what it meant. Then he put his hand on mine for a moment, gave it a quick pat, and asked if I'd ever played hide the key as a child. I nodded and said of course. He smiled and said that I must remember what you say when the searcher is very close to the hiding place. I was about to open my mouth, but stopped when Mirko's eyes widened slightly.

You're getting hotter. Burning hot. That's what you say.

I smiled back at him. "That's the most important part of the game, isn't it?" I said.

"Yes, it is. 'Seek and ye shall find; knock, and it shall be opened unto you.' That's what the Bible says, although that isn't our holy book."

He tapped the paper with a finger, pointing to the symbol as if by accident.

"If you would like to come to a prayer meeting sometime, you're very welcome."

"I would like to come," I said, although I knew that it was a big risk.

Mirko took out a pen and wrote something on the paper. "We're having a prayer meeting today, actually. Here's the address."

I didn't even look at the paper, just put it in my pocket and thanked him.

Mirko got up. We shook hands and went our separate ways. I didn't look at the address until I got home. It was on the outskirts of town, in the area of wooden houses around Kauppi.

I went there that evening. It was an old, run-down building surrounded by a well-kept garden mulched for the winter. I knocked on the door and one of the mascos who'd been at the market square opened it, nodded, and asked me in. I had hardly crossed the threshold when someone grabbed me from behind and held my upper arms tight, pulling my hands behind me.

"Check to see if he's clean."

Three mascos came and patted me down all over. "He's clean."

They let go of me. Mirko came right up in front of me and stood with a big, mean-looking knife in his hand. "Sorry to do this. But we have to be absolutely sure of everyone."

I nodded.

"We're peace-loving people and we don't want to cause problems for anyone. But if you decide to help us you will be magnificently rewarded."

There was something so bombastic about this that it almost made me laugh, but I thought it wise to keep my smile to myself.

"Our mission is to give the fire back to humanity."

After a short discussion I was much the wiser. Mirko went somewhere else in the house and was gone for a long time, and then came back with a plastic bag. "These are our collateral."

He handed me a bag of fresh habaneros.

"For some time now we've been looking for a smart, motivated go-between. You seem to be both. We need money and we can't risk making sales ourselves. The risk will be entirely yours. If you get caught, we have many ways of silencing you before you're even questioned. But if you do your job right, there's plenty more where this came from."

I didn't even think about what exactly was meant by that veiled threat. I knew that some people who'd had dealings with chilis had disappeared. There were rumors of capsos in high places who could use their own channels to handle dealers who took risks. There were whispers about ways to get to a snitch the moment he was put in the paddy wagon. Those might be legends, but the heavy, juicy red bag was there on the table. It was real. Fresh stuff is impossible to fake.

These guys were the real thing. They were serious.

VANNA/VERA

November 2016

I sit at the table. The pan in front of me is holy communion.

I scoop some of the vegetables into my bowl and stir them until they cool a little, but not too much. A fix served in hot food is weird; at first it's impossible to tell what's warming my mouth, the temperature of the food or the precious capsaicin.

The first hit of habanero shakes me. I've already had three or four forkfuls before it starts to come up on me, first in little waves lapping the shore, then, before I know what's happening, it's like a roaring tidal wave curling over me.

A little squeaking shout comes out of me as a hot iron starts pressing the inside of my mouth.

Every sweat gland in my body starts to ooze simultaneously. Burning drops flow down my spine, my forehead, under my eyes, down my arms, over my crotch, making my panties damp as though I've wet myself, and I may actually have wet myself—I hardly would have noticed, because flames are shooting through my digestive tract, hitting me right under my chest like a hatchet.

"Aaaa*aaaa*!" I bend over double, and the fork falls to the floor.

My ears have slammed shut. I can barely hear Jare asking me something, his face worried. He asks again, louder.

"Is everything all right?"

I raise my head from my plate and look at Jare, his shape wavering through the sweat and tears on my lashes.

"All right? This is *unreal.*"

I take the fork in my hand again, scoop up the reddish mixture and shove it in my mouth. I could put the fork right through my tongue and not feel the difference. The fantastic, exploding pain hits my mouth again, like someone smashing my teeth in with a sledgehammer.

The burn has to be cradled like a flickering flame. You have to let it live; you can't smother it with bread or milk or cold water. Because as long as your mouth and gut feel that holy pain your body keeps pumping luscious opiates into your system. The best thing to do is to fan the flame higher and higher, into ever greater frenzy, if you've got enough stuff to do it; the pain receptors in your mouth react to every little bite as if it were a match thrown onto a pile of straw soaked in gasoline. The habanero has intense overtones; its heat is shrill, piercing, like a drill on the nerve of a tooth. The flavor of it is yellow, almost white-yellow, flashing on my optic nerve. This is the best rush ever, ever, ever.

Thankfully, there's lots of food still left when I get up and start to dance to the pop song on the radio. I don't even need music; the chili is squirming and churning inside me, huge, slashing undertones mixed with unspeakably deep, wonderfully agonizing bass notes.

The chills will come soon, but I can keep them in check if I keep moving.

I'm alive.

"THE ENDURING LEGACY OF DIMITRI BELYAYEV"

From *A Short History of the Domestication of Women*
National Publishing (1997)

The modern social system we all enjoy might not exist in the form it does today if not for a brilliant Russian geneticist, Dimitri Belyayev.

Belyayev was born in 1917, the same year that Finland gained its independence—an interesting example of how history is far from random and is in fact filled with beautiful synchronicity! For Dimitri Belyayev and his life's work are uniquely and inextricably intertwined with Finland's destiny.

Belyayev began his well-known series of experiments in domestication in 1959. He chose the silver fox as his test subject. The animals had long been domesticated, but were bred merely for the color and thickness of their fur. Belyayev decided to find out what would happen if humans took the place of natural selection and strove to make the foxes more gentle and docile, able to coexist with humans in the same way that their canine cousins do.

Belyayev's idea was simplicity itself—the only foxes he would allow to reproduce were those that behaved positively toward humans and showed no fear or hostility toward them. The foxes were evaluated as puppies or "kits." If an animal submitted to a human's touch and didn't bite the hand that fed it, it was allowed to produce offspring. At first Belyayev was able to approve only about 10 percent of kits to reproduce the next generation.

One remarkable result of the experiment was that in only three generations the most extreme forms of shyness or skittishness, as well as hostility toward humans, had already been eliminated. A few generations later some of the kits wagged their tails at humans, taking on the characteristics of domestic dogs as if by magic. Some of the kits actually gravitated toward humans, waiting for a pat instead of cringing or running away. Next came signs of affection such as licking the human's face or whining forlornly when humans were absent.

As each new generation was selected and the foxes became more tame and doglike, Belyayev noticed that the new kits were growing more sensitive to what humans expected of them. They were clearly learning to sense what kind of behavior humans preferred, and they were eager to live up to these preferences. They were also quickly learning to read human behavior, gestures, expressions, and touch. And they felt a strong attraction to humans, completely unlike their forefathers—in short, they were biologically conditioned to enjoy human attention.

Another remarkable fact was that the test subjects started to take on doglike physical characteristics such as curled tails, floppy ears, and shorter legs. Pale or even white spots began to appear in their coats. Most noticeable were their shorter, wider snouts, a trait that is common in young mammals but disappears at maturity. In Belyayev's foxes, however, this trait remained until the age of sexual maturity. Belyayev and his assistants had set out to alter, not the outer appearance of the animals, but only their behavior and preferences, but over numerous generations their appearance, or phenotype, was nevertheless changing—specifically, becoming more like the juvenile phase of development. According to the more recent theories of Belyayev's successors, the genes that determine animal behavior function by controlling the chemical structure of the brain, and altering the chemicals in the brain also influences an animal's physical appearance.

This partial retention of the physical attributes of an immature phase of life is called "neoteny." We know that femiwomen also have a youthful physical appearance that lasts well into sexual maturity and even beyond, and inspires in the male tender feelings of protectiveness. Nowadays we understand only too well that social openness, a desire to please, a tendency to seek safety and protection from men, and a playful naïveté are fundamental to the female sex. Before domestication, owing to the distortion of natural selection (or so-called emancipation), traits such as these were diminishing, even disappearing.

From our present point of view it may seem a self-evident assumption that the steady development of neotenic features in femiwomen from generation to generation is living proof that societal efforts to restore women to ways of behaving that are more traditional and characteristic have been in every respect a correct and well-justified decision. Throughout history, a young woman has been a pleasing mate for a man; in some cases, the younger the mate, the more pleasing she has been. The development of the femiwoman has killed two proverbial birds with one stone—creating an ideal companion in both appearance and behavior.

Some Luddites question whether Belyayev's theories should be applied to humans, claiming that the procedures used in the breeding of femiwomen might be "a violation of human rights." But hasn't humanity done the same thing throughout history? When women long ago controlled their sexuality, made it an artificially limited commodity, and used it as a form of extortion, they chose the most outwardly pleasing, muscular, "romantic," or wealthy men and allowed only them to procreate. Belyayevism does exactly the same thing, but instead of working for the selfish individual, its aim is for the greatest possible good—a strong and peaceful society.

Over human history, haven't we as a species always striven to mold future generations by means of good upbringing and moral teachings, by encouraging natural talents, athletic prowess, etc., continuously aiming to improve and develop? There is nothing detrimental to human rights in this. It is as natural as when an animal kills offspring that are unfit and would only be a burden on the rest of the herd.

The domestication of the femiwoman is a step forward for society, and Finland is a bright trailblazer, a nation of forward thinkers. It is only a question of time before other countries follow our example.

Some are skeptical that the domestication of the femiwoman is genuine. Can such a significant genetic change be effected in what is, evolutionarily speaking, an extremely short time, particularly considering the length of a human generation, which is not one or two years, as it was for Belyayev's foxes, but fifteen, and was indeed even longer before the accelerated rate of reproduction brought about by domestication?

Naturally, other methods have been used in the domestication of the femiwoman in addition to reproduction selection. There are two factors that influence the modification of a species: the biological and the cultural. Promoting submissiveness and a desire to please through the use of rewards for desirable behaviors and punishment for undesirable ones, for example, has facilitated a constant development in the right direction. Such a method is recommended by humans' history as social animals, inherently sensitive and responsive to social cues.

Certain hormonal and neurochemical methods have also helped to accelerate domestication considerably. The thyroid hormone thyroxine, given in precise doses at certain developmental stages, has proved to produce an earlier age of reproduction and to increase the occurrence of the optimal physical and behavioral traits associated with domestication. Fortifying foods with melatonin has also helped to lower the age of puberty.

But the most important reason for the success of domestication has been the fact that even before Belyayev's theories and experiments came into common use among Finnish geneticists, our government had already taken many successful preliminary social steps toward femiwomen's domestication.

VANNA/VERA

November 2016

"V, we should get married."

I'm so happy, energetic, positive. The floor of the Cellar is dry and bright—for once there are lights on in there! And then he has to go and say something like that.

"Married?"

"How long have we supposedly been dating. Almost a year?"

This is true. I should have gotten wedding fever and baby fever and whatever other eloi fever a long time ago. Especially now that Jare has these Gaian contacts—all our covers should be as airtight as possible.

I rub my temples in annoyance. "I think this is working fine as it is."

Jare smirks. I can't blame him. Any other eloi would have burst into tears, then laughter, then called all her girlfriends. No, first her mother. And then we all would have run to the bridal shop.

"We can't afford it. I don't have any parents to pay for it. A decent ring alone will cost a ridiculous amount."

Jare has money, of course. But he's saving that money for his own uses. And he can't possibly be thinking of bringing a wife with him when he defects. He would need twice as much money, and that would take a lot of time.

Besides, I wouldn't go. Not when I still don't know what happened to Manna.

"I could ask my mother for her family ring. She would think it was very touching and sweet."

"You need more than a ring for a wedding."

"But if we got married . . . we could move to Neulapää."

Neulapää.

Suddenly I need a fix. My last one wasn't even six hours ago, but the Cellar is suddenly full of water a meter deep. It's pouring in at the corners, rising with a rush.

Manna. Manna. Manna.

I'd frozen the habanero ragout in small batches of a few spoonfuls. There are still fifteen doses left. Just one of them will give me a good high. The rest of the habas we'd dried and divided into small bags, and after the long hiatus Jare's doing an excellent business with them.

I wrench open the freezer, take out some of the ragout, and clunk the frozen chunk down on the counter. Then I slam it into a pan, turn on the tap, send a drizzle of hot water over it, and put the pan on the stove. I'm shaking all over now, and it takes forever for the frozen stew to soften around the edges so I can break it into pieces with a fork. I pick up a piece that's hot on the outside and frozen in the middle, put it in my mouth, and suck so hard that my cheeks cave in. The combination of hot chili and ice almost stuns me.

"I've always been interested in farming. Neulapää would make that possible."

I know now what he's hinting at. My mouth is full of hot, frozen carrot. "Neulapää?" I mutter, the inside of my mouth burning. The merciful sweating has begun.

"It would be the perfect place."

Yeah. In the middle of nowhere.

"It can't have gotten very run-down in the few months since . . . since what happened to Manna. I'm sure the government's looking for someone to rent the farm right now, because you're an eloi and can't inherit and Harri Nissilä can't have it."

I nod. Even a eusistocratic society wouldn't allow that kind of miscarriage of justice.

"If we got married, Neulapää would be transferred to me. To *us*. If the farm is rented to someone, he might assert his right to collect and sell the harvest. It might delay our moving there for as much as a year. A year's a long time."

"Don't you think it'll seem a little strange if a masco with a good job in the Food Bureau wants to take up farming?"

"I could keep working in town part-time."

And keep dealing. Right.

"But you grew up at Neulapää. We would have someone with agricultural experience to serve as the . . ."

"Labor?"

"Exactly. An eloi wife with a farming background. It's perfect."

It does sound logical.

"You're a pure city boy. You would have a lot to learn."

Jare takes a deep breath. "I should have told you about this a long time ago. I've had an experience of deep Gaian enlightenment."

He grins and rolls his eyes.

Ah. He's been *thinking* about this. For a masco, he's sometimes scary smart. Now he's so excited that he starts counting off points on his fingers.

"One. We get married, and Neulapää is transferred as a frozen eloi inheritance into your husband's name. Two. We move there.

Three. My brethren in the faith come to teach me and help me start a bioaura farm. Some of the Gaians can come stay there. There's room in the shed and the sauna house. They live a nomadic life and won't ask for, or even want, anything extravagant or any special treatment."

It's easy to read between the lines. Jare has told me that there are plans for a building project near where the Gaians are growing their chilis. It's just a matter of time before the place is buzzing with plans and permits. Neulapää would be an ideal spot for the farm. As long as we kept a low profile the authorities wouldn't give us any trouble. They wouldn't care about some kooky religious sect moving to the woods to be one with nature. Even if an inspector did wander onto the property, he would look for the obvious things: illegal mushrooms, evidence that we were distilling alcohol or growing tobacco. By growing chilis himself, Jare could earn a nice pile of money in a year or two.

"Think of how peaceful it would be in the countryside. And think of all the organic produce. Bursting with vitamins."

The stuff between the lines was positively screaming for attention. With all the rumors about listening devices in the apartments, we'd learned to speak very carefully indoors or cover our conversations with other noises. At Neulapää we wouldn't have to think about that. Out in the woods there would also be less risk of getting busted for being a morlock, practically no risk at all compared with in the city. But Jare knew it was the reference to produce that was the greatest temptation. *Just think of what it would be like to live every day knowing that you can have as big a fix as you want whenever you want it.*

Even though I'm starting a good buzz, the black water is lapping over the Cellar floor. "Neulapää just . . . brings everything back to mind."

Jare looks at me solemnly. "You'll just have to bear it. You can do it, V."

I remember my close call in the Hedgehog.

Jare doesn't know how close I came to getting busted.

Neulapää could be the solution to the fear bottled up inside me. But I can't make a sudden U-turn without explaining why.

"I'll think about it."

Manna, my dear,

I can still remember your wish list almost by heart. When the masco at the Wedding Planning Bureau tallied the expenses his adding machine tape had to have been a meter long. Embossed invitations, a four-layer cake, live music, wedding candies with love-themed words of wisdom hidden inside. Food with more animal protein and white sugar than a normal citizen eats in a week. You wanted rose-colored balloons with your intertwined initials printed on them. You wanted flower arrangements, pink candles, and, above all, the dress: a dress with a cloud of lace and a shimmer of pearls and a cascade of tulle and a tsunami of a train, all at the same time.

I called the number Aulikki had given me. I met Jare in a popular juice bar on the edge of Laukontori. I was garbed as an eloi should be when she goes to meet a masco, and I noticed that Jare didn't recognize me at first among all the other elois who were trying to stand out from all the other elois by wearing nearly identical clothing and makeup.

We exchanged brief greetings. I asked if he was a model citizen now, and said that if he was, we had nothing more to discuss.

He laughed.

I wasn't in a joking mood. I told him I needed some advice and assistance in a matter that a model citizen would know nothing about. I wanted to know more about the ways of the city, particularly its shady ways. There's always a demand for the forbidden. There have been strange times in the past when people paid for sex, merely because selling sex was illegal. To be more specific: "I want to know how to earn some money under the table."

A lemony aroma hovered around Jare, and he leaned back in his chair and gave me an appraising look. He tapped his fingers together, thinking.

He suggested we go for a walk.

We strolled side by side through the trees lining Hämeenpuisto. I told him about you and your wedding plans. He nodded, remembered you well from his days at Neulapää. I also told him how you had focused your budding eloi feelings on him and how hurt you'd been when you thought there was a romance between us.

I also added quickly that this had been a complete misunderstanding on your part, a childish mistake. Then Jare's face changed and a smell something like turpentine floated around him.

He stopped, sat down on a bench, pulled me down beside him, and threw an arm over my shoulders. He lowered his face close to mine and said that just such a misunderstanding could be an excellent way to mislead people.

It felt peculiar sitting there, right next to a masco. With his lips almost touching my ear, Jare asked in a whisper if I'd ever heard of chilis.

That's how it started, Manna. Jare whispered lots of things that I'd never heard before.

Alcohol, nicotine, cannabis—the ban on importing, growing or processing them was so successful that the black market for them was small, almost nonexistent. But since capsaicin had been made illegal more recently, the borders still had leaks. There weren't effective means of investigation yet. No capsaicin dogs, no methods of detecting capsaicin use in the blood or urine. I learned from Jare that using chilis first produces adrenaline as the body starts to feel threatened, because the sensation is so literally potent, followed by the body's release of its own endorphins. So bodily evidence of capsaicin use is indistinguishable from the effects of athletic activities, provided the chili isn't so strong that it produces visible changes to the inside of the mouth.

Jare had, half by accident, run into a few old army buddies one night in Tampere. Among them were a couple of reckless daredevils who had their own source for small amounts of chili. Jare wasn't tempted to try chilis himself, but when they talked about how exciting it was, how you had to have your wits about you, how it took nerve to take the plunge into the secret underworld of banned substances—a world far from the light of day, where completely different rules applied—he started to get interested.

He'd offered to come along the next time they went to get some. The first time, he just stood guard as his more experienced friends made the deal in a dark courtyard. He saw two men in civilian clothes approach and, thinking that they might be with the Authority, he told them he was lost and asked if they could tell him the way to Hatanpää. The seller and customers were able to slip away from the place and Jare got a lot of praise for his audacity. His reputation grew. He soon gained the trust of a few of the dealers, and gradually he started to learn the ins and outs of the chili trade.

I don't know which came first for him: the excitement, the manly risk-taking, the heart-pounding tightrope walking of the game—or the realization of its amazing financial possibilities.

In any case, he had decided to perform a test of courage greater than any he had tried before.

I was right to think that when a thing is forbidden people will pay for it. The more chili Jare could move before the authorities caught up with him, the better chance he had to carry out his bold plan.

And now he had an idea.

A smart, convincing morlock with nerves of steel who looked like a ditzy eloi would be the perfect partner for selling chili. An eloi wouldn't be suspected of anything worse than angling for a masco's attentions. She could easily retreat with a masco into a dark corner of a dance hall or into the summer shrubbery without anyone thinking twice about it. A masco could put his hands in her clothing, or she in his; they could exchange little packages or bundles of money, and no one would think there was anything going on but what always goes on in the mating market.

I made my first run a couple of days after our conversation about your wedding.

A week later I told you—I'm sure you remember it, you were so thrilled—that I'd gotten a substantial sum from Aulikki. If you and Harri could wait just a little longer, Aulikki could give you even more, once she cashed a few stocks she had in a kitchen drawer.

A week later I told you that the rest of the money had arrived.

You had your wedding. I was so happy that you had your moment of happiness.

I didn't know what it would lead to.

Forgive me.

Good night, dear Manna.

Your Vanna (Vera)

I wish I could a pretty eloi
and not a morlock be
for my true love loves only elois
and never will love me.
  —Finnish folk song (revised circa 1955)

VANNA/VERA

November 2016

They come one at a time, each one bringing a bunch of flowers or a porcelain knickknack or a package of berry sweets or a hair doodad she found at the store that "looked like me." They elbow their way through the door, redolent with perfume and hair spray and creams, their ultrahigh heels clomping, their mouths dewy and glistening, their eyelashes gooey with mascara, their breasts molded into high, shelflike mounds that nearly touch their chins. They screech and giggle, whisper, and kiss each other's spackled cheeks.

They lisp out soft *S*'s and, as if in compensation, crow words like "fantastic" and "awful" and "heavens" in a screeching falsetto. Their names are Hanna, Janna, Sanna, and Leanna, and every one of them wishes in her heart of hearts to be my bridesmaid.

It's a girls' night. I'm serving sweet, fizzy, low-calorie fruit drinks and bite-size sandwiches and heart-shaped apple jam cookies I baked myself, each one with a few slivers of ridiculously expensive dark chocolate on top. The dark chocolate is considered healthy, so you can get it at the pharmacy without a prescription, but the price puts quite a dent in an eloi's state mating market subsidy.

The girls flock around a table decked with rose-colored napkins, flowered dishes, and colorful tumblers and admire the bows I used to tie the seat cushions to the legs of the kitchen chairs. They peek into the bedroom and just *love* my pink bedspread, and they are gratifyingly scandalized at my extravagant use of chocolate.

Hanna, Janna, Sanna, and Leanna purse their lips and open their painted eyes wide as they grill me about my coming nuptials.

"How did he propose?"

"It was so romantic. He asked how many years of home economics I took, and I told him two."

"Well, you nearly did! You've been in school more than a year."

"Food preparation, household budget, home hygiene, child care, body maintenance, and, of course, sexual adaptability courses."

"Did you take any electives?"

"Sewing and entertaining. And interior decorating. When I told Jare that, he said pretty soon I'll be a handy housewife."

Everyone sighs. What a wonderful masco.

"Well, then you *had* to know what was coming!"

"Then he said he thought I was really pretty, and that other mascos probly thought so, too. 'Cause I've given a wink or two to some of his friends, you know."

"Of course you did! That's the smart thing to do."

"Then he said, 'I ought to get a jump on the others before somebody beats me to it,' and I just looked down at the ground and didn't say anything. And then he was like, 'Vanna, let's get married.'"

"*Oooooh!*"

"Oh, Vanna, weren't you *excited*?"

"Give us the scoop on your *dress*! Strapless? Or maybe a

heart-shaped neckline? Everybody says they're all the rage right now!"

"What kind of white'll it be? Snow white or cream?"

"Are you gonna have a full veil?"

I squirm as if I'm feeling self-conscious, all the while sighing and trying to look like I'm drinking up all this milk and honey. "I don't know. I might wear my debutante gown, since it's long and white. I'm sure some of you remember it from the dance. Sort of silver-white."

"Your debutante gown? Nobody gets married in their debutante gown!"

"Well . . . see, it's sort of a . . . secret engagement."

The girls emit a deep collective sigh of expectation. They're about to hear something with the taint of scandal or the bloom of romance, and either possibility produces a delicious itch to hear more. I pause dramatically.

"See, Jare has this ex who went pretty crazy when he called it off. We've decided to do everything on the quiet, nothing elaborate. Otherwise she might get the idea to show up crying and make a scene at the wedding."

An immediate uproar follows. I'm not even sure which painted mouth is hurling which question. It's scandal and romance in one package, and it's irresistible.

"Gosh, that's *horrible*!"

"You mean you're going to have a *civil* wedding? How awful!"

"Exes are such a *pain*!"

I bite my lip, tilt my head, and look at them with pleading eyes.

"Girls, girls, *girls*. You've got to all promise me that this'll be, like, just between us."

They all nod, every one of them prepared to join this great conspiracy. I lean toward them and lower my voice. "Like *nobody* can know about this. You'll all keep quiet about it, right?"

They all swear that they will carry the secret to their graves.

I know that the story will now spread more quickly than the annual flu. Nobody will wonder why they weren't invited, or why I didn't insist on an overstuffed wedding.

"THE TRAINING OF ELOIS"

From *An Eloi in the House:*
Advice for a Harmonious Family Life
National Publishing (2008)

When you've moved in under the same roof with an eloi, it is good to acquaint yourself with an eloi's way of thinking in order to establish rules and help her adjust to them.

You have to learn to appreciate your spouse just as she is, a creature of instinct, driven by hormones. Repetition, rewards, and reinforcement are the cornerstones of an eloi's understanding. In token of her gratitude, your wife will be obedient, loyal, and willing to give unceasing love and devotion.

The key to training an eloi to be a wife is to be methodical, consistent, clear, and patient.

Obedience should be a natural characteristic of an eloi. There may, however, be tremendous variation in inherited characteristics from one individual to the next.

An eloi can't always tell right from wrong; she bases her behavior on associations and whims. This means at its simplest that if a behavior has pleasant consequences, she will repeat that behavior. If, on the other hand, a behavior produces unpleasant consequences, she will avoid it. That is why the use of mere punishments is not the best method of training an eloi; it's also important to reward and reinforce desirable behaviors.

Rewards for good behavior should also be adapted to the case at hand. If an eloi enjoys good food, it is wise to reward her with her favorite treats—in moderate amounts, of course. If an eloi responds positively to praise, then she should be complimented. Physical affection can also be used as a reward. Most elois like to have their hair stroked, have their rear ends patted, and be given a kiss not intended as a prelude to sex. Her smile will tell you when you're on the right track. For especially good behavior you might buy her flowers, jewelry, clothing, etc., but such rewards must be used sparingly in order to be effective.

Training an eloi is easiest when she is motivated. She will appreciate a reward of a food treat the most when she is a bit hungry or hasn't had a sweet or a pastry for a long time. Rewards of praise and attention also work best when it's been some time since she received any.

Undesirable behaviors can also be the cause for limiting access to rewards. This generally works better than punishment, but should negative feedback be needed, a firm reprimand or small physical reminder will usually suffice.

Timing is of the essence. Give her a command, wait for her to react, and if she does what is desired, reward her immediately. If a reward is not immediately provided she may not connect the positive feedback with the behavior. Consistency is also important. Always use the same brief commands.

Train the eloi to be obedient in varying environments and give her plenty of verbal feedback. An eloi will soon learn to recognize the tone of voice of even neutral statements. If negative verbal comments don't work, drawing her attention elsewhere is often effective (for example, in a situation where she wants you to buy her something in a store).

Make sure that your wife's daily routine has sufficient activity so that the boredom of idleness doesn't lead to dysfunctional behaviors.

VANNA/VERA

December 2016

It's impossible to describe Mirko's expression. The scent of his emotional state is a swirling mixture of extreme amazement and intense rage. He stares at me, then tears his eyes away and fixes them on Jare so fiercely that a minus man would have collapsed on the spot.

"Valkinen. You dragged an *eloi* here with you? Have you got something loose in your head?"

Ah. So he hasn't told Mirko everything about me.

"We need a farm. This is no time for a family outing, even if the land does belong to her people. What's your clever plan to keep her mouth shut?"

Jare's enjoying this. He's in no hurry to explain, and now I'm starting to feel steamed.

I walk straight up to Mirko with long, lanky strides, not swinging my hips, no pussyfooting. I stand myself in front of him with my hands on my hips and stare him straight in the eye. He stares at me with his mouth open.

"Can't you tell an eloi from a morlock?" I ask.

Mirko sizes me up, undiluted astonishment swirling around him. He looks at my blond curls, my makeup, my high-heeled shoes, my propped-up shelf of a bosom. Then he looks at Jare, who's smiling broadly now.

"Shall I add some numbers in my head? Or maybe explain the process of photosynthesis?" There are no lisping *S*'s as I say this, no trace of falsetto. Mirko is still staring, not saying a word. I give him a little pat on the cheek and return to where Jare is standing. "For your information," I tell him, "we're not a couple, although we are engaged. We're business partners. We make the deals together. You can take the whole package or forget it."

"I'm sure you realize what an asset Vanna's outward appearance can be?"

Mirko shakes his head. "I believe it. I believe it. But how is it possible?"

I raise my voice. "You can breed dogs to be small and sweet, but once in a while even the most docile parents can produce a testy little mutt. My outside is what it should be but my inside isn't."

"A testy little morlock," Mirko says, smiling contentedly now.

"Yep. A very testy little morlock when I need to be," I say.

Hello, Manna!

Do you have any idea how happy I was when you asked me to be your bridesmaid—your maid of honor? I thought it was proof that the rift between us was repaired, that you'd forgiven me, that our sisterhood could be rebuilt.

The frilly hot-pink frocks that we six bridesmaids wore were in the classic tradition—the bridesmaids should look as frumpy as possible so as not to outshine the bride. The dressmaker had done his work well; we all looked like stout, sparkly little pigs who'd just come from a roll in a pile of bright pink leaves.

All the preparations were beautifully done; the cake, the food, the music, the decorations, the dress, and the flowers were all perfect, extravagant, dripping with romance.

You were positively glowing.

You got your legal fix, your dose of an eloi's favorite drug.

There were only a few guests on the bride's side: Aulikki, me, and a couple of your girlfriends.

Your birthday was chosen as the wedding day. The groom might have had something to do with that decision. Many elois think that choosing the bride's birthday to be the most important day of her life is the height of romance, but there might have been practical reasons to do it that way, because then you can celebrate two annual events with one party, and one gift.

Be that as it may, the symbolism of the day turned out to be horribly wrong. It wasn't the beginning of a new life for you; it was the initiation of a countdown to departure.

Aulikki sat in the wedding chapel, frail, gray, and straight-backed. I had called her before the invitations were sent and told her that Harri's parents were paying for the wedding and that it would be indelicate to mention the matter to anyone—people can be sensitive about traditions. Aulikki laughed and said she understood.

Two days after you became Mrs. Nissilä, Aulikki died.

In one blow I lost two-thirds of what I most loved in life— Aulikki and Neulapää. You were the third.

Literally in one blow.

Aulikki died of a skull fracture. You may recall that it was officially recorded as the result of a fall on the front steps at Neulapää. I'm sure she wouldn't have lived much longer anyway, but somehow . . . somehow I couldn't help thinking how convenient that death was for Harri Nissilä and his wife.

Aulikki had two heirs, you and me. But because we were both elois, ownership of Neulapää passed to the nearest legally competent relative—your husband, Harri, and thus to your benefit.

Don't misunderstand me. I don't think you could have wished Aulikki any ill. You were thoughtless sometimes, thin-skinned, occasionally even lapsing into meanness, but there wasn't a trace of true, calculating cruelty in you.

It was shameful, low, paranoid of me to even think how easy it would have been for Harri to go to Neulapää—a place with no neighbors anywhere nearby—to visit the old woman, get to

*know his ersatz mother-in-law. How he would have seen the land,
calculated its value. Gotten an idea.*

It was after Aulikki died that I first saw the Cellar.

*It was as though a little sun inside me had collapsed into a
black hole, melted the gray matter in my head, and formed a
passage to a chamber somewhere on the other side. Created a
smooth-walled cavity, an open, echoing cave with a darkness
living in it deeper than the space between the stars.*

*The darkness of the Cellar was alive. It got its power from
death.*

*Black water stirred on the floor of the Cellar. And the water
was rising.*

Jare was alarmed at the state I was in, with no speck of joy, never
the slightest of smiles. He urged me to cry away my sorrow but I
couldn't. It was as if all the water in my head was needed to fill
the dark hollow of the Cellar, to make the little black ripples on its
surface rise inside my skull right to the top, to whisper, Pointless,
and Meaningless, and Evil, and Guilty! Guilty!

He was worried not just about my psyche but also about the
fact that I could hardly drag myself to school, let alone work. A
couple of sizable deals went off the rails and his reputation as a
dealer was starting to suffer.

I should have kept working. At Jare's suggestion, I had signed
up for an installment plan with the Wedding Planning Bureau.
It was the only way an eloi could spend that much money without
arousing suspicion. There was still a lot of it to pay off.

It must have been in the early-morning hours. Nothing felt like
anything, but a stray hyena was scratching at something under

my heart, tearing up my insides. I couldn't sleep. I don't know if I even wanted to sleep. My sleep was a kind of stupor that did nothing to refresh me, interrupted by long stretches of lying awake, staring dry-eyed at the ceiling of the darkened room. Nothing mattered. I thought about the knives in the kitchen.

One knife in particular. Because of my kitchen skills class, I knew how to draw a knife across a whetstone at just the right angle. The blade of my best knife was so well sharpened that all you had to do was let it fall on a tomato and the fruit would divide in two with such breathtaking ease that the victim would hardly notice its horrendous wound, the gush of red liquid from between its two halves.

That knife would be my way out. I didn't think about you, or Jare, or what you would think of that solution. My only thought was to get out of the Cellar, to empty that black water out of my head one way or another, even if I had to slit my throat to do it.

I turned on the light in the kitchen. That's how I know it must have been autumn.

I was looking for the knife when I saw the little bottle sitting on the counter with a bright-colored label that said "Pain Is Good."

It was chili sauce smuggled from the United States that Jare had bought and left at my apartment until he found a buyer for it. I'd promised to find a good place to hide it, and once he'd left I had forgotten about it.

I needed to put it somewhere before I got out the knife and did what I had to do. I had nothing left to lose, but if the bottle was found in the apartment after I died, it would cause the Health Authority to investigate Jare.

I thought about what to do with it. The surest solution would be to put it in a bag with a couple of stones for weight and toss it in Näsijärvi. The lake would be frozen over soon. By the time it was found, if it ever was, the trail would be cold, literally.

Why not send myself out the same way? That would make the world inside my head and the world outside my head one and the same: soothing, numbing black water.

I picked up the chili sauce, but my fingers were nearly numb already—clumsy, twitching—and the bottle slipped out of my grasp. I watched in horror, paralyzed, as it turned over in the air and fell straight onto the durable, easy-to-clean tile floor.

The neck of the bottle broke off. Dark brownish-red sauce splashed over the floor and onto my feet. I bent instinctively to pick up the shards of glass and got some sauce on my fingers. Without thinking I shoved my finger in my mouth and licked it clean.

The shock of pain was so awful that it pushed everything else aside. It was like a radiating, rhythmic flogging that penetrated my mouth and my throat and my whole body. It started at the tip of my tongue, crawled its way to the root, and then thundered through my gums and palate in a screaming treble, all the while filling my mouth with a deep, dark red, a twilight of rumbling bass, almost lower than human perception. And as I shouted out loud and groaned and tried with shaking hands to cool my mouth with water, bread, anything to cover up the burning, I realized something amazing.

It was like a hot wind blowing through the Cellar.

As if a door to the Cellar had opened and a little sliver of merciless desert light had passed through it—cruel and hard, but light nevertheless. My heart was pounding, pounding like crazy, pounding like something thrillingly alive, and second by second my thoughts were becoming clearer. I was able to think of more than just the pain in my mouth.

I looked at the puddle of sauce on the floor.

I thought about the knife.

About its meticulously sharpened blade.

About how that flawless blade could scrape up every little drop of the sauce.

And not let it go to waste.

That bottle of Pain Is Good had to be worth thousands of marks. But Jare wasn't even shocked or upset that I'd broken it. His sincere sigh of relief that I was feeling better was like a breath of birch leaves and lakeshore breeze.

At first I didn't think to tell him that I had saved the sauce. I'd gathered several tablespoons of it up in a little cup. The skin on my bare feet was tender as if it were sunburned. I knew now that one drop of the stuff was enough for what I later would come to call a "fix."

I realized that I had to tell him.

I said that I would only use capsaicin now and then, when I needed it, that I could quit any time. I knew a lot of our customers said the same thing—they were just "chillers," occasional users, just having fun.

The feelings Jare was exuding were so complicated that I couldn't quite pick out the different scents. There was tart, citrusy fear and worry, and the smoky smell of surprise, and sometimes a flicker of his familiar lavender-apple-rosemary.

"Like I always say, V, a good dealer never touches the stuff."

I told him it was just a temporary thing.

But I can't lie to you.

It didn't stop there. You probably guessed that.

I love you, my sister.

Vanna (Vera)

JARE SPEAKS

December 2016

While I'm arranging to have Neulapää transferred into my name, business really picks up.

The fresh score I got from the Gaians is starting to run out as they gradually wind down their greenhouses to get ready for the move. It's hard to grow in the colder winter months anyway. But there's as much flake as anyone could possibly want. I get a new batch from them every couple of months. I don't have to pay them anything for it; it's their advance payment for rent at Neulapää.

We're making amazing amounts of money.

Instead of using the bulletin boards, V and I have a new way to find customers that is simple but effective. We use the personals. The ad is always purportedly taken out by an eloi, since we're naturally looking for mascos. The wording varies, but the key point is that the ad always uses the word "hot" or "burning" or "fiery," as in "Beautiful eloi is ready for a fiery relationship with someone ready to take the plunge." We change the name and the coin-operated postbox every time, and V always goes to collect the replies. The authorities aren't interested in the romantic exploits of an eloi. I don't worry much about the security cameras. V's always dripping with makeup and hair spray, in a corset with cleavage, looking like one of the fashion dolls that little elois play with. She wears clothes from FemiDress, the state store. She fits the description of a thousand other elois. Ten thousand.

Of course we get a lot of responses from mascos taking the ad at face value. But the respondents who know what's what play the game right. They write as if they want to get to know her, but they sprinkle their letters with lots of words having to do with heat: talk about being on fire, about a hidden flame, use the kind of code I learned from Mirko. "Do you have the hidden treasure I'm looking for? Will you whisper in my ear, 'You're getting hotter'?" Those are the ones we write back to in a way that will still sound like romantic overtures if the letters fall into the wrong hands, but includes hidden information about bulletin board locations, identifying pictures, key words. When a potential customer shows up at the refreshments bar, a few exchanged words make it clear whether we're on the same page. Only then do we arrange where to meet for the first deal, which often leads to a regular customer relationship.

No one's interested in why an eloi who's engaged, or even married, would be placing ads in the personals. A free, unregulated mating market is to everyone's eusistocratic advantage. An eloi looking for companionship outside of marriage might have extremely loose morals, but if it provides another, unmarried masco some satisfaction, what's the harm in it? At worst it could cause a little scuffle between two men. It's ten times more common for a masco to be looking for next year's model.

Consistent quality is our selling point. It used to be, especially before V was in on the game, that I'd be sold half-fake stuff, adulterated with formic acid or some other substance that stings the mouth to fool inexperienced users into thinking it was capsaicin. When V's tolerance started to increase she realized the potential of the vaginal test. The level of capsaicin doesn't have any connection to the taste, and the real stuff can only work on the mucous membranes in one way. But the Gaian stuff is always good. You don't even have to test it.

My travel fund keeps growing and growing. That's mostly thanks to V. It's still nothing near as much as I need, but at least I can see that the goal is attainable. Over the past couple of years at least two guys I know in a roundabout way have been transferred abroad from the Food Bureau by greasing the right official wheels. One went to Tokyo to spy on the matsutake mushroom market and the other to a factory in Germany where they process Finnish blueberries into health lozenges.

Our newfound wealth doesn't show. Sometimes I buy a book for V; sometimes we go to the movies. Of course V isn't that interested in the short romances and melodramas geared toward the eloi audience, and the war movies full of acts of heroism and patriotism made for the mascos bore her pretty quickly, too. We mainly do it just so that we can be seen in public as a couple.

I've heard that in the hedonist countries drug dealers drive fancy cars and wear tons of jewelry and drink expensive alcoholic drinks and dress like kings.

I wouldn't trade places with them. Right now the most important thing is that V is all right.

Dear Manna,

Do you remember the weekend in October when I was helping to dig up the rutabagas and put them in the cellar?

When Harri came into the living room at Neulapää with a red toy train in his hand?

I still get the shakes when I think about it.

At first I didn't understand why you and Harri wanted to keep Neulapää. I thought Harri would sell it immediately. But then it occurred to me that Neulapää was Harri and Manna Nissilä's country house. A powerful status symbol. A villa, a dacha, almost an estate, at the edge of nature, where the two of you could promenade up and down the paths arm in arm and invite city guests in the summer to enjoy the cool greenery and birdsong, the scent of lilacs and the shade of the apple trees.

I'm sure that's what Neulapää seemed like to you. To be the mistress of Neulapää was like a story in Femigirl *magazine, a place where the lady of the estate could sip chilled mint coolers in the gazebo with friends.* Femigirl *gave you the idea that getting married would change your life into a fairy tale; once a masco came along, control of an eloi's life was outsourced and the crazy, chaotic world became clear and orderly.*

But that's not what happened.

You called me often after your wedding. Almost too often, though I was always happy to hear your voice. It usually had something to do with summer chores. You couldn't remember when it was that the vegetables Aulikki planted should be harvested, or you'd forgotten how to preserve them. Should this go in the cellar or the freezer? How do you make sauerkraut again?

Oh my delicate, wide-eyed, endearingly energetic kitten. Of course I would come on my weekend off to help you out. Brother-in-law Harri strutted around the place like any city masco, knowledgeable enough about pipes and wiring and the secrets of light switches but happy to leave the gardening to us elois.

We weeded and harvested, picked berries and made juice, shelled peas. I offered my advice, gave you little tips, but also took care that I didn't talk too theoretically or knowledgeably when Harri was around, remembering to lisp and end my sentences on a shrill pitch. I acted like a chimpanzee doing tricks she's been taught through frequent repetition. But all my effort went down the drain when Harri walked into the room with that toy train.

I exuded fear as bitter as cranberries.

Harri shook the toy train in front of us as if it were covered in blood, as if it were an amputated hand. He asked you sharply if Aulikki had babysat any masco children.

You shook your platinum curls, sure of yourself for once, at just the wrong time. "Nope! No way! There was no one here but us elois!" you said.

Harri's sandy-colored eyebrows scowled. He'd found other boys' toys in the attic as well. Letter blocks. Even some sort of toy gun.

I started to feel dizzy. What a stupid mistake we'd made, Aulikki and I.

Elois have difficulty lying. You immediately turned to me and said, "I'm sure Vanna knows why."

I looked at Harri with my big blue eloi eyes. "They must be Grandma Aulikki's fiancé's things. She was going to get married once but the masco skipped out on her. When he left she still had all his old things. And she saved everything. She saved her old ballroom gowns, too."

The dresses were a nice little jab. Harri didn't like talking about those dresses, not at all. I had a hunch that selling those dresses hadn't been your idea. Harri looked at me narrowly and the soil smell coming off him was so strong that I thought he might be ready to dispute what I'd said. But there was also a strong smell of lemons, which told me that for now he was simply suspicious.

"Grandma Aulikki was so silly," I said, and giggled, though my heart was frozen through. "She had a fiancé—I mean, like, a real fiancé, not our grandfather—but that was decades ago. And she was going to have a baby with him, but the baby was never born, it was a miscarriage, so Grandma Aulikki never got married because the masco didn't want a wedding if there wasn't any baby," I babbled excitedly, feigning an eloi's relish for gossip. "So she went a little nutty and saved his toys, thinking that he might come back someday and make another baby with her. Isn't that pathetic?"

I flashed a look at you, desperately hoping that you would follow the herd like a good eloi, and you did.

"Yeah. That's what happened. Just like she said. Exactly like that. Pathetic."

Harri's tense shoulders relaxed and he exuded a scent of laundry dried in the sun. He believed us.

"Grandma Aulikki was such a silly head!"

I stretched my face into a grin. You did too, like a mirror image.

"She really was a silly-billy head!" you said.

You saw your reward in my face, took Harri by the arm, and lifted your shockingly beautiful, cherubic face toward his and laughed, happily and loudly. "We had just about the dumbest, silly-billy-headedest granny in the whole world!"

Then you disappeared.

I already had the Cellar inside me, but oh, how it dug itself deeper, how much darker and broader and hollowly echoing it grew.

Its darkness was the darkness between the stars, cold and indifferent. Sometimes there was a flash, a supernova of pure hate, exploding in scorching flames and then dying. But even the roaring brightness of my hatred couldn't light up the suffocating blackness of the Cellar.

And at the bottom of the Cellar flowed more and more swirling, night-colored water.

Your sister,
Vanna (Vera)

Excerpt from *A Short History of the Domestication of Women*

National Publishing (1997)

In the nineteenth century, a wave of unprecedented violence and chaos swept across Finland. This phenomenon began in Ostrobothnia in western Finland, and in retrospect the initiating factors are easy to trace.

The west coast of Finland had become quickly prosperous. Tar was a commodity in great demand and large quantities of timber were cut to produce it. This freed up large areas of arable land, which in turn led to a glut of grain. Grain that isn't sold must be stored, but grain doesn't keep long, so the only effective way to exploit it monetarily and preserve its value was to produce another commodity that was in great demand at the time: alcohol.

Prosperity also led to an increase in population. The number of children per family grew, and in some places the increase in offspring made it impossible for the youngest sons in many families to be allocated land or other means of livelihood as an inheritance. Having no home or occupation of his own made it difficult for a young man to find a wife. The situation was made more difficult by the fact that the inhabitants of Ostrobothnia had traditionally attached a strong social value to a house, a farm, and other acquired possessions.

The idleness of an unmarried state, the ubiquitous availability of alcohol, and young men's competitive nature combined like sulfur, charcoal, and saltpeter to form a volatile mix that needed only a little spark to cause a tremendous explosion.

That spark was struck during the time of the troublemakers, or the knife-fighters, as they were called. It was a period of unprecedented fear and terror. At its worst point there were more than 20 homicides per 100,000 residents in a single year. The period between 1820 and 1880 is a shameful mark on the history of the Finnish people and its social system, and a strong warning to us. It showed us that ordinary, respectable young men can be completely corrupted when their basic rights are neglected. Marriage and the position of natural dominance and regular enjoyment of sexual intercourse—so important to a man's personal well-being—that marriage provides are fundamental rights that the state should have granted and protected for the good of society instead of allowing deviant behaviors to foment to the point of acts of murder.

Luckily the state, in the form of the Finnish Senate, did not fail to act. Thoughtful statesmen such as J. V. Snellman introduced stricter punishments for knife-fighters. But Senator Johan Mauritz Nordenstam, well known and deeply respected for his efforts to restrain the recklessness of many young people, proposed cutting the problem off at its root. Instead of trying to rein in young men's unrest through force, a clause was added to the parish laws fining young women for "unjustified jilting" (an infraction known today by the more contemporary term "willful mating misconduct," though with the advancement of our present Finnish social order it is a clause rarely invoked). Since it was clear that the unrest was largely caused by young men whose proposals had been rejected, it was decided that the fine would be exacted from those young women who for reasons of misplaced pride or sheer obstinacy refused an offer of marriage. Henceforth, the only legally valid reason for a refusal of marriage would be a suitor's infliction of serious physical injury or proof of his criminal background.

This action on behalf of dispossessed young men offered an immediate and noticeable improvement in opportunities for obtaining a wife and family, and through them a meaning and direction in life.

Of course, wealthy households could easily pay the fines, which allowed well-to-do fathers to avoid surrendering their daughters to any suitor who came along. This was, in a way, understandable, since many marriages at that time entailed combining land and possessions. The marriage chances for dispossessed young men who were discriminated against on the mating market nevertheless unquestionably improved, as could be seen fairly quickly in a gradual return to social stability.

At this time another discovery was made that would be very significant for the future. Most of those who obeyed the new law were meek-natured girls who recognized limitations on their own value and desires and were aware that a marriage proposal was an honor for a young woman and in accordance with nature's laws. It was noteworthy that over time this attitude was increasingly passed down to female offspring—partly owing to genetics, but also largely as a result of being raised by mothers who had internalized these moral values. Uncooperative or overly proud young women, particularly those of modest means, often had to compensate for unpaid fines through imprisonment or resort to unseemly means to pay them, which caused them to age prematurely and left them with decreased hopes for matrimony. Those who had the means to pay their fines and avoid imprisonment, on the other hand, might be quickly labeled as "penalty girls" and be assumed to be ill-tempered, coldhearted, or of questionable moral character, and thus they, too, were often left husbandless and unable to pass on their socially damaging characteristics to their female offspring.

This discovery was extremely important to social welfare, and the government made an effort to reinforce this positive development—it began to select meek-tempered girls for matrimony.

A personality test was developed for the purpose, made up of a series of questions about opinions and attitudes and administered by parish pastors in conjunction with confirmation classes. If a girl's answers were appropriately submissive, she would be confirmed and given permission to marry. The personality test made up for the shortcomings of the traditional confirmation exam, which had concentrated on qualities of secondary importance to motherhood and marriage such as literacy and knowledge of the catechism. Because the use of the new test produced consistently positive results in the life satisfaction of marriageable men and promoted social order, it was eventually adopted throughout the country.

This step produced one of the pillars of Finland's eusistocratic system, and with the advent of Francis Galton's eugenic theories at the beginning of the twentieth century, Finland's eusistocratic project was further clarified. The theory of eugenics created completely new and brilliant insights into the future of the Finnish people and all humanity. Positive racial hygiene incorporating both training and genetic selection was understood to be an essential complement to negative racial hygiene, which used a variety of rules and limitations to prevent the birth of weak specimens. Later, a deeper understanding of the work of Gregor Mendel and Dimitri Belyayev and of the mechanisms of genetics served to carry the torch of eusistocracy still further.

Another important pillar of our society was, of course, prohibition, which went into effect in 1919 and was later expanded to include not only alcohol but also many other "recreational substances" dangerous to health and welfare, substances whose unfettered use we still sometimes learn about in school when we study the hedonistic societies.

One might think that prohibition is completely unrelated to the domestication of women, but these two cornerstones of our eusistocracy are inextricably connected. While it is true that public health is protected by restrictions on the availability of dangerous substances, it also must be recognized that human happiness and a balanced life are naturally connected to certain specific chemicals in the brain that promote a feeling of well-being. Physical exercise, regular sexual intercourse, and the satisfaction of serving as the head of a household—or, for the weaker sex, the joys of motherhood—are important sources of these brain chemicals.

The duty of a eusistocratic society is to support the pursuit of this good life and to strive in every way to lower the barriers to its achievement.

Establishing prohibition as a permanent part of Finnish society has not been without its problems, however. In the early days of prohibition alcohol was smuggled into Finland from elsewhere in Europe in large quantities. Systematic prevention and surveillance, and above all substantial toughening of punishments, succeeded in bringing contraband under ever greater control. An absolutely thorough system of border control, applied to both people and goods, essential in the enforcement of prohibition and created for that purpose, later proved a blessing in other ways as well. The Finnish eusistocracy has no need for decadent democracies' luxury goods, for dangerous substances demoralizing to the public health and destructive to human welfare, nor for the soulless human worms who attempt to exploit such substances for personal gain. Strict control of our borders also ensures that deceitful propaganda isn't allowed to undermine the development of our society or rot away the heart of our eusistocratic system.

Wartime, as difficult as it was for the heroic Finnish people, provided a more favorable growing medium for our eusistocratic endeavor than ever before. The unavoidable loss of men on the front brought about a situation in which marriageable women far outnumbered men. It was a time when docile-natured women could more effectively be steered into marriage and procreation, while overly independent women were enlisted into maintenance and auxiliary roles required for the war in organizations such as the Lotta Svärd auxiliaries.

This meant that by the 1950s the female population of Finland was already selected to such an extent that, as awareness of Belyayev's experiments increased over the ensuing decades, it was but a small step to adoption of a systematic and scientific program of domestication.

Manna,

I swear I tried to get in touch with you. I swear by everything most precious to me.

You very rarely called me over the winter. You were living in town so you didn't need any gardening advice, but you called sometimes to ask about recipes or stain removal. I'd stayed in eloi school much longer than you had, after all, and taken courses that you hadn't because of your early graduation.

I almost never saw you in town. I sometimes saw your husband in passing. Once he was even obliged to acknowledge me when I was walking by as he got out of his car.

I expected that at any time I would get that certain news.

Baby news.

But it never came. I knew that if it had happened you would have told me immediately. I've sometimes wondered if everything would have been different if you'd gotten pregnant.

Spring came, then summer. You and Harri were staying at Neulapää while Harri was on vacation, so my phone started to ring again. You called almost every day. The berry bushes had developed a bad case of aphids; the tomatoes were blossoming but not fruiting. What's the best way to stake peas? There was a

catch in your voice when you talked about the failed radish crop,
the tops healthy looking but the roots long, thin, and inedible—
"And Harri likes radishes so much*!"*

I asked if you had thinned them and remembered to water
them, if you had pruned the tomatoes, if you had tried adding
ladybugs to the berry bushes.

You didn't ask me to come and help you, though. Just
the telephone calls. "Harri says I gotta learn to take care of
myself."

In July the calls stopped like they'd hit a wall.

At first I thought that you'd finally started to get the hang of
gardening.

Then I started to feel nervous about your silence. I decided to
call, using your birthday at the beginning of August as an excuse.
Like all elois, you set great store by your birthday—the one time
in the year when an eloi, consumed with housework and giving
birth, can be a princess again, can be the center of attention, dress
up and get presents, if only for a day. I'd been planning to ask
you if you wanted to have your birthday party in your apartment
in Tampere or in my little bachelorette's studio, or whether we
should plan a party at Neulapää. After all, it would be your first
anniversary, too—doubly important.

Harri answered the phone and said that you were out.

Out?

Where could you possibly go? Elois don't drive and public
transportation to and from Neulapää was limited.

I asked if he would call you to the phone.

"I'm sure she can't hear me," he said.

I know now that he was telling the truth for once.

Elois don't pry and they certainly don't question. I thought you might have gone out on the bicycle, maybe to pick up some milk from the kiosk. I asked Harri to tell you I'd called and to call me back as soon as you had a chance.

Two days passed and you didn't call. Of course there was a possibility that you had tried to call when I was at school or at the store or out making a deal. I knew how you liked to throw extravagant, well-planned parties, so I was perplexed. The birthday girl can't arrange the whole thing herself; it has to be a surprise, even if she actually dictates exactly what she wants to her friends and family. It was really strange that you hadn't already come to me with a wish list. When you were younger you used to start planning next year's birthday the moment this year's was over.

I was afraid you were still holding a grudge against me, although I'd thought that things had finally warmed between us. Were you planning to exclude me from the party? Maybe a gaggle of your old classmates was already planning the table setting and baking cookies and wrapping trinkets for you. Or perhaps Harri was planning some big, romantic first anniversary celebration for just the two of you?

I seriously doubted it.

I called Neulapää again. Harri answered, once again irritable and in a great hurry. You were out again. I went straight to the point.

"Has Manna told you she doesn't want to talk to me?"

"Unfortunately that is the case."

And he hung up on me.

I was flooded with worry. I knew that elois sometimes make a show of avoiding a person—it was typical competitive behavior to be "mad" at some of your friends and form alliances with others for one reason or another, whether it was from jealousy or envy or merely a desire to stir the pot. But you had invited me to your wedding, as your maid of honor no less, and I'd been over to Neulapää to help you several times.

Even if you did still have a grudge against me, your behavior was mystifying. When an eloi has an opportunity to be the birthday girl, the center of attention, she makes sure she has an audience for it. Besides, every guest would be bringing a gift, and like all elois, you loved pretty, shiny things. You definitely would have wanted me at your party.

Jare came by to plan our next drop, and I told him about my worry. I was relieved that he didn't laugh at my concern and listened to me seriously. I told him I was afraid because of what had happened to Aulikki.

Jare pointed out that stumbling on the stairs and hitting your head weren't unusual accidents for a woman of Aulikki's age. If Harri had wanted to kill Aulikki so that he could get his hands on Neulapää, wouldn't he have waited for a time when the connection wouldn't have been so obvious?

Be that as it may, I was tortured with worry. The dark water in the Cellar was churning, and I had to keep it from rising. I needed information more than I had ever needed a fix.

I asked Jare if he would take me to Neulapää in his work car. He pondered for a moment and thought of an excuse he could use for taking the car there, but I wouldn't be able to come with him.

It would do. I asked only that if he saw you he would try to find the reason for your coldness.

He agreed.

I knew that you might be shocked to see Jare. But it was the only way I could think of to quickly find out what was wrong.

He told me what he saw when he went to Neulapää. Hopefully someday, if I find you, I can shed some light on at least some of what Jare was thinking, why he acted the way he did. For my sake and yours.

Until next time,
Your sister,
Vanna (Vera)

JARE REMEMBERS

July 2016

I drove straight to Neulapää, parked right in front of the steps to the house, and slammed the door with exaggerated force. Driving a government car is enjoyable in a mean sort of way. People stiffen, get flustered, behave with artificial politeness, even fear. Perfectly law-abiding citizens will start to look around and wonder if they've broken some rule and not realized it.

Before I could even knock Harri Nissilä was already standing in the doorway. His hands were on his hips and his face was a mixture of nervousness and defiance.

"What do you want?"

I introduced myself: Inspector Valkinen from the Food Bureau. I showed him my card and said that because the property had recently transferred ownership, it was my responsibility to make a routine inspection and confirm that no illegal nicotine- or capsaicin-producing crops were being grown there and no alcohol was being produced. The Food Bureau had no resources for any such routine inspections, but how could Harri Nissilä know that?

He relaxed a little and put on his shoes, ready to show me the fields and outbuildings. I looked around. The air was warm and clear. If Manna was at Neulapää, why was she keeping herself indoors?

As we made the rounds Nissilä chattered about how it was just a summer place for him and he grew only enough food for his own needs and his vacation was over the next week and he would be going back to town. I noticed he kept saying "I" and "me," rather than "we" and "us," but I let it pass.

As expected, I didn't find anything illegal going on behind the sauna or in the shed or the barn loft. I said I'd like to look in the house. Nissilä let out a pointed sigh, but he showed me in. I didn't see Manna anywhere. The rooms had changed a great deal since the last time I saw the place. They had an unmistakable eloi's touch.

The room that had been Mrs. Neulapää's bedroom was now filled with a large double bed. Still no sign of Manna. There was a small dressing table in the corner scattered with makeup and lotions and creams. A hairbrush with long strands of platinum-blond hair in it. As if Manna had been there just a moment before brushing her hair and had stood up and stretched and gone to run some errand.

For the sake of appearances, I peeked into the kitchen and Vanna's and Manna's former rooms, one of them turned into a guest room now, the other some kind of manly den with a writing desk and some papers and manuals about heating and air-conditioning.

No trace of Manna.

I leaned back casually against the kitchen table and said, "Is the lady of the house not in?"

I could see immediately that Nissilä didn't like that question one bit.

"My wife has gone shopping."

"Ah. Where does she do her shopping? There must be very few shops out here."

Nissilä opened his mouth, but we both knew that anything that came out of it would be bullshit. I knew the services in the area quite well from my days as a summer farmhand. And the bicycle was parked in the yard.

"Berry picking, I mean. There's been a nice crop of blueberries this year. Picking berries at this time of year is like going to the store without needing any money. Heh heh."

My respect for Nissilä's intelligence rose a notch. Blueberries indeed. They were even in season. But for some reason I knew—without a hint of doubt—that Manna wasn't out there crouching among the tussocks and swatting the bugs away. Elois shun the woods. To them the woods are a chaotic, ever-changing place, lacking the regularity and permanence and familiarity of a street or front yard.

"Aren't you worried she'll get lost?"

"She always stays close by. This area's familiar to her. This is my wife's childhood home."

Another point for Harri. I was impressed. Truth is always the most effective weapon when you want to lie convincingly.

"Is there any other nook or cranny I can show you, or shall we consider this inspection complete?"

He was fucking with me. That meant two things. First, that he had no suspicion I was interrogating him and thought I just happened to inadvertently hit upon a sore subject, and he had, by his reckoning, sailed through it admirably; and second, that he really wanted to get rid of me, and fast.

"Thanks for your time. I'll report that no further investigation is necessary."

Naturally I had every intention of investigating further. There was something rotten going on, rotten in every way. I knew how obsessive elois are about their birthdays. Vanna could call Manna's friends. If Manna hadn't gotten in touch with any of them about a party, then something was terribly wrong. And I suspected that Harri Nissilä's fingers were in it.

166

SUBMISSIVE PERSONALITY TEST FOR YOUNG WOMEN

Excerpt from the Supplementary Confirmation Questionnaire (1912)

How do you greet your husband when he comes home from work or from the fields? Choose only one answer.

1. I ask him to wash up and come eat.
2. I remind him of his chores.
3. I request his participation in household tasks such as chastising the children, preparing the meal, cleaning, etc.
4. I welcome him home and give him a kiss in greeting.

If your husband approaches you with conjugal intent, how do you respond? Choose only one answer.

1. I accept his advances, provided there is no reason to refuse such as monthly troubles or illness.
2. I request that he wait until I have put the children to sleep and have completed my other household duties.
3. I remind him that we already have a considerable number of children and that abstinence might be prudent.
4. I give myself to him willingly and unreservedly.

Who in your opinion is the best person to turn to for guidance and instruction on the road of life?

1. My father, brother, or parish pastor.
2. My mother, sister, or aunt.
3. I believe I know how to make my own decisions about my life.
4. My husband or fiancé.

How to score the test:
Nos. 1 and 4 are correct. No. 2 is acceptable provided the girl is otherwise good-natured. No. 3 is unacceptable.

Dear sister,

Just one year after your wedding, your coffin was lowered into Kalevankangas graveyard.

There weren't many mourners. Harri was still in custody, and for understandable reasons his family didn't come to the funeral. Besides Jare and me, only a few of your bravest, or perhaps softest-hearted, friends dared to come. Elois prefer to avoid any sort of unpleasantness. Some of them were probably attracted by the possibility of gossiping about it afterward with their friends, calling it a tragedy, whispering together and shuddering with horror. Manna's husband. The man she married, a murderer.

I'm sure it would never occur to them that such things happen all the time. An angry, frustrated, or otherwise dissatisfied masco fulfilling his duty to instruct with a slightly too heavy hand. It's so common and tacitly accepted that it's usually punished with a sentence of only a couple of years, and half of that on parole. We could no doubt expect the same for Harri.

Jare and I were the only ones at the funeral who knew the coffin was empty.

I had thought at first that you couldn't have a funeral without a body. But the funeral director told Jare that missing persons cases were common enough that it was a quite normal practice.

And that it was quite understandable that the loved ones of a person presumed dead would want to have a place to remember her, even if there was no body in the grave.

I couldn't help but be fascinated at the idea of the burial of empty coffins. I wondered aloud whether it was done to dupe people, to lead them to believe that defectors were actually dead. Jare shook his head. There might be such cases, but most people who disappeared were elois.

I had called around to all your friends, and every one of them said that you hadn't been in touch with her at all and she'd thought you were "mad" at her and didn't want her to come to your birthday party. You'd vanished from everyone's life, not just mine.

I begged Jare to do something. There was nothing I, as an eloi, could do that would be taken seriously. But because I was miserable and tense and sleepless and nervous and worried about you, we had to take extreme measures. I didn't like it, but it was the only way.

We got engaged.

Forgive me, Manna. I had to do it.

It meant that Jare and I had an official relationship. We were presumed to be soon to marry. And that meant that Jare could go to the authorities to inquire about his fiancée's sister's disappearance and request an investigation. Because the missing person was just an eloi, and a married one, answerable to her husband, the police weren't particularly interested in the case, but they did make a routine visit to Neulapää.

They didn't find you there.

They searched the farm and adjoining woods and didn't find any signs of recent digging. The garden was so full of weeds that if there had been any turning of soil in the previous few weeks it would have been easy to see.

They dredged the well. No body.

At my suggestion, Jare told the police to look in Riihi Swamp, told them you had once almost drowned there. They searched the shore and even brought dogs, but no remains were found.

Then there was a breakthrough. A few of your platinum hairs were found in the trunk of your husband's car. A few drops of something dark were also found, probably in a spot where they hadn't been noticed and wiped up. They were identified as human blood.

That was evidence enough. Because the corpse-sniffing dogs didn't identify the car, it was likely that Nissilä had knocked you unconscious, driven you to some unknown location, killed you there, and hidden the body.

Even under heavy questioning, Nissilä refused to show or tell where your body or remains were. He just accepted his ridiculously lenient sentence, his slap on the wrist. And a year later he would be let out, for all intents and purposes a free man.

Harri Nissilä might have been stupid, but he was no idiot.

He must have learned that the person who had requested the investigation was the very same Food Bureau worker who had inspected the farm. He may have found out that the Food Bureau actually never made inspections like that.

And now that same man was my fiancé.

I'm sure Nissilä smelled something.

He had been perpetrating the perfect crime. He had a wife who had inherited a nice piece of land. The only living relative of this wife was, as far as he knew, a softheaded eloi, a little simpleton, *and once you had coldly shut her out it would be clear to her—to me—that you no longer wanted any contact with me.*

If no one had asked any questions, there would have been no reason to suspect anything. You know better than I do the length and strength of eloi friendships—if you don't see a friend for a week, she's as good as forgotten. And to the rest of the world, what an eloi does or doesn't do is a trivial matter. If Mrs. Nissilä doesn't come to her husband's company party, for instance, nothing could be less remarkable. Many a masco wishes his wife would stay quietly at home where she belongs.

If there hadn't been a police investigation, your husband probably would have waited a short time, sold Neulapää, and then obtained a divorce. It's a simple matter of declaring the marriage terminated and you wouldn't have had anything to say about it.

Then he would have been a divorced man and ready to rejoin the mating market. Manna Nissilä, née Neulapää, wouldn't have been missed by anyone. She no longer had any educational obligations, or offspring, or living parents, or relatives with any legal standing. If she didn't want to apply for state alimony benefits, that was her business; no one was going to force them on her.

Manna Nissilä's official status would have been so invisible that she might as well be dead.

No one would have wondered whether she really was dead.

But are you?

Your body hasn't been found.

Did you run away from Harri? Maybe he mistreated you, was mean and cruel and sadistic. Every time we met you were

*wearing heavy makeup, enough to hide any small bruises you
might have had. You might have tried to get away, maybe
hitchhiked somewhere, could have gotten pretty far if you were
nice to the driver. Maybe somewhere out in the woods there are
kind people who help elois who've run away from their husbands, like people did for runaway slaves in the United States,
feeding them and sheltering them. Maybe you're someplace like
that, hiding. Maybe that's what happened to other elois who
mysteriously disappeared.*

Maybe I'm clutching at straws.

*Hair and blood in the trunk? That seems like indisputable
evidence.*

*But what if you just bumped your head on the trunk when you
were getting groceries out of the car? I mean, I'm sorry, but that
would have been just like you.*

*It's stupid to sustain myself on this utterly unfounded nugget
of hope.*

*After your funeral I sank into the Cellar and stayed there for
days, barely able to keep my nose above the black water.*

If only I hadn't . . . If only. If only.

*If only I hadn't made friends with Jare at Neulapää. You
would have simply had a typical eloi crush on Jare, a first case of
unrequited puppy love. A way to practice your emotions, a small,
inevitable setback in your preparation for life.*

If only I hadn't broken your heart.

If only I hadn't spoiled your coming out.

*Then you never would have rushed recklessly, defiantly into
a marriage with Harri Nissilä.*

If only I hadn't paid for your wedding.

You would have had to wait. You might have changed your mind. Harri might have changed his mind. You might have never been able to scrape the money together.

If only.

The dark Cellar water lapped against my face and nearly drowned me.

Because I was engaged, a blind eye was turned to my recurring absences from school. Jare wrote notes to the school with various excuses for my absence, sometimes illness, sometimes wedding preparations. Otherwise I'm sure I would have ended up in some kind of institution for unstable elois.

Jare was at my apartment frequently. He didn't necessarily try to talk to me or cheer me up. He didn't try to get me to go out. He was just there and tried to answer if I managed to say anything.

After I'd been in the Cellar for almost a week, I got out of bed to go to the toilet.

On the floor in the main room was a little plastic bag. As if it had fallen out of Jare's pocket when he sat down at the table.

The bag was filled with red pieces. It was a basic bag, our standard sell, maybe about two teaspoons.

Flake.

I felt my salivary glands activate as if from an electric shock. It was the first clear sign that I was alive in days, the first step out of the darkness between the stars, spattered with supernovas of hate and the black liquid of guilt.

I remembered how I'd gotten out of the Cellar after Aulikki's death. History was repeating itself. It had a satisfying symmetry.

There was a little pot of soup on the stove. It was canned vegetable soup that Jare had bought for me. I'd even eaten a little bit of it.

I turned on the burner.

I picked up the bag and dumped the contents into the pan.

A watched pot has never taken so long to boil.

When Jare came over after work I had washed the dishes and cleaned and made the bed and was in the middle of washing the windows.

A bright light was burning in the Cellar, and the floor was dry. The Cellar was almost pleasant. You could practically bring a picnic basket in there and spread out a blanket.

I said I was ready to plan our next buy and sell. But one thing was going to be different. My pay.

Just before your funeral I had paid the last installment on my debt for your wedding. I didn't need money for the payments anymore. I didn't need money for anything. I could take my pay in goods.

Jare was my only source for a score. We were partners.

If a business partner intends to start using part of the haul, it's best to be open about it.

I knew that now. I knew that only the fleeting, shimmeringly thin, fragile calm and hope that a fix gave could save me.

I also knew that this decision would bind Jare and me closer together than any engagement or marriage ever could.

Just a few weeks later I was completely caught up in work.

Using the stuff regularly has given me a big advantage as a dealer. I've also learned a nice new trick—the mouth isn't the only part of the body with mucous membranes. You can test the strength of a batch in other ways besides tasting it. But I won't tell you any more about such things, little sister.

I'm very busy these days, but I still make time to visit the cemetery. I bring you flowers and talk to you whenever I stop by your grave. It's a place that's important to me in a lot of ways. And I have a public reason for going there.

We'll see each other again soon, because I've arranged to meet with a new wholesaler I've heard good things about. He claims to have some dried Naga Viper, which is a very hot variety. I'll soon find out whether he's telling the truth.

Although writing to you has really helped me feel better, I have to keep moving forward. But of course that doesn't mean that I'll ever forget you, Manna.

I don't think I'll write to you anymore. I hope that doesn't hurt your feelings. But I'll never forget you. You will always be my sister, and I know that one day I'll find out where you are.

Maybe I'll burn the letters I've written. And the smoke will rise up to the sky. I can pretend that you're there and that you're getting my letters. It's childish and sentimental and stupid, but I'll let myself pretend anyway. I don't feel any terrible affinity for religious beliefs, but I understand how some aspects of religion can be a comfort.

Or maybe . . . I'll get a little waterproof container. I'll put your letters in it.

I'll build a history for you, Manna. I can make a time capsule, put some magazine clippings or school reports or other mementos in it. Make you immortal in at least that way.

I'll hide the container well. I'll bury it. And someday someone will find it, in a world that's changed, and you'll live again in some stranger's thoughts.

I just might do that.

Good-bye, sister.

Vanna (Vera)

P.S. Jare and I have decided to get married. It's purely for practical reasons, so we can have Neulapää. Please believe me.
P.P.S. Finally, I managed to say it.

Yours.

PART II

Core of the Sun

VANNA/VERA

January 2017

Neulapää.

The coldness of the unheated rooms enfolds me like an oppressive cloak.

Our sparse luggage is standing orphaned on the living room floor. Even though I did visit the house during the short period that Harri and Manna lived here, seeing it after all this time I'm struck by how different it is from my real home, remembered from childhood. There's no trace of Aulikki's simple peasant furnishings, rag rugs, and checkered curtains; they've been replaced with deep shag carpets, ruffled pastel lampshades, decorative pillows piled on sofas, and shelves brimming with china figurines.

I peek into Aulikki's old room and recoil from the immense double bed, the rose-printed bedspread, and the ornate brass wall sconces. Manna's hand must have dug deep into Harri's pockets.

I carry my bags into my former bedroom, which has been made into a guest room. "If you have trouble sleeping in Aulikki's old room we can easily make up a bed on the sofa," I tell Jare. "It is the size of a cruise ship, after all."

He smiles and the air fills with that familiar smell that I still can't quite place, the one that reminds me of grilled tomatoes— sweet and charred and tart and sugary. "Sleeping under one blanket would save a lot of firewood," Jare says. I stop and look at him. Is he serious? But he's already examining the woodstove, peeping inside and then laughing drily. "Welp."

The stove's full of burnt paper.

"Oh for heaven's sake," I say. "Nissilä must have had Manna feed the stove. Typical Manna logic—if paper's good for starting fires, then more paper must make the fire burn that much better."

Jare goes to fetch some firewood from the shed. I find the fire shovel and start scooping the powdery gray ash and charred slips of paper into the fire pail. Among the scorched sheets is something that looks familiar.

A round red logo. I've seen it on kiosk signs and cashiers' counters in Tampere. The slips of paper are printed with grids that have X's marked on them. I find a half-destroyed piece with part of Harri Nissilä's name on it.

National Lottery tickets.

Hundreds of them.

There are some tickets with ten X's on them. It's normal to mark six. I know from the National Lottery ads that marking ten is called a "rake card" and it's a really expensive way to play because it almost doubles your chances of winning.

How was Nissilä able to afford all these lottery tickets? They're all paid for—I can see the entry stamps on the ones that aren't completely burned.

And why did he burn them? These weren't burned for warmth or as trash—this was a deliberate attempt to destroy the tickets. But what's the harm in playing the lottery? It's perfectly respectable. Lots of people do it, even elois.

Jare comes in from the shed with an armful of wood fragrant with sap.

"Look at these." I spread the burnt tickets I've found on the metal floor guard in front of the stove. Jare is clearly startled. He looks as if I'd caught him doing something illicit. I smell a sawdust aroma of shame, then a fresh lakeshore breeze of relief. He crouches down, takes some of the singed bits of paper in his hand, turns them over, and wrinkles his brow.

"He must have spent thousands of marks. Maybe tens of thousands."

"Look at the entry stamps. You can still see some of them. Most of them are from last summer. The time before Manna disappeared."

"Nissilä couldn't afford this."

"No, he couldn't."

Silence.

Jare examines the tickets. "He had lucky numbers."

"What does that mean?"

"He always marked the same ten numbers. Once you've chosen some specific set of numbers to play it can hook you for the rest of your life. You know it by heart. I'm sure Nissilä thought that if he changed his numbers or his system, or let even one round go by without playing, that would be the round when his lucky numbers came up."

I don't know what all this means, except that it's clear that Manna's disappearance wasn't very carefully investigated. They didn't even look in the stove. Or if they did, they just saw some ashes and didn't bother to examine them.

I start to shiver uncontrollably, stand up, and rub my shoulders. The Cellar. The Cellar's quite close again, its dark doorway ready to swallow me, chew me up in its night-colored gums.

"Is everything all right?"

That's Jare's code for *Do you need a fix?* It's touching how he never asks it outright, let alone suggests I have a dose. He doesn't want to do anything that supports my habit. He has to let me make all the decisions when it comes to chili.

"What have we got?"

"I'll go look. And there's something I should probably tell you about."

JARE REMEMBERS

August 2013

That summer in Neulapää changed the direction of my life.

I met you, V, and Manna and Aulikki. Old Lady Neulapää, that's what I called her in my mind.

Aulikki paid me a small salary twice a month. I would wait eagerly for payday, those few faded bills in some old used envelope. For some reason Aulikki never wanted to hand me a naked wad of money. Maybe she was protecting my fragile masco pride from the bald reminder that I had a woman for a boss.

I was given full room and board at Neulapää, and summer interns normally were either saving for something specific—putting money aside for car payments or saving up for a flashy leather jacket or a watch—or using their pay to splurge on health-taxed treats like sugar or meat. I always took my pay and got on that old bicycle that was kept next to the shed—yes, V, I know it was a woman's bike, but I swallowed my masco pride, since the alternative was a twenty-kilometer walk—and rode to Kaanaa. There was a little service station there at the crossroads and a sparsely stocked kiosk that sold newspapers, juice drinks, mineral water, and fruit sweets, as well as some basic groceries. I'm sure you remember that I always told Aulikki I was going for a bike ride and asked if she needed anything picked up from the kiosk while I was out. Sometimes she asked me to pick up some flour or salt. But I had a more important reason for going there: the kiosk sold National Lottery tickets and scratch cards.

I'd played the lottery a couple of times with pocket change before I came to Neulapää, and the very first time I played, I won. Not a large amount—four correct numbers—but enough to get paid ten times what I'd spent for the ticket. I'd made a 1,000 percent profit in no time at all! Getting rich was so easy if you just dared to take a little risk! I had a deep feeling of gratitude toward the Eusistocratic Republic of Finland. It was only natural that our fine society gave any bold, capable citizen a chance to grow wealthy without backbreaking labor.

I was intoxicated by the idea that every bill from my slim pay envelope that I sank into the National Lottery could multiply like a rabbit in heat. Tenfold at first, maybe a hundredfold next time, or ten thousand. Why save to buy a car when you can win enough in the lottery to walk right into the dealership and buy the shiniest, most modern car they've got and drive it off the lot and go and buy yourself a leather jacket nicer than anybody else has, buy a house, get a summer cottage, install a swimming pool?

I still remember that first win. I was sitting at home listening to the radio and writing the numbers down as they read them out. I was using a real notebook and a good pen, not just the margin of the newspaper—not for something this important. A few of the numbers immediately sounded familiar. I felt a sweet shiver down my spine as the voice on the radio said each number, like steps on a staircase leading toward a bright, surprising future. My heart pounded, and my vision almost went dim from the excitement. And when I looked at the ticket and saw those very numbers, just as I remembered them, the knowledge that I had won slugged me in the stomach like a fist. The feeling was dazzling, like nothing I'd ever felt before, as if a door had been opened for me leading to an endless land of opportunity.

You really could win at this game! On the very first try! What a special pet of Lady Luck I was! I hadn't won a large sum yet, but I knew that this was just the beginning. I would learn more, figure out ways to choose the right numbers, look for omens, study statistics. I would become the king of the National Lottery. I wouldn't settle for just one jackpot; I was going to win over and over again!

I got my pay every other Friday. I divided it into two parts so I could play every week, telling myself I did it to maximize my chances, but in reality wanting to listen to the drawing every week on the radio and feel the tingle of excitement, the racing pulse, the rising adrenaline in my veins. If I'd spent my entire pay all at once, I wouldn't have had any money to play the following weekend, and I would have been forced to wait another whole week.

Every time I sat down on the edge of my narrow bed in the shed next to the portable radio Aulikki had put there for me, a stamped ticket in my hand, waiting for the drawing to begin, my heart beat itself nearly in two. It was thrilling, like a drug, almost mystical. The future hadn't happened yet; it lay dormant and pure and untouched just beyond the curtain of time. And when the curtain was pulled aside, there was a possibility—undeniable, perfect, just out of reach—that standing on the other side was the luminous goddess of luck, smiling at me. Even though almost every time the curtain was pulled aside there was nothing but dust and darkness, it didn't eat away my hope, because I'd managed to convince myself that every time I lost increased the statistical probability that I would one day win.

Because I was going to win. I was going to win a lot of money. That seemed self-evident. Even if the probability of winning the jackpot was vanishingly small, *someone* won every single time—it might as well be me. And if I didn't play I was turning aside that offering hand, that thrill of possibility.

Summer passed, and there were no new wins. But I was patient. I knew that my perseverance and my gambler's nerves were being tested; I just had to hang tough through my losses and not let them shake me if I wanted to win the big prize. Besides, if I had stopped playing then, after I'd invested so much, it would have meant that all the bets I'd already made had been thrown away.

Over the summer I also learned your real nature and I promised Aulikki that I would serve as a front for your book orders. One Monday I was supposed to go pick up your book delivery at the weekly post truck. I'd always gotten the money for the books from Aulikki, but she'd had some kind of unforeseen expense and wouldn't get any more money until the bank truck came on Thursday. She asked me if I could pay for the package myself—I'd been paid a couple of days earlier—and said she could reimburse me as soon as she'd made her withdrawal.

I had to tell her that I had not a mark in my pockets.

At first she was mostly concerned about how disappointed you would be about not getting your books until the next post truck. That bothered me, too, perhaps more than anything else. But then Aulikki asked in passing where I'd managed to spend all my money, since there wasn't really anything for sale around Neulapää that would interest a young masco. She kindheartedly supposed I was sending money to my parents. Or perhaps someone in my family was sick? I said with an overabundance of bravado that I had already won a considerable sum from the National Lottery and that I intended to repeat that success.

Old Lady Neulapää was quiet for a moment, giving me an appraising look. I could see from her expression that she really wanted to say something, perhaps scold me for my wastefulness—as if it were any of her business; it was my money, earned through hard work she'd seen me do with her own two eyes. Then she shrugged and went back to whatever she had been doing.

That evening, when the work was done and I'd washed up and was lying in bed reading that day's copy of *The Future of the Countryside*, I heard a tentative knock on the shed door. I remember I thought it was you, come to take me to task for the delay with the books, and I yelled, "Come in!" a bit reluctantly. But it was Aulikki.

She sat down on the stool in the corner and didn't hesitate for even a moment, as if she feared that if she didn't speak right away her resolution would fail her.

"Jare, we've trusted you and up till now you've been completely trustworthy. But I still wasn't sure if I should tell you about another secret. I've decided to tell you because we owe you a debt of gratitude—or we will, in any case, because I believe that when you go back to town you will keep your promise not to talk about us. You're a good boy, smart, ambitious, and obviously good-hearted. So I don't want things to go wrong in your life."

On the little table by my bed were the all-important pen and notebook, and a lottery ticket with the numbers drawn that Saturday circled. There were a few random hits here and there. The best result I'd gotten was three correct numbers. Aulikki pointed at the page.

"The first time you played, you won. Not a big win. I'd guess about five or ten times what you paid. After that you haven't won anything."

How the hell did she know that? She saw the look on my face and smiled drily.

"My late son, Vanna and Manna's father, moved in high places. Before he got the transfer to a wood export post in Spain that he so wanted, he used to have little summer parties here at Neulapää and invite the bureau higher-ups and their wives. I was glad to have them. It brought a bit of change to my solitary life. He hadn't yet met his wife, with whom he later moved to Spain, so he hosted the parties alone, and I would help with the serving and clearing the tables and other things not suited to a masco's dignity. It was at one of these parties that I heard a bit of conversation that wasn't meant for me to hear—for anyone to hear, in fact."

She took a deep breath. "If you ever get caught spreading this information, you'll be in big trouble. Bigger than you can imagine."

She got up and grabbed the lottery ticket from the table. "If you win, how will you get the money? There's no address here."

"It's paid into your bank account."

"And how does the Lottery Office know your account number?"

"When you bring in your ticket, you write down your identity number and they find your account with that."

I didn't know what to think. Surely Aulikki wasn't so stupid that she didn't know these basic facts.

"The National Lottery Office has one of the only computers in Finland. It's huge, almost as big as the room it's in," Aulikki said.

I knew that. The lottery was so popular that checking the millions of entries by hand would have been impossible. That was why they'd imported a computer. They kept it in a lead room so the dangerous radiation it emitted wouldn't harm the workers at the Lottery Office. There had been a lot of discussion of the computer in the papers. They said that although computers and cell phones and other technologies of the decadent democracies had been banned in Finland because of their high levels of carcinogenic radiation, with careful safety measures this one computer could be used in ways that supported our eusistocratic system without endangering public health.

Aulikki almost slammed the ticket down on the table.

"Most of the guests at the party had already left. It was late. I gathered up the plates and glasses and took them into the kitchen, and I heard my son talking in the entryway with a high-placed official. The man was just leaving—his wife was already waiting in the car. They thought they were alone. I was standing just inside the partly opened door and they couldn't see me."

"What does this have to do with the National Lottery computer?" I said, starting to feel nervous and wondering if the old woman's head had gone soft.

"From the conversation I heard, I was left absolutely certain of one thing. That the National Lottery is not what it seems."

I could only stare at her.

"The drawings aren't really drawings. They use the computer to search for numbers that will produce small wins for as many first-time players as possible and also keep the large jackpots to a minimum. They use the players' identity numbers to find their purchase histories and the computer determines when to allow them another win—some small amount that will encourage them to keep playing. They particularly give wins to people who've taken a break from playing and then come back. If they don't want to pay out the jackpot then the computer searches for numbers no one has chosen. From what I understand they do that whenever possible."

"You mean if I keep playing, in a year I might get another tenfold win? After I've spent several hundred marks?"

"That's exactly how it works."

I rubbed my face in surprise, or maybe more in anger. "Damn." I looked at the lottery ticket and remembered the feeling I'd had when the man on the radio started reading off the numbers. That feeling of a curtain opening, a feeling in every cell of my body: the pleasurable pain, the racing heartbeat, the buzzing in my temples. A moment when anything was possible.

"All gambling is set up so the house wins." I raised my voice without meaning to, because even though I believed what she'd told me, I still hoped it wasn't true.

"Of course. The National Lottery brings in a lot of money, so the government is keen to hook people on playing. But it also provides the Health Authority with an excellent registry of people who crave risk and excitement. The same people, in fact, who might get involved in all kinds of illegal things. It's not good to be on that registry. And besides, you're not playing for the money; you're playing for the feeling it gives you. If you keep playing it won't be long before there's no room for anything else in your life. You'll just be giving your money right back to the government, leaving you penniless. And harmless."

And she left.

I was horrified, dumbfounded, at how right she was about me.

I've never told anyone about this. The moment I heard what she had to say, I realized it was something I shouldn't spread around.

I realized some other things, too. At first vaguely, then more and more clearly. That there were people who knew more than I did. People in high places, and from those high places they could see things that ordinary people can't see. Not just see them, but do things behind the scenes to influence my life in ways I couldn't predict.

That our eusistocratic society wasn't just a caring, protective big brother.

That there might be something desirable in the decadent democracies.

After that summer in Neulapää I started to listen more and more to rumors and whispers that I'd once thought were silly. Like stories about how to get out of Finland.

I stopped playing the lottery. It was no way to get rich—I knew that now.

Just one year later, right after I finished my military service, I found a new way to make money. A much, much surer and in many ways more exciting way than playing the lottery.

And I knew what I was going to do with the money.

VANNA/VERA

February 2017

There are some customs in the country that I'd forgotten. Of course people who live around Neulapää are going to drop in to say hello to the new "man and lady of the house."

Having guests is always difficult and uncomfortable. I have to pull myself together, put on the engagement ring Jare's mother left—or rather lent—to me, put an eloi's lilt in my voice, bustle around in the kitchen with herbal tea and quiche or soda bread sweetened with beet sugar. I rarely make sweet rolls or other yeast breads because using a yeast ration card too often can raise suspicions that you're keeping a still.

Yet another knock at the door—a local farmer who used to buy Aulikki's vegetables, come to pay his respects. Jare asks him into the living room and shoos me into the kitchen. Naturally there are no baked goods in the house, so I dig some cinnamon rolls and slices of apple pie out of the freezer and warm them up in a covered skillet. The different pastries thaw at different rates, of course, and the burners on the old stove are hard to regulate. When I bring my offering to the table, the slices of pie are nearly charred on the bottom and I'm not sure if the rolls are even warmed through.

I apologize to Jare and the guest for the poor offering. The farmer has decided to be broad-minded. "You'll learn as you get older. The sleigh teaches the filly, you know, that's what the old folks say. A house ought to smell like fresh-baked rolls is what I say." He turns the cinnamon roll over in his hands. "Have you folks heard that down south some people are getting television from Estonia? Those stations aren't allowed, but I suppose you can't help it if you're flipping through the channels and you happen to come across it."

There are exactly two Finnish television channels. There is no way to *accidentally* stumble on any others.

"They're going to hell in a handbasket," Jare chimes in. "Of course, in the Food Bureau, we are well aware of the downward trend in the decadent democracies even without watching their television programs. Grocery counters heaped with red meat, refined sugar everywhere, pastries and candies dripping with fat. It's a wonder the whole country hasn't gone extinct."

The farmer wolfs down his cinnamon roll and I hear a soft crunch. It's still frozen in the middle. He gives the roll a pained look.

"You know, I just thought of something . . . they have those microwave ovens there. A demonic device is what that is."

"I guess they just don't care if the entire population's brains rot," Jare says.

"There's no need for the little lady to apologize," the farmer says, taking another bite of the frozen roll. "Better a frozen roll than a radioactive one."

The constant visits are exhausting. I serve blackcurrant leaf tea or juice, hand out pitiful offerings on tiny plates. I stand at the table behind Jare's chair until everyone else has been served. Then I have permission to sit down.

If the guests are a couple, I converse only with the eloi. This bores me to death. We talk about the weather, the local gossip, and the newest clothes and makeup, and it isn't seemly to listen or pay any attention to what the mascos are talking about. If it's evening and there's a show for elois on television, we watch it: ten-minute romantic minidramas, homemaking shows, and the especially popular wedding montages.

Luckily the visits seem to be coming to an end. No one has made a repeat visit.

The most annoying thing about playing house is the way complete strangers talk about our newlywed status. They congratulate *me*. "You've got yourself a fine husband there, Mrs. Valkinen." "You have lucked out in the mating market, little lady." "Mrs. Valkinen, do you have any idea what a polite, well-mannered fellow this man is?"

I nod and smile and curtsy and look up at Jare adoringly and cling to his arm as we show our visitors out, and Jare is almost too convincing in this theater of devotion, stroking my hair and patting me on the butt with a proprietary air.

"It's such a good thing that no deserving person has to be alone anymore," one of the older mascos says as he gazes upon our youthful happiness. He's between marriages at the moment, but from his talk it seems a third marriage is not far off. A farmer not yet sixty and he's already sent two wives into state guardianship. One was disobedient, the other lazy. "I'll pay child support, of course. I'm an honorable man," he says. "I've got two little elois and one masco in diapers, and once the boy's grown it may be that I'll take him on to keep the farm going. But that's not for some time yet. Right now I need some fresh meat."

Before the door closed behind him I'd already gone to get a fix.

*　*　*

Will the Gaians never come? I liked it better when Jare and I saw each other only now and then, like a dating couple. The air at Neulapää feels thick and heavy. The two of us circle each other like nervous cats.

"OUR LAND"

Finland's National Anthem
Lyrics by Johan Ludvig Runeberg

Our land is poor, and so shall be,
to those who seek for gold.
Those who are strangers would cast it aside,
but in our precious land we will abide,
its wildlands, islands, and its shore
golden forevermore.

The feeling is beyond compare,
all here is as it should be,
no matter what fortune may to us bring
this is our land, our fatherland, we sing.
In all the world no greater grace,
and no more precious place.

Were we e'en up to glory led,
brought to the clouds of gold,
where never falls a single tear,
and joy untold unfolds from year to year,
yet to our land however poor
our hearts would yearn once more.

VANNA/VERA

March 2017

The shed smells like fresh sawdust. Jare and I have spent all winter there putting together the wooden components for the greenhouses. We've also scouted the woods for a good place to put the secret greenhouses. There's no snow on the ground. The carbon output from Finland's eusistocracy is unusually small, but the effects of the warming of the global climate caused by the loose morals of the hedonistic countries can be seen and felt here, too. Sometimes the winters are unusually long and cold and snowy because of the accelerated melting of the arctic ice, but now we're having another one of those winters when it's really only rained and the temperature has started to hold at springlike levels quite early.

Jare became a believer just in time for our wedding. He let it be known at work that he'd experienced Gaian enlightenment, and he was seen publicly with members of the sect. It didn't matter much as long as it didn't affect his work—at most it caused a few raised eyebrows and a twirl of a finger at the temple when he wasn't looking.

The Gaians arrive in two large old trucks. When they drive up and get out of the trucks the only one I recognize is the dark and dramatic-looking Mirko. The other two are strangers to me. Valtteri, who jumps down from the driver's seat, is the absolute physical opposite of Mirko: he's short, slightly chubby, with sandy-blond hair and a persistent, good-natured smile. I don't know if it occurs to me because of his soft looks, but there might be a bit of minus man in him. But I don't doubt his intelligence for a moment. His gaze is clear and alert.

The slight figure getting out of the passenger side of the truck is a surprise to me. At first glance I think that it's an almost stunted-looking minus man, but then I notice barely perceptible breasts under the heavy sweater.

A morlock.

The first one I've ever met.

She might be about forty. It's hard to tell her age, because I don't know what to make of her appearance. In the few years I've spent in Tampere I've learned to recognize the signs of aging in an eloi, things that makeup can't hide—the deepening wrinkles around the eyes and brow and the corners of the mouth, the loosening neck, the prominent veins on the backs of the hands. No one is quicker to notice an eloi's mating marketability than another eloi. It's become a learned reflex. But this person is impossible to measure on the eloi scale. She's suntanned, with visible freckles. She's not wearing any makeup to cover them. But her skin looks healthier and fresher than mine. And even more amazingly, she's obviously not wearing a corset under her clothing.

As if to stand out even more starkly, she's had her dark hair cut short—or perhaps even cut it herself, from the look of it. It just touches the tops of her ears. The Gaian mascos have longer hair than she does. She's also dressed like a masco, in blue pants made of thick fabric and a loose sweater. Her relaxed, unrestricted way of moving in her long pants and flat shoes is almost obscene. She walks right up to Jare and offers him her hand. "Hi. I'm Terhi."

She approaches him without any shyness, as if there were no question that she has a right to. And her name is Terhi! With an *R* in it! That's a letter that's always been reserved for mascos, though I've never known why.

We were once Mira and Vera, Manna and I, a long time ago, in a country where there was nothing strange about those names.

Terhi hardly glances at me, and I understand why. I walk over to her with the same long, swaggering strides that she's just displayed and put out my hand, just like she did, briskly, unabashed, looking her in the eye.

Defiant.

"I'm Vera, but you should use my eloi name, Vanna, just to be safe. I'm the owner of Neulapää."

Terhi's eyebrows shoot up. She looks at the mascos in surprise. Jare and Mirko grin at each other. Terhi looks at me again, a hint of a smile on her lips, and gives me a firm, muscular handshake.

"All right, Vanna. You really don't look like a morlock, but I believe you. Nice to meet you."

As we unload the trucks I hear Terhi and Valtteri talking. Valtteri says, "A morlock in an eloi phenotype body. It's a bit like the bitter almonds that sometimes sprout on long-domesticated almond trees . . ." Mirko has obviously prepared Valtteri for my peculiarity, but they decided to let Terhi have a little surprise. I'm pleased to learn that Gaians have a sense of humor.

There's a carefully constructed hiding place in the covered beds of both trucks that is completely unnoticeable at a glance—the only way to detect it is by comparing the inner and outer measurements of the cargo space. The hiding spaces are crammed with flats full of little seedlings and a few mature plants trimmed short. There are little packages of seeds in cloth sacks, dozens of varieties. Just the names written on the packages start me trembling and make my mouth water. Inferno. Tears of Fire. Thai Dragon. Fatalii. Malagueta. Naga Morich. Trinidad Moruga Scorpion. Deep Impact. Hell's Angel. Harrisburg. The Gaians tell us that some of them are varieties they've crossed and bred and named themselves.

They want to see the proposed site for the secret greenhouses before they've even unpacked. We take them into the woods a good kilometer from the house. We've already brought the wooden pieces for the frames, well concealed by the thick spruce canopy. Mirko gives his approval and we assemble them.

They won't let us pour any foundation "on the skin of the forest," as they put it. We dig holes for strong corner posts, drive them in as deep as we can, and tamp them firmly in place. Then we screw the main ribs to them with suspension brackets. To those we attach clever rope-and-dowel constructions that the Gaians brought with them to form a horizontal framework. The floors are made from loose squares of board that Jare and I made using instructions they sent to us. The whole thing fits together like a puzzle that can be quickly assembled and disassembled. The walls and roofs are covered in strong plastic from a large roll that Jare bought. We attach it to the frames with a nail gun.

We install battery-powered lights to keep the spaces warm as well as to provide extra light. The lights are necessary, since this is actually a ridiculous place for a greenhouse, dense and shady. But that's the point. This way it will be hard to notice them even from the air. You could walk past them just a few meters away and have no idea they were there. Valtteri gets some blinds made of black plastic from the truck and puts them up inside the frames. As long as there are dark nights and dim evenings the artificial lights will have to be hidden. He says that later in the summer, when it's light nearly round the clock, the blinds can be taken down and the lights dimmed, left on just bright enough to make up for the shade of the trees.

We shovel soil and peat into the planting beds. We've brought a wheelbarrow heaped with dirt from Neulapää's fallow fields and from the shores of the swamp, which is rich with humus.

Valtteri says that it's the new moon—apparently the best time to plant. I don't know what they base that belief on, maybe some Gaian theory of the reaction of liquids to the moon's gravitational pull. There's something endearing about the Gaians. Valtteri knows everything about his subject of expertise and is very matter-of-fact about it, and in the next sentence he might say something about "the wisdom of the soil" or "the lower powers," and I can't help smiling to myself.

We sow several kinds of seed in some of the beds and in others we gently, carefully transplant the seedlings they've brought.

I'm starting to feel hungry, but the Gaians don't want to take a break or eat anything until this most important task is finished.

I ask where they got the chili seed. Valtteri says they used to have many correspondents abroad who sent them different kinds of seeds hidden in the spines of books or other innocent-looking packages. But nowadays they produce all the seed themselves because all the mail from hedonistic countries is more and more closely inspected.

The entire time that we're planting the seeds and seedlings, Mirko, Valtteri, and Terhi chant the Transcendental Capsaicinophilic Society's "Litany Against Pain." This prayer, or spell, or whatever it is, is something I've read before, in English, on the side of a bottle of chili sauce, and I already know it by heart:

Teach me, chile, and I shall Learn.
Take me, chile, and I shall Escape.
Focus my eyes, chile, and I shall See.
Consume more chiles.
I feel no pain, for the chile is my teacher.
I feel no pain, for the chile takes me beyond myself.
I feel no pain, for the chile gives me sight.

Ugly old, ugly old morlock hag,
Stuck her head in a burlap bag,
Tried to screw a masco, took him for a stroll,
The joke's on her, 'cause there ain't no hole!
One, two, three and you are it.

—Popular eloi hopscotch rhyme (circa 1980s)

VANNA/VERA

March 2017

Every dent and spot on the white enamel electric stove in the kitchen at Neulapää is familiar to me. Remodeling the kitchen wasn't a high priority for Manna or Harri Nissilä. Manna wouldn't care because guests rarely come into the kitchen, and Harri probably couldn't have cared less what kind of facilities his wife had for her household chores.

Although Harri Nissilä did, in fact, show an interest in some of the kitchen items. There wasn't a single piece of good china left in the cabinet. It had been Aulikki's parents' set, and no doubt valuable.

Oh, Harri. You must have been in a pinch for some quick cash again.

The Gaians don't eat any animal products, not even the kind you don't have to kill the animal for. Nothing made with milk, or eggs, or even honey. I make roasted root vegetables, mashed potatoes—with no butter or milk, so they taste like an old shoe—and thick green sauce from onions and dried peas. Jare and I can eat what we like, of course, but it would be too much trouble to cook two separate meals. Besides, the inexpensive diet helps Jare save more for his travel fund.

I'm the only one here who went to eloi school, so the meals are always my job. The Gaians know how to cook vegetables, of course, but how the food tastes means nothing to them, so I've learned that it's best to offer to do the cooking myself. The mascos and Terhi do help sometimes with peeling or chopping, and they help wash up. And there is a good side to kitchen duty—I can get a little fix every now and then without anyone noticing.

The mascos are coming in from washing off the day's dirt in the sauna. Terhi sets the table. The door is closed against the chilly early spring, the evening growing dark outside the windows. It's so idyllic and homey that it's as if all of our calm, deliberate movements and relaxed conversation were a carefully polished performance for some hidden camera. Look, this group of the faithful is preparing a tasty vegetarian meal and talking about next summer's bioaura-grown squash.

This makes Mirko's question all the more jarring.

"So you're a capso."

It's as if one of the actors reciting his lines had without warning asked another member of the cast if she'd like to go have a juice after the play—it shatters the carefully constructed illusion and violently thrusts the audience into reality, which is complicated, not preordained, and more dangerous than the safe and familiar script.

I'm speechless, which isn't like me. I glare at Jare. He stares back, unflinching.

"Yes. Hi, my name is Vanna and I'm a capsaicin addict."

"I told him, V," Jare says calmly.

"Do you suspect me of stealing your stuff?" I ask as coldly as I can.

Valtteri's smiling, pleasant expression parries my iciness. "No! It's nothing like that. We want you to work with us."

"We had a capso who was our taster and estimated the scoville levels," Mirko says, "and I thought about asking him here when we start to harvest. I mentioned it to Jare, and he told us about you."

I look at Jare accusingly, although I'm beginning to understand what this is about. He still doesn't avoid my gaze.

"Every person who stays at Neulapää costs something. There's only enough room in the outbuildings for three people to sleep comfortably. I'm thinking in purely practical terms. I also don't know how trustworthy he is. I can be absolutely certain of you."

"Gosh, *thanks*."

"Under no circumstances would we—or Jare—insist that you do it," Valtteri hastens to add. "If you did do it, it would be your choice completely. And if you wanted to stop, it wouldn't be a problem for us because we could get in touch with our other contact."

"Jare said that you're a real connoisseur," Mirko says.

I shrug dismissively, but I feel my heart warming, and not just from the whisper of capsaicin inside me.

"I'll think about it."

Think about it. How long would an alcoholic think about whether to take a job as a wine taster?

"We would be very grateful if you did it. I understand you've built up quite a tolerance."

I laugh drily. "You could say that."

"That could be an immense advantage for us. It would help us increase the scoville count in the new varieties we're developing."

I scowl. There seems to be a big, tattered hole in their logic.
"Why?"

"Why what?"

"Why develop stronger chilis? It'll take years and tons of work. The customers are perfectly satisfied with the stuff we foist on them now. The average capso can get an epic high on just the ten thousand scovilles in a serrano. New, stronger stuff will be welcome, of course, and I'm sure it'll sell, but why go to all that trouble when you can make good money with the varieties we have now?"

Mirko and Valtteri exchange a glance, then Mirko sighs.

"We have some other goals besides money. We always need money, of course, but it's not the main thing. It's more about time and energy. We want to concentrate on what's important to us. That's why we outsource the sales. That's why we're spending all this money to rent space here at Neulapää. This place is ideal, and we're very grateful."

"So your goals are scientific?"

"In a way. Or ideological, you might say."

"Do you worship the plants? The stronger they are, the more powerful the wisdom of the soil?" I'm purposely needling him because I want an answer.

JARE SPEAKS

March 2017

Mirko strikes a noble pose, and as I look at his long, dark hair and hooked nose, I can't help thinking that he looks less like a Finn than a mythical "noble savage," a wise, brave, mystical member of the original Native American race. I wouldn't be surprised if his inclinations toward earth-based spirituality were something inspired by growing up looking like that.

"All cultures have at some time in the past known things that have been suppressed by our excessive rationality and the reduction of life's mystery to the merely chemical or physical. Chili came to Europe, and to Finland, because it was supposed to come here. Because it has a mission here." He has obviously made this speech many times—he delivers it so seamlessly. "Some sources claim that the Vikings brought chilis from the New World, that traces of them have been found in grave sites. In any case, they would come eventually, because their arrival was an inevitability. It was the beginning of a change in the world. Because although the north is at the top of the map, it is the route to the Lower Realms."

None of this is new for Terhi and Valtteri, but they nevertheless seem quite rapt. V smiles wryly. I can tell she's still not particularly thrilled that I told the Gaians about her little vice.

"Back in 1609 Garcilaso de la Vega described for Europeans how the Incas worshipped the chili pepper as a god named

Agar-Uchu, or Brother Chili. Agar-Uchu was one of the four mythical brothers in the Incas' creation story."

"And Brother Chili is no doubt on good terms with Mother Gaia. Just one big happy family," V says, oozing sarcasm. This doesn't seem to bother Mirko.

"Brother Chili is on good terms with humanity—the part of humanity that understands chili. Everything has a meaning. Why is chili hot?"

"Elementary. It's the plant's defensive adaptation. So animals won't eat the plant until the seeds have been sowed."

"Then why don't birds avoid chilis?"

V wrinkles her brow. "Because their digestive tracts have adapted to it."

"Right, but it's also an advantage to the chilis. The birds spread the seed. The seeds pass through their digestive systems and are redeposited in faraway places. But which evolutionary advantage came first? The advantage of a source of sustenance that chili tolerance gave the birds, or the reproductive advantage that the birds gave the chili?"

V looks bored. "You're talking about it as if plants and animals actively promote their own evolution. 'I suppose we ought to start feeding our fruits to the birds.' 'Let's start learning to tolerate capsaicin.' That's not how it works."

"I am simplifying, of course. But the relationship between people and chilis is naturally determined in exactly the same way. When a person is interested in chilis as a medicinal or recreational substance, to the chili that person becomes a new kind of bird. An exploiter, but also a spreader of seed, a means of maintaining the species. It doesn't matter to the plant whether its seeds are planted in the ground in a bird's excrement or in a human's greenhouse. The end result is the same: the species survives and multiplies. Both parties benefit. The Incas' rocoto chili, for instance, has been bred and cultivated for eight thousand years. It's been domesticated for so long that it no longer exists in its wild form."

V nods. "Got it. You and the Incas have a cooperation agreement with Brother Chili. What else is in the contract?"

"We call chilis the Fire Within that we wish to tame, the same way our forefathers tamed worldly fire."

Mirko pauses dramatically and Valtteri interjects. "Eusistocratic Finland offers us a unique opportunity for experimentation and evolution. Since all the various intoxicants that affect the central nervous system and the neurochemistry of the brain have been weeded out of society, we can conduct our experiment under pristine conditions."

"We completely understand the ban on alcohol and tobacco," Mirko continues. "They have a particularly large negative effect on society. In the hedonistic states they claim that drinking a little red wine can actually be good for your health, but there's always the risk of slipping into overconsumption. And tobacco is never anything but bad for your body. Even overconsumption of caffeine can cause sleep disturbances, heart palpitations, or digestive irritation. Any substance that can cause confusion or loss of motor control is banned for perfectly understandable reasons, because their effects can also affect people other than the user."

None of this is new to me, but I admit that the ban on chili has always been a riddle to me. After all, it's thought to be exceedingly healthful, full of all kinds of vitamins and antioxidants. A dealer I once met claimed that outside Finland people think that eating chilis can lower your blood pressure and cholesterol, and maybe even prevent cancer. If a person makes a pot of tom yam soup, pants and sweats for a while, and enjoys the feeling it gives him, how is social well-being threatened? Why the heck do the authorities care if somebody gets addicted to chilis if feeding the habit doesn't cause crime or weaken public health? I'm sure there are lots of caffeine addicts in the hedonistic countries who don't rob banks to pay for a cup of espresso. Maybe coffee's illegal in Finland because it causes a trade imbalance, an excess of imports. I can understand that. But why chili? After all, we import expensive oranges into Finland.

Does anyone else in Finland even think about things like this?

And am I only thinking about it because I'm sunk too deep in this swamp?

There must be some variable that I don't know about. But Mirko doesn't seem to have any opinion about that.

"Here the body and mind are undamaged, and thus ready to accept the Fire Within. And through it, the Lower World." Mirko continues his liturgy. "Finland also has a proud past that is more recent than we might think. Those who live in the north of Finland—the majority of them now mixed with the general population—know of methods by which a person can detach from his fragile shell and allow his spirit to move free and unfettered."

I raise my eyebrows. Although I've learned a lot of the Gaians' viewpoint and so-called philosophy by heart so I can use it and have the ring of a true believer, this gibberish is new to me.

"To arrive at this state, Lapp shamans used laborious methods, such as drumming and singing themselves into a trance. They sometimes freed their spirits with mushrooms, which our studies show to be a very imperfect and toxic method that can in fact injure the user. But chili works in a different way. It produces pure pain and pure ecstasy. At high levels, capsaicin produces an invaluable state of receptiveness. It produces tranquillity and sharpens the senses to their maximum sensitivity. *Focus my eyes, chile, and I shall See.* That's exactly what happens."

"Our goal is to breed the strongest possible chili and use it to ignite the Fire Within whenever we wish and spread it among us," Valtteri adds.

V laughs. The sound of it is like a blow. Mirko's eyes flash, his high brow furrows, but V doesn't flinch.

"This is all very interesting, but unfortunately it just doesn't hold water. Even if you set aside all the Lapp shaman mumbo jumbo and concentrate on the physiological effects, why breed a new kind of chili? Why not just use pure capsaicin? Chemically extracted pure capsaicin has a potency rating of sixteen million scovilles. You can get about two million scovilles just by separating the oleoresins from the fruit. Why take the trouble of breeding new chili varieties when you can probably devise a means to extract the alkaloids from the plant much more easily?"

I wait for Mirko to say something angry to this, but he just looks at V, her calm superiority, as if she were a small child who doesn't yet comprehend such things. "In the first place, pure capsaicin is so strong that just a few grams can put the body in shock. Animals who've been exposed to it in tests have sometimes died from respiratory failure. In the second place, a living plant that's grown in the soil has its own unique energy that is destroyed when you attempt to chemically concentrate its essence. I know how unscientific this sounds to you, but think about the vitamin C in a carrot, how its healthful properties fundamentally decrease when it's cooked. Certain forms of processing destroy the deeper essence of some substances. Artificial extraction of capsaicin destroys the natural Fire Within, the bioaura of the plant, leaving nothing but a cold, soulless, mechanistic chemical effect."

"I understand the vitamin analogy, but as you said yourself, that bioaura stuff sounds rather unscientific."

"Just a few hundred years ago electricity was a conjurer's trick done with cat skin and amber. Now you get it from a wall socket. Science doesn't know everything about the powers of nature. Think of a capsaicin molecule as a piece of iron. Just a lifeless piece of metal. But if a piece of iron is magnetized, you can do amazing things with it. You can use it to determine direction. You can use it to attract other pieces of iron. The capsaicin in a living chili fruit is like magnetized iron—it's identical in every other way to the pure chemical compound, but with an invisible element of energy."

Valtteri, who's been attentively following the conversation, clears his throat. "I don't know any other plant that has so many myths and beliefs associated with it. Most folk beliefs are pure superstition and nonsense, but sometimes an old belief has a scientific basis. People knew how to fight anemia by eating nettles and liver even though no one had ever heard the words 'anemia' or 'hemoglobin.' Some practices seem to be purely instinctive, like the way many pregnant women crave calcium-rich foods. People have been drawn to the chili in almost all cultures because they felt it was an almost magically powerful aid and companion. Now we know that it affects dopamine activity in the brain, so it's no wonder that it's been used for centuries for every sort of ailment. Not just physical ailments, but also as a method of fighting witchcraft or the evil eye, or driving out demons."

At this, V's expression changes. She grows serious and presses her lips tight, as if considering. "Fine. It's really none of my business, except that you say you need a tester. Why not just test it yourselves?"

"We don't use chili ourselves. We're waiting until we've developed a perfect variety. There's no sense in increasing our own tolerance—we want to give ourselves to the Fire Within as virgins, when it's ready to take us."

"I can only imagine," V says drily.

"We're searching for a lost, undiluted communion with nature. A state that humans have become separated from due to the effects of so-called civilization. A complete oneness with the world, freed from the fetters of being human. A state that the shamans understood. How much could we learn if we could see reality from outside our limited physical beings, as they did?"

"It certainly sounds lovely."

V's voice drips with derision. Valtteri is visibly angered for the first time. "Let me speak your language, then. It's a state known as trance possession, and very serious research has been done on it. Fakirs and shamans sought a state of trance possession through such means as cutting themselves. But they could have activated their pain receptors almost as effectively with chilis—by irritating the trigeminal cells in the mouth and gut with capsaicin. That releases certain neuropeptides in the body that then stimulate dopamine metabolism. These same neuropeptides may have other chemical effects on the brain, which we are trying to test empirically."

Valtteri and V stare at each other. Valtteri has just scored a point in this sparring match. Suddenly V grins. "What didn't you say so in the first place?"

Valtteri bursts out laughing, but Mirko is still serious.

"*Take me, chile, and I shall Escape.* We are looking for a path, and we intend to take a lot of other people with us," Mirko says, and Terhi adds, "But our escape will be inward, not outward."

Later V asks me to order her a book about shamanism. I order it without asking her any more about it. When I pick up the book at the post truck, I thumb through it. She might be disappointed with it. The only book on the subject that they had at the state bookstore isn't a scientific work. It's about shamanic spells and songs and folk poetry. There's page after page about a couple of guys named Nuwat and Ukwun.

One sentence catches my eye: "My boat is light and swift."

VANNA/VERA

April 2017

April has barely begun but the ground has already thawed enough for tilling. The Gaians brought their own seed potatoes and helped us plant and tend them in the "public" greenhouse near the main house. It's safe now to transplant them outdoors, but we're putting garden cloth over them at night in case of frost. This way we should have new potatoes to sell by midsummer. They'll sell wonderfully at that time of year, since most of the other farms don't have time for fussing with them. They plant their seed potatoes straight in the ground, so most of their harvest doesn't come to market until July.

Jare has tilled the soil with the rototiller. Terhi and I just have to dig holes about half a meter apart, set the seedlings in, and tamp the soil around them. The Gaians' potatoes are heavy producers, so it's best to plant them widely spaced. Terhi is working purposefully on the row next to mine. I glance at her now and then, her bold strides and precise movements, completely devoid of an eloi's flirtatious way of moving or posing her body. She doesn't smile unless she's amused or happy. Elois have an ingratiating smile that rarely disappears from the time they're little. They wear a smile even when there are no mascos around. It never struck me as strange, but it does now. It's as if I have muscles in my face over which I have no conscious control.

Terhi is efficient in her work, quicker and better than I am. Her fingernails are short and unmanicured; you can see heavy physical labor in her hands. She gets to the end of the row before I do, straightens up and stretches, turns her face toward the sun, which is already warm, and closes her eyes. She can let the sunlight strike her face. I always wear a broad-brimmed hat to protect my light, soft eloi skin. I finish my row and stand up.

"What's it like to live as a morlock?" I ask.

Terhi has a very masco-like way of talking. She gets right to the point, doesn't pad her talk with pleasantries or manipulation. It's strangely exhilarating to do the same, like committing a tiny transgression.

Terhi laughs, without a hint of merriment.

"I was so unmistakably a morlock when I was born that I was categorized by the time I was six months old. Did you know even some elois are born with dark hair, but it falls out after the first couple of weeks and grows back blond. That's why they don't make the final gender assignment at birth. They wait until the child is a couple of years old."

I didn't know.

"That's not what happened with me."

She crouches over the potato bed, takes a seedling in its peat pot out of the flat, and pushes her planting trowel into the dirt in one forceful thrust, as if she were trying to stab mother earth right through the heart. I can't see her face, and I sense the sawdust smell of shame and the meadowsweet aroma of confusion, tinged with a touch of the gasoline of bitterness.

"My parents gave me away as soon as it was clear that I was a morlock. I don't even know what their names were. Or whether they ever got the child they wanted. I grew up in a morlock home."

She pushes a potato seedling into its hole and presses the soil around it with her fingers. "There was nothing wrong with the place. People fit to work but not to procreate have to grow up somewhere. Besides, I should consider myself lucky. For some reason a lot of morlocks die in accidents as children."

I don't want to ask, but I ask anyway.

"What about procreation . . . ?"

There's a dark humor in Terhi now. She stands up and brushes the dirt from her face. "Ah. You want to know whether us morlocks have all the bells and whistles? Whether if I were to find some minus man who wasn't too picky we might be able to produce monster children together?"

I don't answer because the subject is unspeakably embarrassing. Has she noticed me stealing glances at her when she cools herself on the porch of the sauna? She takes her saunas with Valtteri, so I haven't seen her naked from up close. My cheeks are burning.

"Yes. Contrary to popular belief, we have all the right cooches and wombs and everything. But they sterilize us while we're still in morlock school—tie up our tubes. *Fwip.* Wouldn't want any more morlocks dirtying up the gene pool. Besides, where would we put the kids while we were working?"

"Valtteri said you met in a hospital."

"You leave the morlock home to go to work when you're still a teenager, if you're a quick learner. I changed sheets at first, but later, when they noticed that I did careful work and had a good memory and could read well, I got to work as the dispensary assistant and then as 'personal assistant' to a doctor. He was an older masco who apparently had an equally elderly wife at home. I think after having six children she'd gotten a little loose in the cooch and the gentleman doctor got in the habit of poking at a morlock now and then on the examination table. I guess there was something like affection in it, since he let me read the books he had in his office on my breaks."

"Sounds strangely familiar."

"We do what we have to for a bite of the tree of the knowledge of good and evil. Valtteri was there for a while as a patient—he'd been poisoned by some pesticide at the market garden. We just got to know each other somehow, and we got along. Of course, when he got out of the hospital I was sure we'd never see each other again. But not even two weeks later I was leaving work and there was Valtteri standing on the steps in front of the hospital. We chatted for a minute and he told me he had quit his job at the market garden and found a new purpose in life. That he'd become a believer."

"And he converted you, too?"

"I've never really been a religious person, although it's something they try to offer in morlock school. Any religion is a boon to a eusistocracy. Religion offers easy answers to your problems, ready-chewed moral guidelines, and it has the bonus of getting people to monitor their own behavior."

"That's why they turn a blind eye even to the Gaians."

"Valtteri told me about the Gaians' migrant lives, about how they were using bioaura methods to grow vegetables to sell and training people to do it all over Finland. He said that if I joined them I would have a chance to use my head and hands for something other than emptying bedpans. At that point it didn't matter whether I believed one jot in the Gaians' concept of the world. Later on, though, I came to the conclusion that they're on the right track about some things."

"Which one of you fell in love? Valtteri?"

Terhi flashes a sharp little smile.

"What kind of eloi question is that? I'd had all I could take of staring at gray-haired morlocks who'd been worked to death, pushing their mops around the halls of the hospital. That would have been my future if it weren't for Valtteri. And you. When I look around me I see trees and grass and I smell sap and wind and dirt. Neulapää is the only real home I've ever had."

My eyes grow wet. I squeeze her arm and can't think of anything to say. Terhi squats back down over the row of potatoes.

We plant the seedlings. The sun beats down and we work like machines, and I find myself thinking, *This is what it would be like if I had a real sister.*

Excerpt from "A Few Words About Sterilization and the Sterilization Law"

Hearth and Home, issue 7, April 11, 1935

Since 1926, when the Council of State first established a committee to thoroughly investigate the feasibility of passing a nationwide statute making it possible to sterilize, for social and humanitarian reasons, those individuals who would weaken society, the question has remained a subject of consideration both publicly and privately. With parliament's recent passage of the sterilization law by an overwhelming majority on March 5, it is likely that the question will sink into obscurity, as conundrums usually do once they have been solved.

A brief explanation of the question before such silence ensues is thus in order, especially in light of the fact that the adopted law is conceived in many quarters as a measure against certain social classes, and because it has been widely acknowledged that both the concept and the necessity of sterilization are extremely poorly understood. This can be seen particularly clearly in some of the speeches made in parliament before the vote. Many who took their turn on the podium propounded the aforementioned question of "class" and even made the claim that the law was uncivilized and contrary to the laws of nature. What the speakers failed to take into account, however, was that our entire modern life, with its long-developed methods of maintaining civilization, has already left the idea of natural laws and "natural selection" far behind when it comes to humanity. Society no longer rids itself of weak individuals by means of a natural instinct for self-preservation, demanding that the weak make way for the strong. The preservation of our species thus must be ensured by other means, the nearest at hand being the prevention of the birth of weak individuals.

Sterilization in the broader sense refers to any medical procedure by which a person's ability to procreate is removed. Since such procedures can be more or less thorough, we distinguish castration, by which we mean the removal or destruction of the gonads causing an inability to procreate, from sterilization in the narrower sense, by which we mean any procedure that impedes the gamete on its natural course without destroying the sex drive.

In approaching a discussion of the reasons for subjecting a person to sterilization, it must first be pointed out that in our own country, as elsewhere, various animal husbandry organizations active for decades and conscious of the fact that not every individual animal is fit to pass on its weaker or poorer traits have examined said traits and carefully chosen suitable individuals for breeding. The results of their work can be clearly seen in Finland.

It was only with the dramatic deterioration of bloodlines that there arose a cry demanding some kind of control over procreation when it came to people as well. The question never would have come into currency, however, if the rise of civilization, with its higher levels of services and all their accompanying costs, hadn't struck a chord and raised concerns.

In studies of birthrates, attention was given to the psychological and physical condition of parents, and it was observed that those segments of the population who passed on the weakest intellectual inheritance to their offspring often had noticeably higher fertility levels. As the weak component in society increased, the burden on responsible members of society increased proportionally. This is the source of the thinking that led to the drafting of the sterilization law.

There are also indeed reasons of so-called racial hygiene that, when presented most cogently, support the regularization of sterilization in law. There are also social arguments, in particular the fact that owing to parental indigence, children are born and left uncared for. So-called neuterwomen aren't fit for marriage, but because pregnancy outside of marriage still continuously occurs among this group of individuals, their children are left with no legal provider, and are thus the doubly unwanted representatives of the weakest social element, reliant upon the charity of the rest of society.

One could argue that the improvement of the race that is the aim of the sterilization law could be achieved in other, more positive ways, such as encouraging genetically eligible individuals to reproduce by raising awareness and passing supportive legislation, but because the results of such methods are spotty and uncertain, they must be supplemented with negative measures, namely the prevention of the birth of substandard individuals.

VANNA/VERA

May 2017

It's late evening and I've gone to use the outhouse. It's at the back of the yard, out of sight behind the other buildings. When I pass the shed I hear Terhi's and Valtteri's voices. Small squeaks and low, breathless talk, and a rhythmic thumping like a piece of furniture hitting the wall. At first I think I should go and ask if anything's wrong, then I realize.

They're having intercourse.

I hear a loud moan and recognize Terhi's voice. In sexual adaptability class they repeatedly remind you of the importance of panting and whimpering. It has something to do with a masco's self-esteem. I can't understand why Terhi's obeying eloi rules, but I suppose it's her business. I stop for a moment, because the sounds are interesting.

The slight excitement I feel isn't just intellectual. There must be something special about what they're doing, or else why would Terhi bother? She's a strong, independent morlock. And I can't believe Valtteri would pressure her to do anything she didn't want to do.

I mean, I know how orgasms occur. It's not exactly quantum physics. But what all is involved when you try to have one with another person? My eloi studies didn't enlighten me on that—you're supposed to complete your instruction once you're married.

I realize that I am curious like an eloi.

Like a little monkey.

A little monkey with ants in her pants.

JARE SPEAKS

May 2017

I open my eyes.

At first I don't understand why V is standing next to my bed. I sit up and try to focus. "Has something happened?"

She puckers up her mouth and turns away, avoiding my gaze, and for a moment there's something painfully eloi-like about her. Something's bothering her and, rare as this is, she can't express it in words.

Then she pulls her nightgown off over her head.

V doesn't wear a nightgown or pajamas to bed, I know that. She doesn't understand why a person covered in blankets needs to wear anything and rub up against rough seams and twisted hems. But she's wearing a nightgown now. She probably got it out of Manna's dresser drawer. It's a typical eloi nightgown, bright red, see-through synthetic fabric with black lace trim.

She throws it on the floor. She put it on just to take it off again, which is such a clear signal that my heart would ache if it wasn't beating a mile a minute.

Of course, I did have some idea of what she would look like without any clothes on, but I have to admit I wasn't prepared for anything like this.

She takes hold of the edge of the blanket, peeks under it. I don't know whether to be proud or ashamed, but I would have to be made of stone not to react to the sight of her.

My whole lower body feels hot and hard as wood.

"Want to have a wedding night?"

VANNA/VERA

June 2017

I'm like a kid with a new toy.

We screw, fuck, hump, copulate at every opportunity, and there are lots of opportunities. But we still haven't moved into the same room; I would rather sleep alone, and besides, the only double bed in the house makes my skin crawl.

Sex is like a game in many ways, each person taking turns being in charge. Sometimes the best strategy is to let the other person lead, but sometimes it's more interesting to take over. It's especially interesting learning what gets a reaction out of Jare and making the same discoveries about myself. Having an orgasm masturbating has always been for me a matter of reaching the goal as efficiently as possible, but with two people the whole end climax part is actually sort of a side issue. The journey is almost more interesting than the destination. I've also learned that sighs and moans aren't just something you do to bolster a masco's self-esteem.

When I manually stimulate myself my body knows what to expect the whole time, but the unpredictability of another person's touch is an entirely different thing. The bright blue of an unexpected light caress, the deep red of a new kind of move-ment, the neon yellow of rising passion, the pulsating ocher of the nearness of skin—they are an exotic landscape that I roam through, drown myself in, dashing and digging around like a happy animal set free. Sometimes I can smell Jare's startled feeling when I come up behind him in the middle of some everyday task and lick his neck—he's not used to this sort of thing—but he's quickly ready to play the game, and before we know it we're in one or the other bed, on the sofa, on the bench in the sauna dressing room, or lying on tufts of brush, within hearing distance of the greenhouse.

Luckily Jare has condoms. He only had a couple, but he bought some more. Since I'm a married eloi I can't get them without a doctor's prescription for valid health reasons, because mascos determine the size of a family. I don't want a baby. It might be a girl.

I've started to realize why there's so much fuss about the whole thing. Why it's such a central part of adult life that going without it could be considered a violation of human rights.

I read anything I can get my hands on about it. Sex releases a flood of neurochemicals in the brain—dopamine, oxytocin. They're what make me snuggle up against Jare's side even when we have no particular intention of doing anything erotic. Sex makes your body and brain alert, but it also makes you sleep deeply. The mesolimbic dopamine pathways, the amygdala, and the ventral tegmental area are my new best friends.

I don't think about getting a fix as much now. I haven't been to the Cellar in ages.

Honestly, sex might be addictive.

It's also easier for me to understand some aspects of the eusistocratic system now. Sure, adrenaline and endorphin pathways can be activated in other legal ways, like exercise or taking a sauna or gambling, but this fix has something absolutely fundamental in it.

I bring the subject up with Mirko. He thinks for a moment.

"No, not all mascos wanted this kind of system. Not even close."

"Then why did it end up this way?"

"Because they didn't ask everyone's opinion about it."

"You mean voting? Like in a decadent democracy?"

He explains patiently:

"They didn't need the support of the majority. Sometimes all that's needed is a group of people loud enough and influential enough to change the world and make it the way they want it to be. It doesn't even have to be a huge group, as long as some of them establish their own personal preferences as the only real truth, and make enough noise to give the impression that the forgotten, neglected masses are behind them. Even for a person who's satisfied with things the way they are, it's easy to give support to an idea if it's going to personally benefit you. A lot of people might be perfectly happy without a car, or think it's reasonable that to get a car they're going to have to work or give up something else. But if enough effort's made to put the idea in people's heads that life without a car is impossible, that not having a car is an infringement of their rights—who's going to turn down a free car if the government's handing them out?"

Excerpt from *Emancipation and the Sex Life of the Human Male*

National Publishing (1956)

As far back as 1885, Gustaf Johansson, the bishop of Kuopio, wrote in a letter to the clergy of his diocese that the emancipation of women was contrary to God's natural order and dangerous to both the female sex and society as a whole.

Further light can be shed on our modern concept of a proper and harmonious society by the Swedish author G. af Geijerstam, writing around the same time, who brought to public attention the fact that women have difficulty understanding the problems that a demand for abstinence can cause in a man. Geijerstam understood that men have an intrinsic and compulsive sex drive that is outside their rational control.

In the process of intercourse and procreation, man is active and initiating, woman passive and receptive. Men's and women's roles in the continuation of our species and our country are easily distinguishable and reflect the division of labor in our society. This idea was confirmed by the physiology professor Max Oker-Blom in his 1906 description of the differences between men's and women's sex drives. The libido of the male chiefly consists of a drive for ejaculation, while that of the female seeks adoration and surrender.

Many of Oker-Blom's contemporaries stressed that a woman's sex drive is at its base a wish to marry—instead of basic sexual satisfaction, she has a lust for the joy of motherhood. This entails a female desire to surrender to male control and thus find a fitting place within society. This quintessential female characteristic has been a protected and encouraged trait throughout the history of eusistocracy, because it produces unparalleled peace and well-being in the family.

The esteemed Professor Oker-Blom stated as early as 1904 that "the grand and wonderful task of mothering and raising children that is given to women by the Creator places on them a responsibility not just to themselves but also to family, society, and future generations."

VANNA/VERA

June 2017

The greenhouses are like the tropical jungles I've seen in books, lush with green foliage, with a sweet and sour smell of chlorophyll and dirt, damp and muggy, the sun shining from high in the sky down through the spruce trees onto the transparent roof. Some of the plants are already taller than a man, with white or violet or mottled brown flowers among the branches. I walk behind Valtteri between the rows until we step in front of one dense-leaved plant.

"In nature, bees or other nectar-seeking insects would take care of this. Because it doesn't matter to them whether they mix the pollen of two varieties or strains, they create natural hybrids. If there doesn't happen to be a pollinator around, the chili flower can fertilize itself, and the offspring of the fruit will be identical to the mother plant. But since we're trying to develop new varieties, we want to control the plants' reproduction. That's why we don't grow them outdoors, even though it's quite possible to do that for part of the year in Finland. Some random buzzy bee might come along and spoil our painstaking work. We also don't want the plants to self-pollinate, so we have to intervene before that happens."

Valtteri has an assortment of tools in the pockets of his utility vest: a small brown glass bottle, tweezers with tapered tips, a magnifying glass, pens, rubber bands, slips of cardboard cut from empty food packages, and a blue-covered school notebook.

"I'm looking for a flower that hasn't had a chance to be naughty yet. Like a masco looking for a virgin wife so he can be sure their children carry his genes." He soon shows me a plump white flower bud. "This is just right. If I left it alone it would open on its own in a couple of days."

He takes out the tweezers and carefully pries open the sepals and petals and plucks them off. He looks at the flower through the magnifying glass now and then to make sure his work is precise. Then he removes the stamen. It looks to me like forcible rape of the flower. I say so. Valtteri laughs.

"More like a castration. It leaves only the female sex organ, the pistil, behind. Now let's find a daddy for this baby." He checks the information on a tag attached with a rubber band to the stem of another plant, then chooses an already open flower and removes one of its stamens. He touches it to the castrated flower's pistil, then writes the father plant's number and the date on a plant tag and attaches it to the mother's stem. He writes the same information on the father plant's tag. "You can transfer the pollen with a swab, but we don't want to consume too many natural resources or produce any waste, so we prefer this technique. Of course, the tweezers have to be disinfected each time before we use them for another crossing."

"With that?" I ask, pointing at the little brown bottle.

Valtteri grins. "Yes. It's alcohol, actually."

"I had no idea you could buy it."

"Yes, you can get it for sterilizing instruments and for other hygienic purposes. But it's denatured alcohol. Just one drink of it could kill a horse."

He fertilizes a few more flowers. "If the cross-pollination doesn't work the flower will wilt and fall off within a week. If it does work it will produce a fruit with seeds that we can use to grow a new plant, and then we can see how well the desired characteristics have been passed on."

"But it doesn't always work?"

"Of course there are dead ends and setbacks. But if we have enough patience and perseverance, we should start to see the varieties we want begin to establish themselves within four or five generations. By the eighth generation we might already have a relatively stable strain. Sooner or later the traits we want will be showing up in nearly a hundred percent of the daughter plants."

Excerpt from *A Short History of the Domestication of Women*

National Publishing (1997)

The juvenilization or paedomorphism associated with the domestication of women is biologically a straightforward and one might even say inevitable process. Juvenilization is nature's way of retreating from the evolutionary dead end that women's excess of independence and autonomy was leading to.

The sexual dimorphism between men and women nearly disappeared from our species until a concerted effort was made to control reproduction to favor neotenic features in the female. A human female's task is to compete for males, but the cultural characteristics of the human species do not lend themselves to a situation in which the female is merely seeking an inseminator. The physically and intellectually weaker female also needs a breadwinner. In such a case, childlike features that arouse a feeling of protectiveness are a female's best tool in her relations with the male of the species. It's a formula that works: in females' competition for males we have an almost ideal meeting of supply and demand, for sexual satisfaction on the one side and security on the other.

VANNA/VERA

July 2017

Valtteri cuts a piece of freshly picked chili, plastic gloves covering his hands. The slice of pepper is vanishingly thin. From that slice he cuts another, a bit of chili about as big as a nail clipping from a baby's finger. The working name of the fruit is Nuclear Meltdown; it's a cross of Valtteri's own Harrisburg with Naga Jolokia. Valtteri is nervously excited, muttering to himself, "Let's see how this works . . . I'm also growing another entirely new hybrid, the fourth one I've bred myself. It's hard sometimes to find the right combination of characteristics because not all varieties that you cross are productive; some hybrids just produce mules."

He tells me in a rush how the *annuum* variety crosses very readily with the *chinense*, which is high in capsaicin. I'm surprised, because I thought chili was native to South America.

"The name *chinense* was an error. Some early botanist screwed up." He laughs. "Yes, it's from the Amazon region." He says that the name *annuum* was a mistake, too. It means "annual," and chilis are perennials.

"Some people claim that the name of the genus, *Capsicum*, supposedly came from the Greek word *kapto*, which means 'I bite.' Personally I think it has to do with the shape of the fruit, that it's from the Latin *capsa*, meaning 'purse' or 'pocket.'"

He spears the tiny slice of chili on the end of his knife and offers it to me. "Let's see if this little devil bites."

I put out my tongue and take the piece in my mouth.

I let it rest on my tongue for a moment. Then I chew to spread the capsaicin through my mouth. I breathe out through my nose—the taste buds on the tongue are dullards; they can taste only the most basic flavors. The smell receptors are more discriminating. Of course the point now isn't the flavor, but the heat. Capsaicin itself is tasteless and odorless, but it wakes up the inside of my mouth, and the chili's own flavors start to come out, too. The flavor will matter if they plan to sell this chili.

The tip of my tongue goes numb, which is a good sign. Then I start to cough. My airway fills with something that feels like it might have been used as a weapon in World War II.

"Do you need some water? Yogurt? Bread?" It's Jare, always the worrier. I'm not listening to him, or rather not hearing him, because my ears have closed up.

My heart breaks into a frenzied pounding; my mouth is full of molten metal. I swallow and hot lava crawls down my esophagus.

I try to move my tongue inside my mouth and every movement releases a school of microscopic piranhas that bite the membranes of my mouth with greedy, needle-sharp teeth, followed by tiny atomic explosions that scorch my jaws until they feel as if they're about to be burned to a crisp and crumble down my front. Sweat from my forehead mixes with the liquid that is pouring uncontrollably out of my nose.

"How does it taste?"

Valtteri's voice comes from behind some kind of wall. Stupid, stupid masco. I'm above all of them right now, can hardly be bothered to spit out a few words to them.

"Dark. Very dark bass notes—so low they're almost black. Ultraviolet black . . . but it also has some high, shrill overtones, like impossibly high flutes. They have a lot of violet in them, too, and the color's so cold that it's hot! Like iron going through the spectrum as it melts."

Through the fog of tears in my eyes I can see Valtteri's and Mirko's perplexed faces.

Now I'm shaking. Jare fetches a wool blanket from the sofa in the living room and puts it around my shoulders. All of my senses are intensely alert; the outlines of people and objects are excruciatingly sharp on my retinas. The screech of the legs of Valtteri's chair as it slides across the floor almost bursts my eardrums, though my ears are still half sealed up.

"I don't understand any of this," Mirko says, his sharp tone ringing in my ear canals. "It's a simple question. What's the degree of heat compared with, say, a habanero? If a habanero is a ten, what would you say this is?"

"This is how V always talks about chilis," Jare says almost apologetically, but I can also smell his desire to defend me, that malty scent. "I always thought it was some weird morlock thing."

Terhi slowly shakes her head.

"She's gone totally bonkers," Mirko says. "We'll call our regular taster tomorrow."

My head is spinning, there's a buzzing inside my skull, and as I look at them all helplessly, it's only Terhi's face that shows some kind of understanding, and I get a whiff of epiphany.

She's speaking excitedly in a low voice. The only word I catch is "synesthesia."

I look at her through the veil of sweat. It's rare for me to hear somebody use a word that I don't know the meaning of.

"Quick, Vanna—without thinking about it, what color is the letter *A*?"

"Red."

"What color's the number *5*?"

"Light green, a little yellowish."

"What does a habanero sound like in your mouth?"

"A high counterpoint, like a violin at the top of the scale. But there are lower sounds, too . . . like muted trumpets . . . that come later, once the taste reaches the back of my tongue, especially if I move my tongue in my mouth and the burn starts again."

"This is all very interesting, but that's not what we're talking about. What's the strength of the sample?" The odor around Mirko is almost angry now.

"Let me put it this way. If the Authority had some kind of simple scoville meter set to test basic varieties, the indicator would have spun off the dial and the whole device would have exploded in a puff of smoke with springs and screws flying everywhere."

Mirko looks at me with an air of contained amusement. "All our regular taster can say is 'strong,' 'quite strong,' and 'not all that strong,'" he says.

"Nuclear Meltdown is a very accurate name," I say, trying to turn the conversation to something other than my own embarrassing peculiarities, which are one more reminder that I'm a freak in every possible way. "I don't really know if it'll make a good selling name, though. Not many people appreciate irony. The average chiller isn't exactly hyperaware of nuclear power issues in the decadent democracies. Why not give it a Finnish name, since your customers are Finnish?"

Valtteri raises his eyebrows and laughs.

"That's what happens when you follow old habits like a goat on a tether. I guess I just have the English names stuck in my head, but of course there are names in other languages, too. Quite well-known names. Like Naga, the Indian snake god. A Finnish name would fit perfectly, since it's not just the heat I'm working on with this one. I'm also trying to develop a hybrid that's cold hardy. If it works we could grow them outdoors for a longer season and wouldn't have to bring them in except for the coldest part of the winter."

Mirko straightens up. "The Incas associated chilis with lightning strikes and with those mysterious rock formations said to be found in places where lightning has struck. The old Finnish name for them is Ukko's darts, for the Finnish god of thunder. Let's name this one Ukko's Dart."

MINISTRY OF HEALTH
PUBLICATION SERIES ON
DANGEROUS SUBSTANCES
TO BE AVOIDED

Capsaicin is an alkaloid made up of various capsaicinoids. Scientist **L. T. Thresh** gave the name to the crystal extract of the fruit of the chili plant in 1846.

Capsaicin alone is tasteless and colorless. Its effect is caused by stimulation of the pain receptors in the mouth and nose. When the pain signal reaches the brain, it begins to release a variety of chemicals into the body. These chemicals may cause a false feeling of euphoria, but some of their side effects are quite dire. In large doses capsaicin is a neurotoxin—it causes damage to the nerve cells. Side effects of capsaicin use include sweating; stomach pain; heart palpitations; damage to the digestive tract; serious inflammation of the urinary tract, mouth, and other mucous membranes; irrational behavior; and sometimes hallucinations. Capsaicin is powerfully addictive and even experimenting with small doses quickly leads to increased levels of use.

The danger of capsaicin is indicated by the fact that it is in the same family of plants as the *Solanaceae*, or nightshades, which include such toxic plants as *belladonna* (deadly nightshade) and *datura* (devil's trumpet). Just a few belladonna berries are enough to kill a person. The toxins in both plants cause powerful hallucinations and delirium. Another extremely dangerous plant, tobacco, is a member of this same family of plants.

One milligram of pure capsaicin on bare skin feels like a hot iron and causes visible damage.

Because chili peppers and the capsaicin they contain can be preserved for long periods by means such as drying, freezing, or various cooking methods, the task of tracing and destroying this terrible substance is a challenge. However, through its tireless determination, the Ministry of Health has almost completely eradicated the drug from Finland.

VANNA/VERA

August 2017

This summer has been like a plant reaching up out of the soil. It seemed to develop slowly, like a seedling, unhurried, and yet also to come in a rush, like a garden at the height of the season, bursting to send out sprouts and fruits as fast as it can. The chili production and the Gaians' methods for growing vegetables have given me a lot to learn; every day something new and exciting happens, and I feel as if I've packed a hundred hours into the day before it starts to fade into the limpid darkness of a summer night. But then I'm suddenly startled to notice that the time has stealthily flowed away like water sinking into sand, and seeds that seem to have been sown just yesterday have already pushed their first leaves out of the ground, and now here I am pulling up bright orange carrots twice as long as my hand.

Sometimes I even forget about Manna. Now that I basically have unlimited access to the hottest chilis to be found in Finland, and maybe in the whole world, I don't need a fix as often. The mere knowledge that I can get a fantastic high at a moment's notice whenever I feel like it keeps the Cellar door closed and the water low. I can go days without one, since the stuff is literally within arm's reach all the time.

And I have Jare, too. His skin and his hands saturating my senses with colors, a burning landscape that I can step into whenever I want.

* * *

The time sinking into the sand hasn't passed to no effect. Time and sun and rain have given us tomatoes and lettuce and root crops and herbs and squashes, onions and potatoes, leeks and peas. Jare and I drive a truck of vegetables to the Tammela Market every Saturday. We openly refer to them as "bioaura-dynamically grown," although I find it a bit embarrassing, and even though we ask a little higher price for them they sell well. That's not surprising because the Gaians are very skillful farmers and teachers, and the plants and seeds they brought with them are of an extremely high quality. Our crops are abundant, beautiful to look at, and flavorful. The tomatoes are vine ripened and most of what we sell was picked the same day, early in the morning, practically still wet with dew.

By July we were already overhearing market shoppers say things like, "I never buy my turnips from anyplace but Neulapää now—they have some flavor to them," or "Have you tried the Neulapää potatoes? There's really nothing like them. They make the Sieglindes pale in comparison."

Time has worked its changes on the growing operation in the woods, too. The place is voluptuous. The green branches hang heavy with drops of yellow and orange and red and brown and pale green and purple in different sizes and shapes and aromas. When we close up at the market around noon, we go out to do some dealing.

At first the customers were shocked, then excited. Word has spread and demand is many times greater than our supply. That's why we purposely keep the sales of the fresh stuff to a minimum. Nobody sells diamonds by the kilo. We bring out individual Harrisburgs or Ukko's Darts as if they were rare jewels, when we actually have great piles of them, enough that we're drying part of the harvest and grinding them up—even learning to smoke some of them for the real aficionados—because the dried flake is much easier to store, hide, transport, and slip to another person than whole dried peppers would be, never mind fresh ones. We've been putting the flake in that familiar old hiding place under the living room floor.

There's also a lot of cash there. We've switched containers from a briefcase to a suitcase.

Jare will soon have enough.

I ought to be thinking about that moment, preparing myself for Jare to leave, figuring out what I'll do after that. Neulapää doesn't belong just to me anymore; it belongs to Jare and me. But the only way I can hold on to Neulapää and prevent it from being transferred to the state would be for Jare to sell it to Mirko for a nominal sum before he leaves—some negligible price between brothers in the faith that wouldn't arouse any suspicion—and include the condition that once Jare has left the country Mirko will marry me. That would give me a legal guardian I could at least trust a little. And why not? The Gaians like it here, the place feels safe, and I'm getting better at farming all the time.

But since we sell at a high price, we sell slowly. We don't use any middlemen at all, so we get the highest possible street price. We make only a handful of deals, but they add up to a lot. Jare is very careful not to let our prosperity show. He never buys expensive clothes or luxury goods and makes his car payments only when he can afford to with the money from his part-time work for the Food Bureau or from selling vegetables.

Sometimes he hints that I could go with him. After we started sharing a bed he hinted at it more often.

But I can't even think of leaving until I know what happened to Manna.

At Neulapää I might be able to find out. *Because she's partly here. I don't know where. But to me she's not dead until I see her body.*

Maybe knowing would light up the Cellar. Maybe I could finally find a way out of there.

I remember what I thought when I was planting potatoes with Terhi: *This is what it would be like if I had a real sister.* The shame of that stabs me so deep.

Manna was my real sister. We have the smell of the same litter, a smell that will never rub off. How could I be so heartless, so traitorous, that I could even think otherwise?

And then there's Jare. The only thing Manna ever wanted that I wasn't able to give her.

Do I think I can make up for my betrayal by refusing to leave, by giving Jare up forever?

I need a fix. After thinking thoughts like that, I need a hell of a fix.

Jare is in Tampere making a deal, and though I ought to be helping Terhi dig potatoes, I run off to the secret greenhouses. The smell, the warmth, and the brilliance of the varied shades of green and red draw me to them irresistibly. It beats the potato patch hands down.

I step inside the smaller greenhouse. Valtteri and Mirko are in the back corner in fervent discussion about something. They see me and look at each other, and Mirko's eyebrows rise a bit. I stop. The tar smell of suspicion pierces the tropical aroma of the room, but Valtteri nods to Mirko and then beckons me over.

They're standing next to a rather sparsely stemmed plant with tapered leaves. There are numerous cardboard tags attached to it. I can see that the first fruits are ripening; a few of them look ripe already. The chilis are shaped like elongated hearts and are such a dark red that they're nearly brown in places.

Valtteri points at one.

"These are the brand-new hybrid I was talking about, and they'll be ready for testing soon. I'll warn you ahead of time that these babies are nothing to mess around with."

"As strong as Ukko's Darts?"

"If we've succeeded, then Ukko's Darts will be oatmeal compared with these things."

Oho.

"More than two million scovilles?"

"Maybe."

Mirko looks at the chilis, the fruity aromas of hope and excitement positively swirling around him, though he's trying to look stiff and serious.

"When do we taste them?" I ask, trying to look businesslike and coolly professional.

Valtteri hesitates, glances at Mirko. Mirko clears his throat.

"Not quite yet, perhaps. We have to be careful, not rush things. It could be a breakthrough."

A breakthrough to what?

"Does it have a name yet?"

Valtteri perks up.

"It has a working name. I started with the chili's botanical name, the order *Solanales* and the family *Solanaceae*. I think that etymologically it's from the Latin for 'sun,' and somehow this variety seems to me—to us—to suggest the idea of an extreme, life-sustaining, everlasting fire. If there were anything more powerful than the sun, it would be the source of the sun's power, its center, the deepest, perhaps nearly divine part of the sun."

"The core of the sun," I say.

"Exactly."

* * *

The potatoes have been dug and I should be making dinner, but I linger around the greenhouses as if under the pull of a magnet. The Gaians have another large sowing and transplanting operation going on in the other greenhouse. I can hear their hymn through the glass.

> *Teach me, chile, and I shall Learn.*
> *Take me, chile, and I shall Escape.*
> *Focus my eyes, chile, and I shall See.*
> *Consume more chiles.*
> *I feel no pain, for the chile is my teacher.*
> *I feel no pain, for the chile takes me beyond myself.*
> *I feel no pain, for the chile gives me sight.*

I know that some of those chilis are ripe. Ready to be picked.

Why should Valtteri and Mirko and Terhi make all the decisions? About matters in which I am the undisputed expert?

Even if they have brought all the lights and growing boxes and seeds and plants, they are dependent on me. My abilities. My inheritance.

I slip into the empty greenhouse. I go to the back corner and stand for a moment in front of the plant Valtteri showed to me. My heart is pounding, as if I were doing something wrong, even though that's not the case at all.

I have a right.

I take hold of a branch and pluck off one, just one ripe chili from the Core of the Sun.

I'm a morlock. I want to know.

I'm not curious the way elois are—I have a pure, clear, sincere thirst for knowledge. Those are two very different things.

I shove the Core of the Sun into my apron pocket.

JARE SPEAKS

August 2017

Sometimes with new customers it's better if V isn't with me, especially when it's a totally fresh contact. They might be nervous around her because they assume, of course, that she's an impetuous blabbermouth like most elois. I get them used to her gradually. I assure them that she's my wife, that she's so loyal she would never tell anything to an outsider, that she's as nutty about me as an eloi can possibly be—so worked up into a frenzy of love that she'd walk through fire for me. I joke about how easy it is to manipulate an eloi with little romantic gestures until all you have to do is wave your hand and she'll do whatever you tell her to, like an obedient machine. The customers nod—they know how elois are, we're on the same wavelength, sometimes a carrot's better than a stick, heh heh. And V will be standing right behind them grimacing and rolling her eyes. Once she stuck out her tongue and it was all I could do not to laugh at a totally inappropriate moment.

I promised this new mark that I would have something very special for him. And I do—a fresh sample of Ukko's Dart. I plan to give him a taste of it—just a paper-thin slice, but I'll show him the whole chili to assure him that it's real, and as wordless proof that there's more where that came from, if we can agree on a price.

We agreed to meet at a juice bar on Hämeenkatu. I go in, sit at a table, and order a mineral water. I put the personal ad page on the table nonchalantly and start reading a paperback. The book is the sign—the password is "seven" so, clever as I am, I brought a copy of Aleksis Kivi's *Seven Brothers.*

I notice with amusement that there's a government poster on the wall. It shows a map of Finland with all the countries outside its borders on fire, covered in red and yellow flames, and the tips of the flames are reaching threateningly toward our country. If you look closer you see that the flames are stylized chili peppers. A brave crowd outlined in silhouette is manning the borders in a bucket brigade. At the top it says in large letters FIGHT THE FIRES OF DESTRUCTION and at the bottom, in smaller letters, DON'T GET BURNED—REPORT EVEN THE SMALLEST SIGN OF CHILI TO THE AUTHORITIES!

I feel a rush of excitement in my veins. My scalp is tingling.

After a minute a man comes into the bar carrying a brown briefcase. He orders a tomato juice, opens his briefcase, and takes out the same issue of the personals and puts it on his table. Our eyes meet; he sees the book I'm reading, its title. I raise one eyebrow a little. He does the same. He drinks his tomato juice in a couple of gulps, then goes into the men's room.

I finish my mineral water at a leisurely pace, absorbed in *Seven Brothers,* until a safe period of time has passed, and then I get up, stretch, and walk calmly to the men's room.

The contact is waiting there, obviously impatient. We glance around, slip into a stall, and lock the door. He holds out his hand. "I'm Erkki."

"Call me Petri."

"What have you got?"

"The best stuff in Finland." I recite the list of varieties and drink in his expression. "A lot of those you won't get from anyone but us. Easily more than a million scovilles, some of it."

He takes in his breath.

"Flake?"

"Flake. But also fresh. Serranos, habas, Nagas."

This always works. It makes them gasp, startles them, electrifies them. Erkki absorbs this information with obvious surprise, but not the wild amazement most customers show.

"I only have a small sample of the fresh on me. We only sell the fresh by special order. But the dope I've got on me is an unusual kind. A new hybrid. Million and a half scovilles. It's called Ukko's Dart, a Finnish variety. Want a taste?"

Erkki nods. I take out a pair of disposable latex gloves. This is always a fine moment, as the mark's eyes widen when he realizes why I need the gloves. I take a small plastic bag from the small pocket sewn into my jacket lining and remove the Ukko's Dart. I show the pepper to him, dangling it by its stem. I turn it over beneath his greedy gaze, like a trapper displaying a rare pelt. I take out my pocketknife and cut off a teeny-tiny slice from the tip, then spear it on the tip of the blade and hold it out to him. "Keep in mind when you taste this that it's from the tip of the fruit, the mildest part. The real strength is at the base of the stem, where the seeds are attached—"

The blow stuns me. All my attention is on the chili, and the man's movement is quick as a cobra's, the blade of his hand striking the side of my neck. My arms flop helplessly, my knife and the pepper fall to the floor. The man makes a swift kick and the knife skids across the floor out of reach.

Another wave of pain rushes over the first as a fist hits me hard in the diaphragm. My lungs empty so fast that I almost lose consciousness, doubled over in pain, wheezing as I try to get some air. Erkki clicks open the lock on the stall before I've straightened up again, grabbing the Ukko's Dart from the floor as he runs out.

I cough and try to get some breath, but can't move, and when I finally get my legs to work I know he's already long gone.

I have enough sense, at least, to flush my gloves down the toilet. I pick up my knife from the floor next to the tiled wall and slide the tiny sliver of pepper down the floor drain with the side of my shoe.

Five minutes later I'm driving back to Neulapää. I try to obey the speed limit. I'm in a hell of a hurry, but the last thing I need right now is to attract the attention of a traffic cop.

A greedy capso who wanted to keep the chili and the money? Not unheard of, like the one V met at the cemetery. But this guy knew something about martial arts. He didn't seem like an ordinary mark.

Then an extremely chilling thought occurs to me, entirely too late. If the guy was a capso looking for a score, why would he just steal the fresh chili from me—why not beat me unconscious or kill me and empty my pockets, which he knew would be full of dozens of grams of flake and a wallet to boot?

The Authority.

He has a description of me now. And if he is with the Health Authority, he also knows that we use the personals.

I've been greedy and reckless.

The snoops will know right away that the growing operation is somewhere not far from Tampere because the pepper was very fresh, picked with the morning dew. It's obvious it wasn't carried in a suitcase with a false bottom from somewhere out in Ahvenanmaa, never mind Thailand. And even if the authorities' knowledge of chili is limited, they won't need liquid chromatography or a team of botanists to tell them that Ukko's Dart is an entirely new variety, and that it's hotter than hell.

But why would a guy from the Health Authority just take the chili and run?

Why not show me his badge, slap some handcuffs on me, and take me to a paddy wagon waiting around the corner?

Another appalling idea hits me, and it, too, comes much too late.

They wanted to let me go so they could follow me. Or track my movements, sooner or later, to the farm itself.

Hopefully later. Hopefully.

I've made a terrible mistake, but what's most important now is how I can keep V out of this mess.

An idea flashes into my mind—to find a public phone and call Neulapää to warn them—but I can't afford to waste any time. Besides, there won't necessarily be anyone in the house. They might all be at the greenhouses.

When I get to the little back road that leads to Neulapää, a virtually deserted ten-kilometer stretch, I step on the gas. I'm sure there's no traffic radar here. I've got to drive like a bat out of hell.

VANNA/VERA

August 2017

I close the door to my room behind me. I rearranged the room a little to suit my tastes when I moved in, although it pained me a bit to take the ruffled pink curtains and bedspread that Manna had picked out up to the attic. *Here I go again, the cruel morlock big sister, meddling in your life.*

I take the Core of the Sun out of my apron pocket and look at it, holding it by the stem to avoid touching the fruit itself with my bare fingers, turning it this way and that. Normally you can handle a chili without gloves as long as you don't puncture the skin. The thin but tough skin keeps the capsaicin nicely inside. But with this one you can't be too careful. The way of the chili is not the way of the finger.

Is this what it feels like to handle an unexploded bomb?

On the desk in front of me is a pair of disposable gloves from the stash under the living room floor. They're not exactly disposable for us; we use them as long as they don't have any holes in them and wash them with hot water, wearing a face mask, always outside, since the hot water can cause such a cloud of capsaicin fumes that your eyes water and you cough and you get a little buzz just from the steam.

Next to the gloves is a little cutting board from the kitchen that we used for slicing cheese back when there was still cheese in the house, and one knife that I've carefully sharpened.

The knife is so sharp that I have no trouble cutting a slice as thin as a hair from the Core of the Sun. It doesn't have the usual penetrating, fruity, almost citrus smell that a habanero might have. But it does have that same tropical scent, plus something more aromatic, a smokiness. My nostrils quiver. I sneeze violently and gasp for breath.

This baby's so full of capsaicin I can apparently feel it from a meter away.

Are you sure this is a good idea? I ask myself as I stare at the nearly invisible sliver lying on the wooden board.

Pshaw.

I grab the piece of pepper and toss it in my mouth.

I chew.

I wait.

I don't feel anything.

But something is happening because my heart is starting to gallop and time is slowing to a crawl . . .

An absolute white light goes right through my head. It's so bright that I think it must show through the seams in my skull.

It is such a white white that there isn't even a word for it; it's on the other side of whiteness; new-fallen snow on the brightest winter day is gray by comparison. It's ultrawhite, lacerating white, blinding white, the combination and negation of all the other colors in the world, and an impossibly high-pitched tinnitus starts ringing in my head, as if I'm suddenly able to hear a dog whistle, a dog whistle so shrill, so close to the very edge of perception, that it's as if the light of a distant star has become sound.

Then the sound turns so high that I can't hear it anymore.

I stand there and my vision starts to return and time has stopped. Although my mouth is full of saliva and my whole body's covered in sweat, my tongue isn't burning, and there's no lava in my throat, no convulsing iron band around my stomach.

This stuff is off the sense receptor scale.

Because the needle's gone off the dial, my brain doesn't know how to react. Since it doesn't know what to do with such a powerful sensation, it's decided not to do anything.

My brain has thrown in the towel.

There's a swishing in my head and I feel light, so full of endorphins that I'm starting to rise into the air. I actually do rise into the air, and it feels quite pleasant, to be substanceless, almost carried by the wind. I see a layer of dust on top of the wardrobe. It probably doesn't get dusted because it's so tall, almost reaches the ceiling. There's a spider's corpse lying in the dust, and below me an eloi standing motionless, with a little cutting board and knife and a dark-colored chili in front of her.

It takes me a moment to realize, *Oh, that's me.*

I try to move and realize that if I wanted to I could slip through the partly open window. I sense the rush of life on the other side of the glass, the birch trees and spruces and grass and roses and earthworms and beetles and gnats, and there's a fox skulking somewhere and a brown hare loping along, and I could hop along with it, become part of its brain, ride inside it into the sunset. I could hear what it hears, see what it sees.

Somewhere at the edge of the world of my senses hovers a cluster of ghostly white noise, like distant echoes. It must be the Gaians.

A fly buzzes at the window, its sound echoing, piercing, hypnotic. I move, just a small motion, and in a split second I'm inside something else and that *something else* is a darting, precise, persistent little clockwork that sees the world in a pattern of flickering, dizzying points of light—then I pull away, nimble as air.

This is the breakthrough.

The Core of the Sun works.

Oneness with nature. It isn't just mystical mumbo jumbo after all. It's a clear, straightforward, practical goal.

Merging with the world. Escaping the shackles of the body.

Our escape will be inward, not outward.

JARE SPEAKS

August 2017

I drive right up to the front door at Neulapää, like I did when I posed as a Food Bureau inspector; hit the brakes hard, leaving tire tracks on the driveway; and get out at a run, scanning the area, wondering where everybody is. In the forest greenhouses, of course. I stand in the door and yell V's name, but there's no answer. She might be in the house though, too absorbed in reading to hear me. I run to the door of her room and yank it open without bothering to knock.

V is standing motionless in front of her desk. There's a little wooden cutting board in front of her, and a knife and a dark red chili like a splash of coagulated blood. I recognize it immediately.

Core of the Sun. V, oh V, what have you gone and done?

I grab her by the shoulders and shake her. "V! V!"

She doesn't answer. Her eyes are glassy with the empty look of brain damage.

VANNA/VERA

August 2017

Jare comes running into my room. It's interesting, like watching a silent movie in slow motion. His movements are big, exaggerated. The room fills with tartness and rosemary, a smell that's almost suffocating, and—

My perspective jerks so suddenly that it almost hurts. I'm looking at my own face, my own waxy, frozen expression, from very close, almost like looking in a mirror, but it isn't a mirror.

I'm looking at myself through Jare's eyes.

And at the same time, I'm *here*, *inside*, and I sense pale colors, bluish and reddish and greenish, but they're just hints, a drop of watercolor in a tumbler of water. Everything else is bright gray, the shade of heavy crystallized snow in late spring, and like snow it refracts the light from every imperfection, every crystal facet; but the light isn't coming from the sky—it's a glow from inside.

I'm in a completely different world. On an alien planet. But it's not a planet, there is no direction, no gravity. I'm swimming, floating among strange mountains and leafy tendrils. The shapes that surround me are rough, semitransparent, rising up on every side randomly, chaotically, but with an underlying logic, emerging from above, below, and beside me. They remind me of snowdrifts, the south side of snow-covered furrows when the sun at the end of

March warms the snow and melts sharp, beveled, granular shapes into it, as if the melting of the snow uncovered the rough scales of a dragon sleeping beneath it. Tapered points, crystalline towers, jagged stalactites repeating just as they do in drifts of snow: all from the same root, a result of the same process, and yet every form as individual as a ledge of coral in a vast reef.

I'm moving in a way that I can't understand—maybe my brain is telling me to swim, or fly—and I'm soaring through rushing scales of snow and crystal towers and somewhere ahead I see a darkish spot and I speed toward it, or rather I will myself to go to it, or rather it sucks me toward it and I'm not floating anymore, I'm streaking toward it, and it gets bigger and bigger, it's like a well, or an open jaw, and I fall into the abyss, or maybe I'm shooting upward, like a diver forced up toward the surface, but I'm going toward something that looks dark but isn't dark, it's a friendly blackness, a warm, starry night, and there's something there.

It's smooth and firm and slippery and squirming; it's pulsating, panicked, hard-shelled, cautious; it's alive and supple and soft and unyielding; it changes its shape and yet stays the same; it's unpredictable and safe and it's calling my name. I can't hear it but I sense it, like a dream where you can tell that a thing looks like one thing but means something else. It's saying V, but it means Vera, and it pulses toward me and engulfs me in itself, and it no longer matters who or what is pushing the coral- and snow-scale-shaped rosemary and lavender and apple and citrus and cranberry into me, the light, colors, forming something to grasp, something to understand, something that I don't know how to feel but it knows how, something akin to the smell of fresh-cut grass that floated around Manna so that the air was full of it, back when she had her crush on Jare, and this is the same smell but it's ripened into rosemary, adult, plaintive, saturating everything, every single thing that can fit right now in Jare's head, and all of it mixed with the sour of worry . . .

I know what that smell is now.

Oh no oh no oh no.

I come out of the shock with a jerk and it takes a fraction of a second before my eyes can focus. There he is. Jare, his face a couple of centimeters from mine, his hands shaking my shoulders and his mouth shouting something into my sealed ears. *V, V, V, V, V, what's wrong, what happened, what—*

Another jerk, and although I can't hear anything, I sense the change in air pressure in my clogged ear canals—someone else has come into the room, and Terhi steps into my narrowed field of vision and immediately starts to open her mouth, vehement, and exchanges gestures with Jare and they're talking about me. I sense that it's lunchtime and that's why they've come in from the farm, but that doesn't matter because I'm still floating half outside of myself and *nothing* seems to particularly matter much. Jare and Terhi lead me between them into the living room and over to the sofa and they sit me down and put two blankets over me, and Jare brings me hot sugar water and half forces me to drink it. The hot liquid hurts my mouth, burns like fire, and for a moment I think that it has capsaicin in it, too, but that's just because my mouth is tender and sore. Once I'm wrapped up and have a warm drink the trembling in my body starts to gradually subside.

Through the sweat and the shivering and the soreness in my mouth I'm aware of Jare and Terhi and Valtteri and Mirko looming around me. A real tribal council.

"You had to try it," Terhi's voice says.

I don't answer. I might not be able to, because at the moment my teeth are chattering uncontrollably.

Terhi looks at Jare. "Did you know about this?"

Jare is extremely agitated—I can easily sense it. On overdrive. Why? This isn't some great crime, is it?

"Vanna's not an eloi. She doesn't have a masco who's personally responsible for her! I didn't know!"

"No need to get you knickers in a bunch. Just asking."

Terhi sits on the edge of the sofa. The blankets and sugar water and time since the Core of the Sun began its work have all calmed the worst of the shakes. Terhi reaches under the blanket and takes my hand.

"Vanna, you're like ice."

I nod; her hand feels burning hot in mine. As if all the blood in the veins under my skin had retracted into my organs to extinguish the raging fire inside me. The look of genuine worry on Terhi's face and what I've just learned about Jare and the sensitivity the capsaicin has lent to all my senses and the pain in my mouth fading to a dull throb—it's all too much, and I start to cry.

Terhi pulls me against her chest and holds on to me, not squeezing, not patting me, just holds me in her arms. When I close my eyes I'm with Aulikki for a moment.

"Congratulations," I mutter.

Although my face is half pressed against Terhi's chest, I can tell by the movements of her muscles that she's looking at the others. At Mirko and Valtteri.

"I left my body."

Terhi pushes me back by the shoulders and looks at my face to see if I'm serious. Her cheeks start to redden. "What happened?"

"I saw myself from the outside, from the ceiling. Look on top of the wardrobe. Is there a dead spider there? I can't reach it, but I saw it."

265

Valtteri and Mirko both let out a sound like a sigh mixed with a whine, then they burst into talk at the same time, and Terhi joins the chorus.

"Trance possession!"

"But what if it's just some kind of . . . self-hypnosis?" Jare says doubtfully.

"No, it couldn't be. It's a state that has real neurophysiological changes that can be measured with an EEG. And there are physical signs, just like the ones Vanna had: convulsions, tremors, shivering. In former times the shamans' possession trances were a precursor to a loss of consciousness. With practice you can succeed in deepening the experience to the point that your connection to waking life is cut off completely."

Valtteri looks into my mouth with a little pocket flashlight. "You have inflammation in your mouth. The insides of your lips are quite swollen. But that's to be expected, of course. It will go away in a few days."

"We have to remember Vanna's tolerance. If it works for her, . . ." Mirko says, almost to himself.

"It's a breakthrough."

"It's a *definite* breakthrough."

"We can concentrate on just this variety—"

"We have to get the variety stabilized as soon as we can—"

"It's just a matter of time."

"We've got it."

"We've got the Core of the Sun!"

They ask some more questions, and I'm filled with immense energy, my knowledge boundless—I own all of Europe and I rule half of the rest of the world, too—telling them about my experience in clever turns of phrase, how it felt as if I could move into an earthworm, a little bird, or a lynx slinking around Neulapää. I haven't even gotten to the fly, not to mention Jare, when I realize that something about the mood has changed. The Gaians look at one another, at Jare, at me. There's a whiff of tar and smoke.

That's when Jare takes a deep breath and clears his throat and everyone gets quiet. There's something so significant in that sound, and I look at Jare and his eyes are filled with hopelessness, and even though I'm as far away from the Cellar as I could be, an icy avalanche of fear flashes through my belly.

"I should have told you right away, but V . . . well, now that she seems to be OK, listen. We've got a hell of an urgent situation."

JARE SPEAKS

August 2017

We have to leave, too, V. You're my wife; you'll come with me. You've said you can't go until you know what happened to Manna, but I won't take that for an answer anymore. You've burrowed your way into me, built a nest in my brain. I'd just as soon cut off my hands, or cut out my heart, as leave you here. I know you can get along without me—that's what's painful about this. You can get through anything you set your mind to, and that independence from me is the worst part of it.

Because I'm hooked on you.

I have to convince you. This isn't just about your obsession with your sister's disappearance. At one point you mentioned your precious books, how you supposedly couldn't ever leave them behind, but I've heard about amazing things in the decadent states, like tiny portable devices where a person can store a thousand books—a thousand books filled with information that's completely up-to-date. I've heard about data networks that can give you the answer to any question that's on your mind at the press of a button. I can offer that world to you. It's something you can't do by yourself.

You're my adrenaline, my new game of chance.

I can see that you're starting to give in, deep inside. You are going to come with me. You've got to.

VANNA/VERA

August 2017

Jare and I are covered in sweat, carrying the lights and the seedling boxes out of the forest. There's no way we can fit all the full-grown plants into the hidden cargo hold; all we can do is put a couple of the most precious adult plants there. We'll harvest the rest of the ripe fruit for seed.

Mirko, Valtteri, and Terhi take down the forest greenhouses and carry the parts to the yard. They can haul them in the visible portion of the truck beds. There's nothing we can do about the impressions left in the ground, but we can disguise the traces of where the floors and corner posts were to some extent with brush and sticks.

I think it would have made more sense to wait a little while in case the authorities showed up right behind Jare. There might have been some small chance they wouldn't find any evidence. If somebody comes now our guilt will be as obvious as if we'd been standing over a dead body with a smoking gun in our hands. But for some reason the Gaians want to leave immediately.

As if they were fleeing more than just the authorities.

Jare suggests that Valtteri sink the leftover stems and roots of the plants in Riihi Swamp. He should be able to shove them into the black water under the moss until there's almost no trace of them, and even if they were found it would be hard to tell them from all the other plant debris in various stages of decay.

"But why would the Authority be so ineffectual?" I wonder out loud. "If it really was a bust and they let you get away so they could follow you, they would have already thrown us in the slammer. And if they lost you at some point, I'm sure they could have just looked up your license number. It doesn't make sense."

"Maybe they're collecting more evidence. Want to be sure."

I nod toward the plastic bags glowing red and yellow and green that Mirko and Terhi are carrying to the car in both hands. "There couldn't be any more abundant evidence than that." I hand some boards up to Jare where he's standing in the truck bed. "And what if this so-called Erkki wasn't a bad mark *or* a cop? What if he's a free agent?"

"Free agent?"

"A private detective. Or a bounty hunter. Somebody who's paid to find things out and report back. All he needed was to grab a piece of evidence and run. And even if he went straight to the Authority and sold them the Ukko's Dart for a good price, they wouldn't have any more hard evidence than the chili itself. They'd have Erkki's description of you, maybe a grainy surveillance video from someplace near the bar, the fact that you said your name was Petri, and I guess now our method for making contacts, but it's a big step from that to connecting the crime to Jare Valkinen, Gaian devotee and vegetable vendor."

Jare's tension eases a bit. "There just might be a heck of a lot of sense in that. But it gives us only a little more time. We have to get at least twenty-five thousand together really fast; that's how much we're short in the kitty. There's more than enough stuff to do it, and we can sell it cheap if we can find somebody to buy it wholesale. To hell with maximizing our returns."

"With half the drug agents in Tampere on the lookout for dealers?"

We look at each other. Jare jumps down from the loading bed and goes over to the other truck. "Mirko, can you spare another half a kilo? It doesn't matter what kind; just give us whichever one you have plenty of seed or seedlings for."

Mirko grabs one of the bags and tosses it to Jare without a glance. Jare snatches it out of the air. Mirko's coolness might be a reaction to Jare's recklessness, and the fact that he worried about me first and about the emergency second. But I don't think so. Something else is bothering him.

Jare walks back over to me and holds up the bag. "These and the flake under the floor should be enough." He goes to stash the bag in the house.

"Last boxes!" Terhi yells to Mirko. Valtteri returns from his trip to the swamp, red and panting, his shoes wet from the bog moss.

The Gaians don't waste their time getting emotional. When the trucks are loaded, when the divider separating the secret section of the cargo hold is in place and their few personal belongings are gathered up, they're ready to go.

"Where are you headed?"

"Northeast. The Kainuu woods. The growing season there is starting to get long enough, now that exceptionally cold winters are happening less often. People in the countryside are used to the Gaians' nomadic ways. No one will think anything of it when we show up and unpack. We'll find a little fallow piece of land to rent. Keep a low profile."

I start to feel relieved. If we thoroughly clean up all traces of the Gaians' stay here, we can claim that we just had a couple of them come to teach us bioaura farming at the beginning of the growing season, and nothing more. Luckily they've been so busy growing chilis that the amount of vegetables we've been bringing to the market to sell has been about as much as two hardworking people could manage to grow on their own.

Valtteri and Terhi jump into one truck, Mirko into the other. Mirko waves and drives out the gate. Valtteri starts his engine, too. The wheels are already starting to roll away when the truck stops, the door swings open, and Terhi hops out of the cab. She runs to me, takes something out of her pocket, puts it in my hand, and folds my fingers around it.

"I told Valtteri that I forgot to thank you. Use it wisely."

She runs with quick, long strides back to the truck, jumps in, and slams the door in one smooth movement. The engine roars.

The two trucks pull out onto the gravel road and disappear around a curve into the spruce woods.

I open my fist. Lying on my palm is a ripe pepper about as long as my finger, the color of clotted blood. The Core of the Sun.

"I can't leave until I know—"

"Shut your trap."

I'm stunned into silence. Jare has never talked to me like that before.

"Listen. It's possible, though very unlikely, that Manna's body will still be found. But what satisfaction will that give you?"

"I would be sure."

"We just don't have time. Whoever it was who stole the Ukko's Dart from me won't leave it at that."

I'm still shaking my head.

"Do you remember I told you about those two guys who managed to float out of the country on a big pile of money? One of them took his wife with him. It doesn't cost much more."

"I won't leave Manna."

Jare is silent, his hands in fists, his knuckles white.

"Out there—in some other place—you could be Vera."

Vera. The name is precious and remote to me at the same time. It's a name that belongs to someone I am and am not. I read in a book once that my original name comes from the Latin word for "truth."

I would be real. I would be true.

"Vanna Valkinen would become Vera Neulapää. Because even if we do go together . . . where we're going you'll be free to do what you want, of course."

I look at Jare and suddenly an immense weariness flows through all my limbs. I could shed my eloi shell? Drop all the years of pretending away like a snake in a skin that's grown too small?

He sees the look on my face, sees me giving in, sees me crumble. He takes my hand and quickly kisses it.

"We have to act fast. We have to get the rest of the money together quickly, take risks—we've got nothing to lose now. I have a regular customer who buys a lot, buys often. We've arranged that when I have something to sell I call his downtown office from a public phone. My code name is Paloheimo, a car dealer, so my call is always about a car I want to show him, and if he's interested we agree on a time and place to meet. He's a wealthy man and he knows the going rates. If I made him an offer—all the fresh and flake we've got for twenty-five thousand—he might jump at it. Or maybe thirty thousand—that would give us a nest egg. It would be enough chili to last him the rest of his life. He could have the biggest down-low chiller blowout Finland's ever seen with just a couple of Ukko's Darts."

"But what if they know enough to suspect you? Or if you're on their list of suspects? Won't they be on the lookout for you? You'll get caught. No. It's no good."

"What do you mean 'no good'?"

"I have to make the sale."

Jare looks at me for a long time. Twice he opens his mouth, but he doesn't say anything.

"No one will suspect me. You can make the call, be Mr. Paloheimo, but Miss Paloheimo should be the one to meet him."

Jare Valkinen and his cute little wife, Vanna Valkinen, his little lady in all her eloi regalia, are on an innocent shopping trip in downtown Tampere.

In the trunk of the car are three suitcases. Two of them contain all our personal possessions—a few clothes; enough cosmetics and other requisite eloi supplies to make me believable in my eloi role, at least as far as the border. The third case is full of money.

Jare comes out of the phone booth and gets into the car with me.

"It's all decided. If I bring the money to the man at the Trade Ministry he can get me the papers, tickets, and travel permit all at once. We can't get passports, of course, just a travel permit with your name added, which means that in principle we can't go anywhere but the target country, but the important thing at this point is to get over the border and then think about what to do next. They say you can even buy passports in the hedonist countries."

"Will we be able to leave right away? Where to?"

"There's just one flight out of Tampere on Wednesday afternoons. It goes to Tallinn. Once we get there we'll get a connecting flight. I'll leave the car at the airport, let the government repossess it. The man at the Trade Ministry was still working out what would be a plausible place for him to be sending urgent expert assistance. He's guessing we might end up in Spain, marketing

Finland's unusually clean-grown oat bran. Crushes cholesterol with the very first spoonful."

Spain!

"What about . . . the other phone call?"

"I wouldn't have called the Trade Ministry if I hadn't made the deal. I called as Mr. Paloheimo and said I'd like to introduce him to a friend of mine, said that it's a meeting I know he'll really enjoy. I said this friend of mine was hot to make a deal, one that could also be lucrative for him. I'm hoping, counting on him to understand and bring along plenty of cash, but if he does buy the whole stash like I hope he will, I'm sure he's going to need to make a trip to the bank."

Jare describes the mark to me and tells me when and where we're meeting. The masco's name is Järvi, and we're supposed to behave like a couple in the first phase of mating and exchange the money and packages in some appropriately secluded makeout spot.

"Just do your parrot act."

I nod. The fresh peppers are in two flat, transparent plastic bags taped to my thighs under my skirt. The dried chili is in a shopping bag. It's packed into two paper packages, an emptied sugar bag and flour bag, both with their tops rolled and glued to look just as they did from the store. About fifty grams that we couldn't fit in the paper bags are in a smaller plastic bag, wrapped in paper to look like something bought in bulk—a piece of cheese or a couple of herring filets. To complete the disguise, Jare scrawled a price of a few marks across the paper, to make it look like something bought from the grocer's. The contents of the shopping bag look absolutely normal. Anyone passing by who looked into my bag would assume I was an ordinary eloi out doing some shopping.

I spot Järvi the moment I walk into the station. A man in his fifties, short, potbellied, and ruddy. Obviously a great partaker in life's pleasures. I'm willing to bet he's also indulged in meat and sugar, might not even be a stranger to alcohol.

He's leaning against a pillar in the waiting room, looking bored, reading a newspaper, his leather briefcase next to him. I stand beside him and greet him in an eloi manner, curtsying with my eyes downcast at first. "Good day. I'm Miss Paloheimo."

Järvi raises his eyebrows, letting out a whiff of surprise, then remembers the unusual arrangement and smiles unctuously and plays along. "Miss Paloheimo, of course. I've been expecting you . . . It's very nice to meet you."

We exchange a little empty small talk for the surveillance cameras about the weather and the approaching spring, then I suggest, shyly but with firm insistence, that perhaps the gentleman knows a place we could go to get to know each other better. He does indeed. I take hold of his arm and we walk into the park next to the station. We sit on a bench under a silver willow that droops so that we're half out of sight under its hanging branches. I get straight to business.

"Mr. Paloheimo told me to tell you that he's got a good batch of fresh to sell, half a kilo undried, plus two kilos of flake. The fresh is, um, really good stuff, and some of it's more than a million sco-scovilles. And the flake is all the strongest kinds and it's just dried peppers and there's no fillers in it. Mr. Paloheimo'll only sell it to you if you buy the whole batch—no divvying it up. And he wants thirty thousand marks for the whole deal."

The gears start turning in his head. Thirty thousand is a lot of money—many times the annual salary of the average working masco—but he can afford it. On the street you could add a zero to the end of it, and a one to the beginning, and it would still be a good deal.

"Can I see it?"

I nod. I get up from the bench and head deeper into the willow thicket, with Järvi trailing behind me. I press my back against the trunk of the tree and lift my skirt. Anyone passing by would at most see a couple messing around in the bushes. An eloi lifting her skirt in the bushes—it happens sometimes.

Järvi lets out a gasp when he sees the peppers, but he quickly recovers.

"And the flake?"

I let go of my skirt and open my shopping bag. I show him the sugar and flour packages.

"What's that?" he says, pointing to the smaller paper package.

Suddenly I'm struck with a terrible feeling of insecurity. I'm about to let go of a score. I have no idea where I'm going to get my next fix.

For God's sake, there's *no way* they're going to search us at the airport! Why would anyone in her right mind be trying to smuggle something *out* of Finland?

"Oh, that? That's just a piece of cheese."

"And how do I know it's just chili in those bags, with no sawdust or anything?"

"Mr. Paloheimo told me to say that you can open the bags and look at them and taste them, but he said I should tell you that, um, it would be, like, safer for you to carry it if you left the bags closed, so they look real."

"Hmm. I suppose Mr. Paloheimo would hardly risk me checking the bags and catching him trying to cheat me. I would just cancel the deal. I believe the stuff is what you say it is. He has always been a very trustworthy supplier."

"Mr. Paloheimo also told me to tell you that thirty thousand for the fresh stuff alone would be a steal. You could dry it or freeze it and it would give you years of really, really good cap-saicin."

I purposely stumble a bit over the word and notice Järvi's secret amusement. "May I ask why Mr. Paloheimo wants to give me such a good deal?"

"He's, like, going out of business."

"I didn't think to bring such a large sum of money with me."

OK, here it comes. The trip to the bank. If he's working with the Authority, if he's a decoy, the net's about to fall. I feign calm.

"I can wait here."

I go back to the bench and sit down and Järvi heads to the bank. My mind darts from thought to thought—every masco walking by might be a plainclothes cop—and I remember the few grams I kept for myself. I quickly go back to the shelter of the bushes and remove the paper from the smaller plastic bag. I fold the paper wrapper and put it in my pocket. The plastic bag I stuff into my bra. There's another bulge on the other side of my bra.

Oh yeah. The Core of the Sun. I need to find a place to hide that, too.

One Core of the Sun is enough for at least a hundred good fixes, but for once I'm thinking further ahead than my next high. If I save the seeds, I could plant them in a box on a balcony or in a little garden bed at our place in Spain. It's more important to me now to preserve the Core of the Sun than it is to eat it. And the fruit itself is the best possible way to transport the seeds. Besides, I couldn't cut it up now anyway—in my hurry to leave it didn't occur to me to bring any gloves.

I have to think of a better hiding place, but there's no time now. I go back to the bench and I'm startled to see that the mark is already at the other end of the path, on his way back to where I'm sitting. A suspiciously quick visit to the bank. Should I run? But it's too late to think, because Järvi's standing in front of me, puffing.

"Let's go over there again and get to know each other better."

When we're back under the branches, I lift my skirt and pull the tape away from my thighs. I put the bags of fresh peppers and the sugar and flour bag on the ground and straddle them with my legs. If he tries to bend over and take them without paying I can kick him right in the face.

"Now I want to see the cash."

He smiles and takes three thick bundles of bills out of his breast pocket. They're wrapped in a paper strip that says BANK OF FINLAND. He shows them to me, flips through the bills with his thumb. No newspaper tucked between them. I have no other way to verify that they're real, so I nod.

"We switch at the same time," I say.

Järvi hands me the bills and I step back so he can pick up the bags and stuff them into his briefcase. I put the bills in the side pocket of the shopping bag, which has a clasp to close it.

"It was a pleasure doing business with you, Miss Paloheimo."

"Thanks, you too."

"I happen to have an extra thousand marks in my pocket. If you agree to anal intercourse here and now, it's yours."

I must look confused, because he explains gently, "I'm sorry. Those are probably big words for you. I mean a fuck in the ass."

I almost burst into hysterical laughter.

"Mr. Paloheimo told me to come straight back."

I shove my way through the bushes. Järvi waits coyly for ten seconds before coming out behind me, and by then I'm long gone.

Jare is waiting in the car, which reeks of sweat and nervousness. I slide in beside him.

"What took you so long?"

"The bank, just as we expected. Thirty grand. We can keep the five thousand extra for ourselves." I take the bills out of the shopping bag and lay them in his lap. He puts some of them in his wallet, then opens the suitcase of money and puts the rest in there. It's so full that it's difficult to get it closed.

"I'll go straight to the ministry. It might take a while. A lot of papers and forms and signatures and all that."

"If I'm not in the car I'll be walking somewhere near here. I can't sit still. I'm sure I'll be back before you're done. I'll keep the shopping bag with me so I look as though I'm on some errand."

"There shouldn't be any hurry for at least an hour."

"It would be nice if we had one of those amazing telephones, like the ones in the decadent democracies. You could call me in the middle of the street as soon as you were on your way back to the car."

"We'll have one of those telephones soon enough."

Jare looks at me and the smell of rosemary and lavender and apple surrounds him such that I'm practically looking through a cloud of it to see him.

"Come back soon."

"I will."

One hour.

One of our last hours in Finland.

There's something I haven't told Jare about. It completely escaped me in all the chaos and confusion. When I remembered it, just before we left Neulapää, I broke out in a sweat from pure shame. How could I forget?

It's August. The beginning of August.

All those times I betrayed Manna, and now I'm leaving on her birthday.

There's still time to visit Kalevankangas cemetery and say good-bye to my sister. It's the least I can do. Up the hill from the station, a short walk down Kalevantie, and I'm there. I'm sure it won't take more than an hour.

I have a present for her. It's been in the other pocket of my shopping bag the whole time. Manna loves presents.

Once I'm at the cemetery I can also figure out what to do with the Core of the Sun and the little packet of flake. It'll be safer to make adjustments under the shade of the trees at the cemetery than in the restroom at a department store or a refreshments bar.

The Core of the Sun is the most important thing to hide. It would be smartest to destroy the flake that I kept for myself. One clever way to do that would be to soak some of the dried flakes in water in the women's room at the cemetery and chew them up. Otherwise my visit to Manna's grave might shove me back into the Cellar, and I don't want to be in the Cellar on what may be the most important trip of my life. Once I've had a farewell dose I can flush the rest of it down the toilet. Perfect.

I smile at the thought of being ready to throw away that much chili. Before the Gaians came it would have lasted me half a year.

I find the restroom at the cemetery, go into a stall, and take the bag of flake out of my bra. But what about the Core of the Sun?

I can't let anyone find it, for a lot of reasons. And I have to bring it with me.

There's only one solution.

I lift my skirt, pull down my panties, and push the Core of the Sun into my vagina, tip first. It slides smoothly inside me, much easier than a cotton tampon ever did. The stem is left slightly protruding, just enough that I can pull it out again, like the string on a tampon. Perfect.

I quickly prepare a fix from the flake. I'm about to pour the rest of it into the toilet when my hand stops. What if I need a bumper dose before I get on the plane?

I put the bag back in my bra. It feels like a completely sensible decision. I'll visit the restroom at the airport before check-in, take one more dose, and only then destroy the rest.

I step out into the sunshine. There's a pleasant burn in my mouth, a light sweat breaking out on my temples. I feel alert and free.

Just the right mood to say my final good-byes to my sister.

I guess I should have brought some wildflowers from Neulapää so the visit would look even more natural. But I would have had to explain them to Jare. I could have bought some cut flowers from the kiosk, of course, but Jare has all the money—all I have in my purse are a few coins.

But the flowers aren't important. The main thing is to ritually cut the umbilical cord that still ties me to Finland.

The main thing is to remember Manna.

I go to borrow a little trowel from the caretaker's booth. I crouch at the grave and start to dig. I've brought a few perennials to the grave since moving back to Neulapää because I wasn't able to come here as often as I would have liked. The geraniums and lobelia seem to be doing well, but I need to pull up the chickweed and dandelion sprouts.

I turn the soil and toss the weeds into a little pile, but in the process I'm secretly digging a small hole. I slip a flat metal cookie tin out of the zipper pocket in the shopping bag and put it in the hole. Manna loved the picture of a kitten on the lid. Inside are my letters to her and a collection of other papers and clippings, even some pages torn from books—what does it matter now, since I'm leaving and can't take my books with me? I've wrapped the box tightly in plastic, too, for good measure.

I cover Manna's history with dirt and pat the earth firmly over it.

I'm cutting the thread of my own history.

I stand up and look at the gravestone.

MANNA NISSILÄ

(NÉE NEULAPÄÄ)

2001–2016

And, as if the mere sight of Manna's legal name could create an uncannily realistic illusion, a figure steps out of the shadows.

Harri Nissilä.

He steps right in front of me. He has a gun in his hand and it's pointed at me. The barrel is almost touching my stomach.

From a distance it must look as though a masco is talking with an eloi and the conversation has turned intimate.

"Predictable. Just like an eloi." Nissilä laughs, and his amusement chills me. "It's not hard to guess where to find you on your sister's birthday. I took a chance that you'd come without your darling snitch of a husband ."

He jerks his head toward the men's room, which is just a few dozen meters away. "If you yell or try to call for help in any way or try to escape, I won't hesitate to shoot you. I already have a killer's papers—one more body won't make much difference."

I can smell that he's deadly serious. The empty shopping bag and the trowel are lying on the stone border of the grave. I don't know what else to do but walk in front of him as he follows close behind with the gun pressed against the small of my back. I quickly consider shoving him, kicking him, somehow distracting him and running away, but of course I'm wearing eloi shoes with stiletto heels. I wouldn't get anywhere before he shot me in the back or caught up to me in a couple of strides.

The open door of the brick men's restroom looms in front of me like a tomb. Nissilä shoves me inside and closes the door behind us. There are no stalls, just a porcelain urinal and a wash-basin. With the gun's muzzle, he waves me over to stand between them. There's a toilet in the corner by the door and he stands next to it. *Oh no. It's a restroom for one person at a time. He can lock the door.*

And that's what he does. *Click.*

"We probably don't want any visitors, do we?"

I don't say anything. I keep my body language passive as an eloi, looking at the floor so he can't see my expression. My thoughts are racing in circles. *What does he know?* He smells like suspicion and deep hatred, but also a little uncertain.

"There's something really weird about you," he says. "Something that doesn't smell right. That story about the toy train. I asked Manna about it again a couple of days later and she said that she didn't know anything about your grandmother's fiancé. She'd probably never heard of him. I know elois have short memories, but if she knew all about it one day and nothing at all the next, then who fed her that story, and why?"

Nissilä tastes these words. He's not really asking me, just mulling over his own thoughts. I wonder whether I could knock the gun out of his hand if I made a surprise attack—something he would never expect from an eloi—but I would have to get the gun from him. Otherwise I wouldn't be able to get out the door before he picked it up again. And just as if he's read my thoughts he gives the gun a little jerk as if to say, *Stay right where you are.*

"I didn't kill her, by the way."

I flinch visibly and Nissilä loves that he's gotten a reaction out of me.

"I think I know what it is that's wrong with you. You're obviously smarter than an eloi should be. But that's the hand that gets dealt sometimes. And I'm sure you wouldn't want such a thing to be known. Jare Valkinen must really be under your thumb. What other reason could he have for sticking his nose into Manna's case? You talked him into it. He should have minded his own business! That's always been the code of the mascos—stay out of other guys' eloi troubles. If a bitch is barren, everybody knows you shouldn't have to settle for second-rate merchandise. But let's get to the point, shall we?"

JARE SPEAKS

August 2017

The trip to the Trade Ministry took only forty-five minutes. I got all the papers I needed in what must have been record time. My contact was obviously more interested in my suitcase full of money than he was in bureaucratic red tape. I go back to the car to wait. There's still plenty of time to make the flight, and the drive to the Tampere airport is quick, since it's not far from downtown.

I wait five minutes. No sign of her.

Ten minutes pass.

I start to get nervous, but I don't want to go looking for her because we might miss each other.

Fifteen minutes. Twenty. Twenty-five.

The agreed-upon hour has passed.

The time ticks by.

This is when one of those decadent state wonder phones would really come in handy.

VANNA/VERA

August 2017

"I've got some stuff here that will make you go to sleep. It won't hurt at all. Then you can go to your sister. That's what you've wanted all along, isn't it?"

His voice bounces around the echoing room and my senses are like glass needles piercing everything, sharper than sharp. My body is tingling, and there's a distant, roaring furnace inside me. A bright dizziness sweeps through my head.

The Core of the Sun.

It's glowing inside me, its fierce, relentless, extreme power penetrating the thin skin of the fruit and seeping into me like streaks of fire.

The lower lip doesn't lie.

Harri Nissilä notices my distracted expression. "Not interested? What if I told you that things might not go so great for that dear hubby of yours?"

This makes me focus on him, and he chuckles. "A person can get quite a lot done from prison. People sitting in jail have a good network—insider information. I asked around about that overly curious fellow of yours and sent an emissary to keep an eye on him, and sure enough I got a tip that he was mixed up in some very illegal activity. I laid a trap and managed to get some evidence that could lose him his head. A very hot piece of evidence, you might say."

Although my head is spinning and buzzing, everything clicks into place now. Of course. The stolen Ukko's Dart.

"That evidence will go straight to the Authority as soon as I've taken care of you. Jare Valkinen will spend the rest of his life paying for his social responsibility crimes and for his wife's murder, although her body will never be found. He might even come to his end when they arrest him, because the Authority doesn't take too kindly to dealers. Tit for tat, with interest."

He fishes something out of his pocket. A little bottle and a cotton handkerchief. Chloroform, or something like it. Smart move, Nissilä. Can't just knock me out in the middle of the cemetery walkway.

But why go to the trouble of knocking me out? Why not kill me right away, since we're out of sight?

An ice-cold thought rises in my mind.

There must be some reason that I'm more valuable to him alive, at least temporarily.

He can carry me from here to his car, unconscious. In his arms, my face against his shoulder, looking like a damsel in distress, a girl whose feet started to hurt on our visit to the cemetery. Mascos passing by won't bother to wonder and elois will be jealous, if anything, at the romantic gesture.

Does he plan to use me to extort something from Jare? That doesn't make sense. Even if he does suspect my real nature, he probably just sees me the way he's always seen me, as an ordinary, disposable eloi, a piece of biomass, with plenty more to replace her if anything should happen to her.

And why so slow with the rag and the chloroform? Of course, he has to keep the gun pointed at me, but he's deft at setting the cloth on the back of the toilet and unscrewing the lid of the bottle, watching me the whole time, the barrel of the gun never wavering. He's practiced opening the bottle with one hand. So why are his movements so slow and heavy, like a film in slow motion? . . .

There's something going on, something very familiar, though I can't put my finger on what it is.

Déjà vu.

There's a swishing in my head and I feel light, so full of endorphins that I'm starting to rise into the air.

The Core of the Sun. Trance possession.

It's easy now that I've done it once already.

The colors are a murky, rough world, half in darkness; the snow scales, stalactites, and towers crooked, twisted; the coral gray and tired. There's something ugly in this landscape, squid-like, slimy, and I know it's just my idea of Harri Nissilä, and there he is, an opening filled with a shuddering, convulsing, heaving chunk of something that can only be his pitch-black soul, or mind, or whatever it is, and I'm diving, diving into it like a sperm to an egg, and I'm looking. *Looking.*

A flash like an impulse, a series of frozen images that I sense more than see. *Manna, Manna, Manna.* Manna's hair. She's sitting at the table at Neulapää, his hand is visible, a cotton cloth, then her head hitting the metal lid of the trunk as she's stuffed inside, a flash of her curled up there, limp as a corpse, and the trunk closing. *Click.* The road rushing through the windshield, Harri Nissilä's hands on the steering wheel, the smell of greed and triumph. Some unknown place. It's night. Manna lifted out of the trunk, her eyes blinking—she's alive! Harri Nissilä's hands, other hands holding out a thick wad of money.

Money.

A hell of a lot of money.

A clink. I snap out of Nissilä's head. The clink was the bottom of the bottle. He's poured the liquid onto the cloth and set the bottle back down on the toilet. He takes a step toward me.

"Can I . . . can I have a drink of water?" My voice is trembling, and Nissilä's eyes narrow.

"Well, hurry up. I don't have all day."

That's a mistake.

That's a big mistake, Harri Nissilä.

I pretend to raise my hand in fear, to place it on a pounding heart, but I stick it in my bra and lean over the sink. I take hold of the spigot and turn it, whimpering, *"What are you going to do to me, please don't hurt me, please be nice to me,"* because that's what he wants to hear, mortal terror, his place of power, oh, he enjoys it, I can smell it, that's why he's not in any hurry, his penis is no doubt swelling as he relishes my feeble, submissive pleas, savors the tingle of it as I bend over the sink, lower, lower, and thank God for these long, polished eloi fingernails, because now there's a long gash in the plastic bag that I have hidden in my bra, and he hasn't yet noticed, not yet, as I drop the torn bag of flake straight from my collar into the sink and yank the hot water all the way up.

As hot as it can get.

I stand up, take a deep breath, and hold it.

Now Nissilä realizes there's something in the sink, something red under the gushing, steaming, almost boiling hot water, and he's startled, but he doesn't shoot, of course he doesn't, I'm more valuable alive, and he steps closer to see what I dropped in the sink, and by then it's already too late.

Capsaicin steam fills the air, strong, stinging, and in spite of my tolerance my eyes burn and water as if there were acid in the air. I can't make the mistake of breathing even a tiny bit, not even through my nose. *Don't breathe, don't breathe,* but Nissilä does just what I want him to do, he gasps in surprise, sucking a cloud of capsaicin into his lungs, and his eyes and mouth and nose are in a fog of fire but his autonomic nervous system—dear, *dear* autonomic nervous system—forces his diaphragm and lungs to gulp for air again.

Nissilä bends over double and coughs as if he would cough his lungs right out through his throat. One quick step, a kick at his hand with my pointy eloi shoes, and the gun clatters to the floor. I grab it—I'm going to have to breathe soon—and I pick up the chloroform bottle and hurl it to the floor, and it lands with a luscious smash right under his sputtering face, and then I go to the door and *click* and I sail out of the restroom and close the door tightly behind me. Tightly, tightly.

I fill my lungs with the lime-tree-scented August air of Kalevankangas.

I hear spasmodic coughing that ends suddenly, as if cut off with a knife. Something heavy hits the floor.

It's time to focus.

The Core of the Sun is still producing a fusion reaction inside me. Let it.

I dive into Harri Nissilä's unconscious mind.

The snow scales and frost stalactites float around me, different now, half melted. The internal glow of the forms is blurred, flickering, fluttering dreamily. I'm soaring. I know the way, dive into the pitch black of his consciousness. *Can you ride a human being? I'm going to have to.*

He's an animal. He's an animal. He's a sly, greedy little animal.

I straddle Harri Nissilä's little weasel-like, lizard-like inner self. I press my calves against his sides. I grab the side of his mouth. The creature is limp. This is a mercy, really.

I give a sharp tug. *Click.*

And his pitch-black soul's neck is broken.

The piece of paper wrapper is in my skirt pocket, some eyeliner in my makeup pocket. I write in masco-like block letters OUT OF ORDER and wedge it between the restroom's rain-swollen door and the door frame.

It looks very amateurish, but it might delay them finding him.

If and when somebody does open the men's room door and sees a masco lying on the tile floor—maybe, hopefully, dead—and the hot water running and a torn plastic bag and the dregs of the chili in the sink and a broken bottle of sedative on the floor, it'll be something for the sleuths to chew on.

All I can do is hope that by the time the investigation begins we'll be long gone.

And I run as fast as I can in my eloi shoes.

JARE SPEAKS

August 2017

Finally I see her at the end of the street. I slump in relief. For the first time ever, V has behaved like an empty-headed eloi, now of all times. What's she been doing, trying on dresses?

When she gets closer my relief shifts to irritation. I can see from her eyes and the sweat on her upper lip and forehead that she's had a fix, and not a small one. What in God's name does she think she's doing? A fix, at a time like this?

She opens the car door and slides into the front seat.

"Where the hell have you—"

"Where indeed."

"What? What happened?"

"Harri Nissilä happened."

I gasp. "No, God no. I've got the tickets. The plane is leaving in less than an hour."

"He won't give us any trouble. Not anymore. Probably. But we can't leave. I mean, you can, but I can't."

I'm so astonished I can't get any words out.

"I don't understand a word you're saying."

"Manna's alive. Somewhere. I have to find her."

"What the hell are you babbling about?"

V starts to talk, stammering and stumbling over her story.

VANNA/VERA

August 2017

"I'm going now."
I look him in the eye, once, and depart.
My boat is light and swift.

JARE SPEAKS

August 2017

Her eyes roll in her head and her whole body goes strangely stiff.
She's hardly breathing.

We should be on our way to the airport.

This can't, cannot, be happening.

VANNA/VERA

August 2017

Manna, I'm coming.

The Core of the Sun pulses deep inside me and spreads its ancient fire through me.

It's because of this. This is why chili's forbidden.

It's because of this that the Gaians were in such a hurry. Because they didn't want us to know too much about their ultimate goal.

Leaving my body was just part of the breakthrough. This is what they're after. Spirit travel. Penetrating the consciousness of others.

I almost laugh out loud when I realize how simple it is. How could I not have understood it immediately the first time I tried the Core of the Sun?

Of course the Authority knows. Of course they have some inkling of it, of the fact that a large enough dose of capsaicin gives a person . . . powers.

Dangerous powers.

Revolutionary powers.

Powers that aren't conducive to social order.

It's like giving a terrorist organization a nuclear weapon.

Shaman Nuwat, Shaman Ukwun, I know you only from the pages of a book, for you left your earthly forms long ago. But your words survive, and I grasp them with my mind.

My boat is light and swift!
Core of the Sun,
grant me your fire that I may depart on a long journey;
I wish to rush through every country,
go to the lands where suns are moons.
On the shore of the land of sorrowful evening
is a circle of eternal darkness.
There the light of the moon displaces the sun
and there is my sister,
for whom I've searched nine lands and nine skies.

The earth races under my belly, my wings devour the air, a bird's mind is inside my mind like a ticking little heart. I soar on my mount toward my goal, a place where I know I'll find Manna, her mind glowing dimly in the distant darkness like a slim radio signal: I urge my hollow-boned, luminous-feathered friend onward until my mount begins to fear it's losing strength, and I slide out fluid as a fish, then tether myself to a trotting elk, and the next moment I'm a racing wolf in the woods.

A gray owl combing the canyons for prey!
I fly on its wings, searching.
Searching nine lands, nine skies for my sister.
Where are you? Where are you?
Show yourself, show yourself, show yourself!

When I finally arrive where Manna is, it takes all my strength not to snap back to where I came from.

I don't know if it's been a minute, an hour, a week, or a month since I left myself.

I don't know if one without a body can vomit.

* * *

Harri Nissilä has done some business.

Harri Nissilä has found a niche market.

Harri Nissilä has made lots of money.

Lots and lots of money to play the state lottery.

For some mascos it's not enough to see elois as lower creatures than themselves. Elois have to be *much* lower creatures.

They have to be creatures debased.

Creatures with no possibility of rebellion.

Creatures who pay for the most twisted urges of others out of their own skins.

When nothing is enough, nothing ever will be enough.

A domesticated animal like any other. This is how it's always done. They get smaller, their horns shorter, their snouts flattened, their teeth shrunken, their fur paler, their behavior docile, gentle, meek, affectionate. Dogs, pigs, cows, goats, water buffalo, rabbits, elois.

Every creature that has a use.

And what if they rebel? What then?

They can be beaten into silence. Pierced and chained. Branded.

Bought and sold.

Locked up in a dark place where they lie in their own excrement and do nothing but wait, numb and helpless, to be used again.

Used in any way that can be imagined. Any way at all. Anything is possible.

For the pleasure of those who take pleasure from complete debasement.

Oh, eusistocracy.

To keep the loudest ones happy you brought a known drug
into the reach of the many.

You thought you were liberating sex.

But you liberated something else.

Power.

One taste of it just leads to larger and larger doses.

Ridiculously large doses.

Incomprehensible amounts.

Sickening amounts.

Doses so large that the brain can't comprehend them.

The mind just explodes in white light.

> *My boat is light and swift.*
> *I float over the edge of worlds.*
> *My feet wander along the spine of the sky.*
> *My eyes see the dying suns of netherworlds.*
> *Invisible I wander,*
> *dangerous, traversing dangerous country.*
> *I see the waning moon*
> *collide with the waxing moon,*
> *see it die*
> *and fall.*
> *I see the east and west*
> *fight over who will run*
> *over a hole filled with sharp pieces of bone.*
> *The snow under their feet*
> *shines in the fiery light.*

I take her by the hair
and pull her up from under the moss,
the black water deeper than death.

I'm rocking, rocking Manna.

Oh, my tender little sister. Sister with a heart of chocolate, hands full of comfort, a brain of pink froth. My fair-haired, sweet-souled sister.

Your round head covered in platinum curls, your cute little turned-up nose, your narrow shoulders, full breasts, curving waist, tush like a peach. They're all gone. They don't matter anymore.

Rocking and rocking Manna. *"Aa-aa,"* I say.

There's only one thing I can do for her now.

With one small tug, a barely noticeable motion, I break the slight, hair-thin, gleaming thread that ties her to her tortured body, and I enfold her in myself.

I know where to bring her.

We can be together in the Cellar.

We'll be there forever.

No one can harm us there. The Cellar's walls are so strong, dug so deep. We can both float there in the warm black water, the eternal night.

I don't know if I'm walking or flying or lying on the ground, but I'm moving my wings, the wings of the Core of the Sun, and rocking and rocking Manna.

No. Not Manna.

Mira.

Vera and Mira. Sisters who are the truth, who are a miracle.

VERA/MIRA NOW

I wake to noise and shaking and someone dabbing my forehead.

I'm sitting in a chair like a bus seat, strapped in. It's not like a car seat belt, doesn't go over my shoulder, just across my lap.

There are a lot of people, and little, round windows.

Outside the windows I see glimpses of racing clouds.

A woman in a uniform, dark, with a large nose and short hair—obviously a morlock, but wearing makeup for some reason—is bending over me. Jare is sitting beside me holding my hand. In his other hand he holds a soft paper napkin and dabs my face with it. He's wiping the sweat away.

I'm still on a hell of a high.

Then I sense her. Clear as sight.

Mira is curled up in the Cellar. In a dark, warm, sheltered corner of my mind, nestled like a child in the womb.

Where no one from the outside can ever reach her again.

Safe. Finally safe.

I owe such a debt to you. Without you, without you to be my model, I would have strayed from my designated role and been destroyed. All through our childhood and all through our youth , you were teaching me. You focused my eyes so I could see.

You gave me a means of escape.

You were my sun, and now you are my core.

I don't know if you'll live in the Cellar from now on or if you'll be there only when I use the Fire Within to summon you, but you always have the right to be there. You played an unintentional part in building the Cellar, and now it's yours.

I whisper: "Happy birthday, Mira."

The Core of the Sun hums in my veins.

> *My boat is light and swift!*
> *Its flight guides the birds.*
> *The smaller bird is called Mira,*
> *and it carries her, too.*
> *My two souls say,*
> *Let us keep hold of both sides of the boat*
> *and we will fly to unknown lands.*
> *I fly invisibly, seeing all that is*
> *and carrying the knowledge in my breast*
> *like a bird carrying food to its nest.*

"Is everything all right now?" the woman asks, speaking half to me and half to Jare, and Mira's whisper echoes in the Cellar: *Everything's all right now,* and she curls up still tighter and safer in her fetal position, and falls asleep.

"Yes, she's all right again now," Jare says, and squeezes my hand. "The little lady's just a bit nervous. She's not used to flying."

Excerpt from Åke Wallenquist's
Astronomy and the World Today

National Publishing (1954)

The sun's photosphere—its visible surface—is amazingly thin. The fragile brightness of this heavenly object can make you forget what dark, matter-smashing forces hide deep within its core.

AFTERWORD

One of the inspirations for this book was Tiina Raevaara's wonderful nonfiction book *Koiraksi ihmiselle* (On Dogs and Humans, Teos, 2001), where I first learned of Belyayev's domestication experiments. Belyayev's observations were also presented in the March 2011 issue of *National Geographic*. Many thanks to Tiina for directing me to articles on neoteny and the significance of sex in evolution.

Warm thanks to Jukka "Fatalii" Kilpinen for adding to my chili pepper knowledge, for giving me the opportunity to visit his chili farm and greenhouses, and for his other assistance with the book.

The stream-of-consciousness fragments on pages 296–300 are based in large part on the spirit journey songs of Chukchi shamans Nuwat and Ukwun. The original texts can be found in Anna-Leena Siikala's book *Suomalainen samanismi: Mielikuvien historiaa* (*Mythic Images and Shamanism: A Perspective on Kalevala Poetry*, SKS, 1992).

The article on human sterilization excerpted on pages 223–225 is, with the exception of a very few word changes, taken from an actual article in the second April 1935 issue of *Kotiliesi* (*Hearth and Home*) magazine.

Wallenquist's *Astronomy and the World Today* is an actual book. The quote on page 303, however, is not actually taken from it.

The Transcendental Capsaicinophilic Society is a real, though somewhat tongue-in-cheek, group that can be found on the Internet. The "Litany Against Pain" is borrowed directly from the society.

Any errors, misconstructions, or other inaccuracies are naturally my own.

ABOUT THE AUTHOR

Johanna Sinisalo is the author of the novels *Troll: A Love Story*, *Birdbrain* and *The Blood of Angels*. In addition to the Finlandia Prize, she has won the James Tiptree, Jr. Award. *The Core of the Sun* was nominated for the Tähtivaeltaja ('Star Traveller') Award. Sinisalo's works have been translated into nineteen languages. She lives in Tampere, Finland.